To Helena,

Thanks for reading it

knowing you were going to read this helped me finish the editting, proofreading and design stages (Actually I'm still in the proofreading stage as I write this!)

Thanks so much,

Hope you enjoy it,

Love from Catherine x

Compassion-on-Sea

Catherine West-McGrath

Parks & Mews

First published in 2024 by
Parks and Mews

All characters in this publication are fictitious
and any resemblance to real persons, living or dead,
is purely coincidental.

Hardback ISBN 978-1-7391133-8-4

A CIP catalogue record of this book is available from the British Library.

For my siblings: Anne Marie, Martin and Adrian

Also by Catherine West-McGrath

Poetry and Lyric Collections:
- Homesick for the North and Other Poetry
- Lapsed Capitalist: A Poetry Collection
- Optimistic Activist: Poetry and Verse
- British Values: A Poetry Collection
- What She Really Means and Other Poetry
- Try This, It Might Help: Poetry and Verse

Illustrated Children's Book:
- Ceecee's Treasure Chest

Healing Places: A Journal (published by Lepidoptera Learning)

One

Tuesday 24th January 2017

Thornsea Women's Business Group meets every month at the Golf Club. I'm late for this one, as usual, so when I find a space in the car park, I breathe a sigh of relief. Once in the foyer, I open the glass door to the President's Room, careful not to disturb the audience. Every table is full, so I loiter at the back. When the speaker sees me, she stops mid-sentence.

'There's a seat here,' she calls out, pointing to the front.

I squeeze between tightly packed chairs, careful not to hit anyone with my handbag. When I reach the empty chair, I lower myself, hoping I won't block someone's view. Jean, my mother-in-law, is sitting beside me.

She leans across and whispers. 'How was Marbella?'

'Wonderful,' I reply, 'and thanks for babysitting.'

But the holiday's over and my two teenagers aren't babies anymore. I'm back to the routine of work. Before my first coffee, I checked last night's takings, three bar manager reports and our staff rotas. Before I had a shower, I made sure Ellie and Daniel were ready for school and college. As I got dressed, I listened to my husband, Mike, updating me on the new Liverpool bar. At eight o'clock, we walked to the Beach Road bar together, a hundred yards from home. In my office, on the second floor, I approved a few holiday requests before driving here. All Jean had to do this morning was get dressed - a perk of being a wealthy retiree. The speaker claps her hands, silencing the chatter.

'I have some exciting news to share,' she says, picking up her clicker.

Jean leans towards me and whispers. 'I already know what it is.'

'I'm pleased to announce,' the speaker says, 'Thornsea will be hosting our first Leader at the Microphone event this year.' There are shouts of 'Brilliant' and 'Fantastic.' A photo of a purple microphone appears on the screen under the date: *18th March 2017.*

Almost everyone cheers. Some Leader at the Microphone videos attract thousands of views on *YouTube.* It's a big deal for our little seaside town to be organising our own event.

When the room's quiet, she continues. Anyone wanting to be on stage in March will need to provide the theme of their talk and a brief biography. If selected, and only eight will be, they'll need to prepare a 10-minute talk.

'And one more thing,' she says, 'we're looking for people who haven't done this kind of thing before.'

I make a mental list of who I think will be applying to speak. My name's not on it.

After the presentation, while some rush to the front, Jean and I join the queue for drinks at the back.

'You should apply,' Jean says, tapping me on the arm, 'you'd be perfect.'

The last time I gave a talk on stage was in October 1987. I was 17. I wanted to be president of the student council at St Ursula's College. But I couldn't read my scribbled notes, my hands were shaking so much. Afterwards, I ran off stage before anyone could ask questions. I came last out of six candidates and swore I'd never attempt to speak on stage again.

Jean's done her fair share of public speaking. Her last talk recalled the 30 years she spent running her bridal wear shop. I told her I enjoyed it. Jean's always been a great storyteller, it must be where Mike gets it from.

'Not a chance,' I say, pouring myself a strong black coffee, 'plus what would I talk about?'

Back at our table, I check my phone for work messages. Jean's looking out through the bay window, where a groundsman is inspecting the grass.

'I've got it,' she says, tapping the table. 'What you've learned from meeting top sports stars.' She nods, agreeing with her own idea. 'That could be a winner.'

When sports stars come into our bars, I'm usually upstairs in the office or at home. It's Mike's face in the photos all over the bar walls: Mike with a footballer, Mike with a cricketer, Mike with a golfer.

'I'm not applying,' I say, hoping she'll move on to another topic.

But she persists. 'Mike will help,' she says, 'he's good at this.' Mike has no problem talking. He'll chat to anyone if it means they'll buy another round of drinks or give us good terms on a contract. 'C'mon Ruth,' she says, 'this will be great publicity for us.'

'No,' I say firmly.

'You know David Fitzroy,' she says, 'you must have learned something from him.' She does mean that David Fitzroy, the ex-Premiership footballer. When he spent a season managing Thornsea United, four years ago, he and Mike became good friends.

'I'm not doing a talk about David,' I say, 'can we forget it?'

But Jean's looking out of the window again, and I suspect she's making plans.

During lunch, the speaker comes over to our table. Jean stands to give her a warm embrace. She's the smaller of the two women, petite and slim with a short pixie haircut and black-rimmed glasses. The speaker, a foot taller and with fiery red curls, towers over her.

Jean puts her arm on my shoulder. 'Let me introduce you to my daughter-in-law.'

I give the speaker a polite smile and we shake hands.

'Lovely to meet you,' she says, placing her business card by my plate:

Olivia Partington

Work, Life & Voice Coach

Become a More Confident You

'Olivia gave me some coaching last year,' Jean tells me, 'I told her you could do with some too.'

'Yes,' Olivia says, smiling at me, 'I can help with your confidence.' I notice everyone on our table is quiet and all eyes are on me. My cheeks must be the same shade as the tomatoes on my plate.

'I'm okay thanks,' I say, politely, 'I'm fine.'

'I've told her to apply,' Jean says, putting her hand on my arm.

Olivia smiles. 'And that's a lovely accent too,' she says, 'so warm. Where's it from?' I sense I'm being flattered, but I'm still not applying to speak.

Jean winks at me. 'She moved over here for love.'

'Came here on holiday,' I explain, 'when I was 18.'

Jean nods. 'Mike was the chef, at the hotel she stayed at.' Olivia smiles. I push the card towards Jean.

'Anyway, thanks,' I say, 'but no thanks.' Olivia picks up the card and presses it firmly into my hand.

'Please have a think about it,' she says, 'you're just who we're looking for.'

'She'd be perfect for this,' Jean tells Mike, over dinner that evening, 'but she won't apply.'

I'm bringing a dish of roast potatoes to the table. 'It's not that Jean,' I say, 'it's just-'. I look at Mike, hoping he'll back me up.

'She's too shy Mum,' he says, opening a bottle of Rioja, 'she'll never do it.' I settle in my chair and pour a glass of water from the jug.

'It's just I'm not good at that type of thing.' Ellie, my youngest, touches my arm.

'Yet,' she says, 'you're not good at that type of thing, yet. That's what you always tell us.' Jean smiles and Mike pats Ellie on the back.

'She's right,' he says, 'you should set an example to your children.'

I protest. 'But she's 15 and I'm 46.'

Daniel, my eldest, turns to his sister. 'She means it doesn't apply to her.'

Ellie stands and taps a fork on her glass. 'This house believes Mum should apply to speak,' she declares, in a clear loud voice. I sigh, regretting I paid for her Debating Club membership. Daniel raises his hand.

'Okay, let's have a vote,' he says, laughing, 'who thinks Mum should apply to be a speaker?' Everyone, except me, raises their hand.

'Thanks, Daniel,' I say, giving him a gentle nudge. I look at my family. Each one still has their hand in the air. 'Okay, you win,' I say, 'I'll apply. But it doesn't mean I'll get a place.'

Jean claps her hands. 'Brilliant,' she says, then, putting her hand on Mike's arm, 'she'll need your help on this.'

As soon as we've finished eating, Jean hands me her *iPad*.

'No time like the present,' she says, 'I've found the form. You can fill it in now.' Scanning the table, I meet the gazes of my husband, daughter and son in turn. Each one, waiting for me to accept Jean's assistance.

'Okay,' I say, taking the *iPad* reluctantly. I tap in my details. 'And what am I speaking about?'

'What..I've..learned..from..meeting..top..sports..stars,'

Jean says, slowly and deliberately. I type in the words, exactly as she's said and get stuck at the next question.

'And why do I want to speak about this?'

'Because you run sports bars,' Mike says, 'and you meet sports stars all the time.'

'But I don't,' I say, 'you do.'

Mike waves his hand, as if squatting a fly. 'They don't need to know that.' I can only hope the organisers have so many applications they don't bother to look at mine. And if they do, I hope they'll agree no one wants to hear me talk about this. I fill in the rest of the form and press send.

'All done,' I say, handing the *iPad* back to Jean. 'Happy now?' I sound like Ellie, telling me she's finished her homework.

'Wait till I tell David,' Mike says, filling his wine glass. 'He'll be delighted.'

Two

I've only been to David Fitzroy's house once, to celebrate our new business partnership last year. This time David wants us to meet his new girlfriend. This is the most magnificent house I've stayed in, without paying. It has acres of land; every inch is beautifully landscaped and manicured. There's a tennis court, a paddock and an outdoor swimming pool. Inside there's a cinema room, a snooker room and a trophy room. To the left of the house, a shuttered garage door rolls up and we drive into the underground car park. David and Cara meet us at the lift. Cara's everything I expected she'd be: tall and slim. I guess she's a dress size six. Her straight blonde hair reaches her waist and she has perfectly straight white teeth. I give David a bottle of *Bolney Estate Pino Gris*.

'Just a little gift,' I say, remembering I spent ages choosing it.

David inspects the label. 'That's perfect. We can have it with the starter.'

We take the lift to the main hall where David shows us through to the lounge. As we pick at blinis with cream cheese and smoked salmon, Cara tells us she met David at an awards ceremony.

'There's something about Danish girls.' David says, putting his arm around her tiny waist. Cara giggles and they rub noses. Mike nods. I look around the room and rest my eyes on a statue of a gold elephant on a windowsill.

After the hors d'oeuvres, David shows us through to the dining room.

'So, how's our bar coming along?' he asks Mike, as we take our seats.

Mike smiles. 'A few delays I'm afraid,' he says, apologetically, 'builders found some problems.'

David leans forward to Mike, his eyebrows raised. 'What kind of problems?'

'Nothing serious,' Mike says, smiling again, 'just puts us back a couple of days.'

'And the cost?' David asks. 'Still in budget?'

'Just about,' Mike says, looking at me, 'just about.' I smile at Mike, willing him to tell David the truth about the budget, but he looks away.

'Cara,' David says, stroking her arm, 'why don't you show Ruth your dressing room?'

'Of course darling,' then smiling at me, 'shall we?' I

follow Cara upstairs, along a corridor into the master bedroom. One wall is nothing but glass, no curtains or blinds, overlooking fields. The only building I can see is a farmhouse in the far distance.

'This is amazing,' I say, following her into a smaller room.

'My dressing room, she says, 'just had this built.' She moves her hand along a rail of long dresses. The air is filled with the scent of vanilla and jasmine. Open rails on each side display neatly pressed clothes draped over wooden hangers. Shelves hold folded knitwear, shoes, and bags. A table in the middle holds a mirror and jewellery boxes. I'm drawn to a long thin shelf displaying three handbags, each illuminated by its own lamp. I point to the bag in the middle.

'Can I?' My hand hovers, waiting for permission to touch the soft leather.

'Sure' she says, 'that's a *Loewe*.' She hangs a black tote over her arm. 'This is a *Balmain*.' She points to a cream clutch with gold detail. 'And that's a *Balenciaga*.' I stroke the tan leather and the silver zipper.

'This is amazing, you must love it here.'

'I know we're lucky, but David's worked hard for all this.'

We go back to the dining room just as the first course is

being served: Isle of Skye scallops with lemon and an olive oil sabayon. David takes a sip of the wine we brought.

'Goes perfectly,' he says, 'great choice Ruth.' I smile, relieved. Mike moves his hand towards my leg and gently squeezes my knee.

This is the first time we've stayed at David's.

'This room must be the size of our entire second floor,' I say to Mike, as we're getting ready for bed.

'We'll have a place like this soon,' he says, taking off his shirt.

I laugh. 'I love our house, but this place is something else.'

In bed Mike reaches for my hand under the covers. 'But let's not settle, eh?' he says. 'When we could have all this too.'

When Mike told me he and David were going to be business partners I had my reservations.

'This is going to be hard work,' I'd said, 'is it worth it?'

But Mike could only see opportunities. 'If we don't try,' he'd said, 'we'll never know.'

In the morning, breakfast is served in the kitchen.

Cara's made a colourful fruit salad served with thick Greek yoghurt. I'm not hungry so I ask for a piece of dry toast. Mike gives me a '*You're being awkward*' look.

Cara smiles and says, 'No problem.'

When we get in the car, to drive home, I still have a sick feeling in my stomach.

'Do you really think it's going to work out?' I ask, watching the drive gates close behind us.

'It has to,' Mike says, 'there's too much riding on it.'

For the rest of the journey, I stay silent, listening to the morning phone-in show on the local radio. It's only when we reach home that I ask Mike.

'Did you tell David we're running out of money?'

Three

When we get back to Thornsea we drive straight to the Beach Road bar. In Mike's office, we pour over spreadsheets for signs of waste or potential savings on David's new bar. But it's no good, if it's to open in March, there needs to be a new injection of cash.

Mike's sitting on the black leather settee, against the back wall, balancing a laptop on his knee. 'We'll have to go to Plan B,' he says, staring at the screen.

I'm standing at the window, looking out towards the seafront. 'Put in our own money? Why don't we just tell David?'

'Not yet,' Mike says, 'he'll think we can't manage the budget.' Outside, the sea's rough and the clouds are heavy with rain.

'So we're risking our own money instead?'

'It'll be worth it,' Mike says. I wish I shared his confidence. He comes to the window and puts his arms around my waist. I lift my hands to his shoulders and feel a needle-sharp pain stabbing into my neck.

I take a sharp intake of breath. 'Ahhgghh.'

He pulls his hands from my waist and steps back. 'You okay?'

'Wow, that hurt,' I say, rubbing the back of my neck.

'It's probably the pillows last night,' he says, taking his laptop back to his desk, 'sleeping in a different bed, that's all.' I sit down on the leather settee and massage my neck.

'I don't feel too good,' I say, 'really not good.'

'And all that rich food, last night,' he says, sitting at his desk, 'that's all.'

I lift my head, the room's slowly spinning. I take a few deep breaths and put my head down again. My head hurts so bad. When I'm able to stand I go to my office at the other end of the corridor. There's a box of paracetamol in the bottom drawer of my desk. I'm relieved to find two still left in the blister pack.

Four

A week later I have an email from the organisers of the Leader at the Microphone event. It's a Friday morning and Mike and I are still in bed, waiting for the alarm to go off.

'I don't believe it,' I say, 'I've got a place. They want me to speak.'

'Brilliant,' he says, reading the details over my shoulder. I go into the en suite and splash my face with cold water. Looking at my reflection I try to see a confident speaker.

'But I don't want to do it,' I say. 'I'll tell them I've changed my mind.' I go back into the bedroom and reach for my phone on the pillow. Mike grabs it before I can get to it.

'No,' he says, 'this is just what we need.' I try to get my phone back but he swaps it from one hand to the other.

'I can't do it,' I say, 'with David's bar and everything else.' He pushes past me, still holding my phone.

'Promoting ourselves on *YouTube*,' he calls out from

the en suite, 'you can't turn that down.'

'Okay I'll do it,' I call back in desperation, 'please.'

He opens the door and sticks his hand out. I take my phone and go down to the kitchen.

At the calendar, on the side of the fridge, I turn the page to March. There's no way I can do it, no way at all. David's new bar must open on time and there's too much to do before that. I have no time to rehearse.

While I'm making coffee Mike comes into the kitchen and takes a cup from the dishwasher. I lean against the worktop and type my response to the organisers: *Thank you for the opportunity to be part of your event. However, I will be unable to take up the offer at this time.*

Mike's behind me. 'What are you doing?'

'I can't do it,' I say, 'I'm letting them know.' He grabs the phone out of my hand.

'C'mon,' he says, 'you'll be fine. I'll write it. It can't be that hard.' I put my hand out and he hands me the phone. The reply I'd started now deleted. Ellie comes in and puts a bagel in the toaster. 'Mum's been accepted,' he says, 'she's going to be speak-'.

'Hang on,' I interrupt. 'I'm still deciding.'

Ellie claps her hands. 'You're going to be famous mum?'

'No,' I say, 'I'm not going to be famous. No one will

watch it.'

Mike nods. 'She could be. If she does it right.' Ellie stands behind me and puts her arms around my neck. I feel my shoulders stiffen.

'Do it Mum,' she says, 'say you'll do it.' I don't want to let my children down. I'm always telling them to accept opportunities and be brave. Now it's my turn.

'Okay,' I say, turning to Ellie, 'I'll do it.'

While I'm taking a shower, I imagine myself speaking on stage, in March, in the Grand Ballroom of the Railway Hotel. Will I remember what to say? Will I trip over my words? Will I look awkward? Will I be laughed at? No. Yes. Yes. Probably.

When I go back into the kitchen, Mike's putting his cup in the dishwasher.

'David's says Good Luck,' he says, 'he thinks you'll smash it.'

'You've told David already?' I say, in disbelief. 'Why?'

'Of course I've told him,' he says, 'it's publicity for the bars.'

My phone buzzes. I have a message from Olivia Partington: *Congratulations on getting a place. Give me a call anytime.* I call her back straight away.

'But I've not done anything like this for years,' I say, 'and the last time I did, it didn't go well.'

'Let's get you booked in for some coaching,' she says, 'when are you free?'

After our call, I find a thick black pen and go to the calendar. On the square for Saturday 18th March, I write *MUM'S TALK.* Mike puts his arm on my shoulder.

'Well done,' he says, 'I'm proud of you.' I put the pen in the drawer.

'You'll help me, won't you? I have no idea what I'm going to say.'

'Of course I'll help,' he says, 'don't worry. I'm good at this.'

When he goes upstairs I open the medicine drawer and find two tablets. I put a note in my phone to pick up some more paracetamol later and gulp them down with my cold coffee.

Five

I meet Olivia in the bar of the Railway Hotel. The orange juice I've been served tastes strange; bitter instead of the usual sweetness. I pull a face as I put the glass on a coaster.

'Is something wrong?' she asks. I've taken another two paracetamol but they're having no effect. I read the label on the bottle.

'I don't know,' I say, 'this tastes odd, funny.' She offers to take it back and get me another one. 'No, it's probably me,' I say, 'everything tastes odd lately.'

When we finish our drinks I follow Olivia across the foyer into the Grand Ballroom. It's a magnificent room with two giant crystal chandeliers, art deco ceiling roses and wall panels. Following her instructions, I take the steps to the stage and go between the black curtains of the wings. I'm ready to present my homework: ten bullet points on ten white cards.

'Ladies and gentlemen,' she shouts from the dance

floor, 'it gives me great pleasure to introduce...Ruth Barrett.' I walk out from the wings, eyes fixed on the white x marked in chalk in the middle of the stage and clear my throat. 'Go ahead,' she shouts from the back. Her tone is encouraging but, as my shoulders relax, I feel a sharp pain.

'Aow!' My hand reaches for the back of my neck.

She walks towards the stage. 'You okay?'

'I think so.' I grimace, moving my head from side to side.

'Sure?' she asks, walking forward again, 'you don't look it.' I look behind and see a single chair at the back of the stage. Sitting on the chair I put my head between my knees. I hear the click of Olivia's heels climbing the steps. 'We can stop,' she says, resting her hand on my back, 'if you're not well.'

I picture the digital calendar on my laptop. Every square, from 8 am to 6 pm, shaded out for the next four weeks. We have three rehearsals after this one. I lift my head and smile.

'No,' I say, getting to my feet, 'let's carry on.' I take a sip from my water bottle.

'Okay,' she says, 'if you're sure.'

She leaves the stage and walks to the back wall. 'Ready when you are,' she shouts.

I take another sip of water. 'I'm here to tell you...erm...what... erm...I've learned from meeting...erm...top sports stars.' I know I'll need more rehearsals but I wait for her feedback.

'Can you try it again?' she shouts from the back. 'With a bit more enthusiasm?'

But I've already returned the cards to my pocket. 'I'm sorry Olivia, I'm just not feeling it today.' She walks toward the stage.

'You do look a little pale,' she says, 'are you sure you're okay?'

I switch off the microphone. 'I'm fine,' I say, 'just a bit of stage fright.' She climbs the steps and puts her hand on my arm.

'You're doing great,' she says, 'you'll be fine.'

'But does it sound okay?'

'We've loads of time to get you ready.'

I follow her down to the dance floor. 'I don't think I'll remember it.'

'You'll remember it,' she says, smiling, 'you'll rehearse it so many times you'll be saying it in your sleep.'

'You think so?'

'But let's call it a day anyway,' she says, 'you'll feel better next week.' I'm relieved, and grateful, she's been so kind. Perhaps, knowing she was a friend of Jean's, and that fiery red hair, gave me the wrong impression. But now I'm getting to know her, I can tell she genuinely cares about her pupils, even the quiet ones.

Outside the hotel, we navigate our way past two workmen putting up a '*Celebrate Valentine's Day Here*' sign. It's a freezing day and the tall buildings create a fierce wind tunnel.

'A busy day ahead?' she asks, tucking a cashmere scarf into her woollen overcoat.

'Opening our first bar with David Fitzroy next month,' I say, 'still loads to do.'

'How exciting!' she says.

'How exhausting,' I reply.

When I leave Olivia, I carry on towards the Beach Road bar. My first rehearsal hasn't gone well. Worse than that, I feel embarrassed. I make up my mind I'm not going to do the talk.

Back in my office, I prepare interview questions for a new bar manager. We need a good one for David's Liverpool bar. But I'm distracted, thinking about my decision not to do the talk. I'm sure Olivia will be kind when I tell her. I feel bad for letting her down, especially as she's giving me a discount on her fees. But I'm sure she'll agree I'm not public speaker material. Jean will probably laugh and say *I knew you wouldn't go through with it.*

And Mike? Mike will be annoyed, especially now he's told David. He probably won't speak to me for a day.

In the evening, in between making a casserole and emptying the dishwasher, I call Olivia.

'I'm having second thoughts,' I say, 'maybe I shouldn't do this talk.'

'What's the matter Ruth?' she says, sympathetically, 'you did really well today.'

I wasn't expecting positive feedback. 'You think so?'

'Absolutely,' she says, 'you can do this. Don't give up so soon.'

I'm standing by the hob, watching the casserole bubbling, still on the call. Daniel and Ellie come into the kitchen and I imagine how I'm going to tell them, especially Ellie. I know she'll be disappointed in me. I close my eyes and take a deep breath.

'Okay Olivia you've persuaded me,' I say, 'I'll do it.' I give Ellie a big grin and she gives me a *Mum you're being weird* look.

'Brilliant!' Olivia sounds pleased. 'You won't regret it. See you next week.' When I end the call Daniel and Ellie are throwing a tennis ball to each other across the island.

I raise my arms. 'No throwing in the kitch—Aghhh!' My high-pitched scream accompanied by a sharp stab from my jaw to my shoulders.

Daniel stops the game. 'You okay Mum?'

'It's nothing,' I say, 'I'll be fine.'

Ellie comes over. 'You've gone pale Mum.' She moves me away from the hob. 'You need to lie down.' The casserole's bubbling away nicely. It can be left for another 40 minutes.

'Wake me in half an hour,' I say, going to my bed.

I wake to banging on the door.

'Mum!' Ellie's calling. 'The dinner's burnt!' I follow her downstairs. Daniel's standing at the hob in the kitchen, looking into the pot.

'Sorry Mum,' he says, 'we were in the lounge.'

I sniff the air. 'I can't smell any burning.' What's left of the casserole is stuck to the bottom of the pot.

'I think it's ruined,' Ellie says.

'Let's see.' I scoop up some of the less burnt bits with a spoon. 'I might be able to save it.'

Ellie waits for my verdict. 'Well?'

'Sorry,' I say, 'I can't taste anything.' Daniel scrapes the contents of the pot into the bin. Ellie takes a pizza from the freezer and I sit at the island, resting my head on folded arms.

Ellie brings a blanket and puts it around my shoulders.

'Will you be okay?'

'Hope so,' I say.

She taps her phone and Mike answers. 'Mum's not well. Can you come home Dad? Quick!'

I hear Mike on the loudspeaker. 'I'm on my way.'

I'm resting my head on a cushion when Mike comes running into the kitchen.

'What's the matter?' he says, putting his hand on my back.

I lift my head. 'Can you take me to hospital? I've not been feeling too good for a while.'

He presses his palm on my forehead. 'You're freezing.' He helps me down from the stool and I shuffle to the front door, leaning on his arm. Ellie brings my coat and Daniel helps me put it on. I'm helped to get into the car. 'You didn't mention anything,' he says, taking a blanket from the back seat and putting it over my knees.

'Sorry,' I say, breathing in as he fixes my seatbelt, 'we've both been busy.'

At the reception desk of Thornsea General Accident and Emergency, a woman behind a glass screen takes my details.

'Name?'

'Ruth...Elizabeth...Barrett.'

'Address?'

'107...Beach Road...Thornsea.'

'Age?'

'46.'

'Date of Birth?'

'11th...March...1970.'

'Doctor?'

'Doctor Berry.'

'Religion?' I turn to Mike. He shrugs his shoulders and I turn back to the screen. These days we only go to the Parish Church every Christmas Eve but I still want it noted, just in case I need a chaplain.

'Church of England.'

'Next of kin?' I step to the side so she can get a proper look.

'Mike Barrett.'

'What's the matter?' she asks.

'I'm in a lot of pain,' I say, 'in my neck, my chest, between my shoulders. And I can't smell or taste anything. I just don't feel too good.' Within minutes I'm ushered into a room where a nurse takes my blood pressure.

I'm soon back in the waiting area with Mike. We sit for two long hours, watching people come in and a few go out. It's busy tonight.

Mike squeezes my hand. 'Shouldn't be long now.' A paramedic rushes in, pushing an elderly man in a wheelchair. They go straight through the double doors.

I turn to Mike. 'What if I've had a heart attack?'

'Don't be silly,' he says, 'there's no way you've had a heart attack.'

I lay my head on his shoulder. 'Hope I'll be okay for the interviews.'

He strokes my hair. 'You will,' he says, 'you'll have to be. Can't afford more delays.' The double doors swing open and a nurse with a clipboard calls out my name. I lean on Mike to get to my feet. He rubs my arm. 'Will you be okay?'

I try to reassure him. 'Hopefully,' I say, 'probably nothing.' I follow the nurse into a brightly lit ward. There are doctors and nurses, huddled around computer screens or moving between bays and the large desk. We pass several bays, hidden behind blue curtains. At the bottom of the ward, the nurse stops. He points to a bed. I take off my coat, careful not to make any sudden movements.

'I'll do your bloods,' he says, 'just roll up your sleeve.' He has a calm tone. I look left, towards the wall, and close my eyes, waiting for the procedure to be over. When he's done, and leaves the bay, I lie down, closing my eyes to the glare of fluorescent lights above.

I'm dozing off when I hear the curtains open.

'Ruth Barrett?'

'That's me,' I say, pulling myself up. A doctor writes on a clipboard. 'What's brought you here?'

'A pain in my neck, my chest, between my shoulders.' I move my hand around my body. 'Can't smell or taste anything either.'

'Well, your blood pressure's high,' she says, 'so I'm going to give you something for that.'

'Are you keeping me in?' I ask. 'I've got interviews tomorrow.'

She smiles again. 'We'll do an ECG,' she says, 'check your heart.'

Another nurse comes with an ECG machine, attaching pads and wires to my chest. 'Have I had a heart attack?' I ask. 'You'll tell me if I've had a heart attack, won't you?'

'I'll send your results to the doctor,' she says, not giving anything away. 'Try not to worry.' When she's gone I lie down again, wondering if Ellie's remembered to get her football kit ready for tomorrow and if Daniel has his Grade 8 piano exam this week, or is it next week? I know I've still not sorted anything for his birthday.

The doctor comes back. 'Well Mrs Barrett, your bloods are fine and your heart's normal.'

'So what happens now?'

'You're free to go home,' she says. 'See your GP in a couple of days, get some rest.' I sigh, relieved I've not had a heart attack and I can still do the interviews.

'Will this take the pain away?' I ask, taking a prescription from her.

'Hopefully it will help.' She opens the curtain and, before I've stepped down from the bed, she's gone.

Back in the waiting area, Mike's at a vending machine.

'I'm okay,' I say. He hugs me. 'Just a bit of blood pressure, that's all.'

He wipes his forehead and heaves a sigh. 'That's good, let's get you home.'

Six

The brief relief I felt at the hospital is replaced in the morning by a dull ache. I check my calendar and remember today's interviews.

'You won't tell David?' I ask Mike, when we're having breakfast.

'Of course not,' he says, 'he doesn't need to know anything.'

After Mike leaves for work, I phone Doctor Berry's surgery. The receptionist tells me I can't see Doctor Berry but I can have an appointment with a locum, at 10 am.

In the surgery waiting room, I read a poster about the benefits of getting outside in the winter months. The screen on the wall displays my name and I go to Room 2. The doctor, sitting in Doctor Berry's chair, smiles at me.

'I went to A&E last night,' I explain, 'in a lot of pain.'

'And what did they tell you?' He's staring at his screen and speaks in a serious tone, it's different to Dr Berry's Irish lilt.

'Everything's fine,' I sigh, 'but I have high blood pressure.'

The doctor taps his keyboard, still looking at the screen. 'And you're taking the tablets?'

'Yes.' My chair's uncomfortable, whichever way I sit, no position eases my discomfort.

'Do you want a note for work?' he asks. 'Take a week off?'

'I can't take any time off,' I say, 'we're too busy.' He pushes back his chair, jabbing his pen at me.

'You seem a little anxious to me, Mrs Barrett.' He looks at his screen. 'Would you agree?' Am I anxious? I wonder. Busy? definitely. Anxious? I don't think so.

'I just don't feel very well,' I say, 'and the pain's not going away.' He turns to me.

'I'll give you something for your anxiety,' he says, 'and you can take some time off.'

'I can't do that,' I say, 'I can't take any time off.' He taps on his keyboard and a printer rolls out a neat length of paper.

He hands me the prescription. 'Take this to the chemist next door.' I read the text but don't recognise the medication prescribed.

'What will this do?'

'Give it a couple of weeks,' he says, 'you'll notice a

difference.'

'Can't you investigate?' I ask. 'Find out where the pain's coming from?' He shakes his head.

'You're anxious,' he says, 'the tablets will help.' I put my jacket on and head for the door. 'And another thing,' he says, just as I'm about to leave.

I turn back. 'Yes?'

He smiles again. 'Try not to ruminate. It will only make things worse.'

I look at the prescription. 'I've never taken anything like this before.'

He turns back to the screen. 'There's a first time for everything.'

In the corridor, I stuff the prescription in my pocket. Outside, on Railway Street, I pass the chemist without going in. If things get worse I might take the tablets he's prescribed, but not yet.

When I get back to the bar, I go straight to Mike's office.

He gets up from his desk and hugs me. 'Everything okay?'

'Fine,' I say, 'nothing to worry about.'

'So you can still do the interviews this afternoon?'

I nod. 'Of course.'

'Great,' he says, 'David will meet us there.'

'You won't tell him I'm not well, will you?'

'No,' he says, 'don't worry.'

I go back into my office and lay my head on the desk. I wish I could have seen Dr Berry, at least he knows me. He's been my doctor since I moved to Thornsea when I was 18. He confirmed both pregnancies. I saw him last March. The new medication made me feel much better. When I went back for a repeat prescription, in December, he said I couldn't have it anymore.

'You'll have to get used to this now,' he said, 'it's just part of getting older.'

In the afternoon Mike and I drive to Liverpool for the bar manager interviews. I'm nervous David will notice I'm not well. I'm wearing more makeup than usual: brown eyeshadow and pink blusher as well as the usual tinted moisturiser, mascara and lip tint.

'Do you think David will suspect anything?' I ask Mike, inspecting my face in the passenger mirror.

'No,' he says, 'you look terrific.'

When we get to the bar David's waiting outside.

'Ruth,' he says, smiling and kissing me on the cheek, 'you're looking well.'

I look at Mike. 'Thanks,' I say, hoping these interviews

will be over quickly.

During the interviews David and Mike do most of the talking while I sit, quietly, taking notes and checking documents. When all three candidates have left I let David and Mike discuss the merits of each one.

David's pleased we've found a good manager for his bar.

'Let me treat you both to dinner,' he says, as we're locking up, 'we need to celebrate.' I look at Mike willing him to decline the offer.

Mike grabs my hand. 'Great idea. Where do you have in mind?'

David takes us to a fine dining restaurant where he knows the maitre'd. We go upstairs to a private dining room. David orders a bottle of *Dom Perignon*, to toast another milestone for the partnership.

'You know what I like about you two?' David says, as we're clinking glasses. 'You're both grafters, like me. You work hard so you can play hard.'

'That's us,' Mike says, 'we've never been afraid of hard work, have we love?'

I smile. I want to get back home so I can get to bed.

When we're on our way home Mike can't stop smiling, beaming from ear to ear.

'You look happy,' I say.

'Of course I am,' he says, 'I'm excited. Aren't you?'

I have a sick feeling in my stomach and my whole back is a mass of dull aching. 'I guess so.'

'I mean look at David's life,' Mike says, 'all that's about to be ours.'

Seven

At 4 am I wake, with a headache and coughing. Mike has his back to me but, from the sound of his breathing, he's in a deep sleep. Swallowing hurts. Careful not to disturb him, I go downstairs to the kitchen. In the medicine drawer, I find cough syrup, a year out of date. At the back of a cupboard, a half jar of honey. In the fridge, a single lemon. Under the island, I find an unopened bottle of Irish whiskey, left over from Christmas. I pour a generous amount into hot water and drop in three lemon slices. It warms my throat.

It's no use going back to bed. I go to my coat and fish out the prescription from yesterday. I try to pronounce the name, three times, but I still can't get it right. I'm not anxious, just in pain and I need to ease it. Didn't Jean used to have one of those lavender wheat pillows you put in the microwave? If I get one of those it might do the trick. Or I could see a chiropractor. A new one has opened near the train station. I take the prescription to the kitchen bin.

With my slipper on the peddle I rip the paper into tiny pieces and drop it over three avocado stones.

There's a lot to do today: call the new bar manager to arrange their start date, book interviews for the rest of the staff and do the payroll. I check last night's takings at our bars. It's all good and no one's reported in sick, yet. At seven Mike comes downstairs. I'm on my second coffee.

'How you feeling today?' he asks, smiling.

I lie. 'Not bad.'

When I'm at the sink, Mike puts his arms around my waist. 'Our dreams are coming true babe,' he says, 'we're about to hit the big time.'

'We're not there yet,' I say, 'David's expecting a good return.'

Mike goes to the coffee machine. 'I know that,' he says, 'and he'll get it.'

Daniel and Ellie come downstairs, make their own breakfasts and go into the lounge. Mike and I sit in silence. He taps on his phone, sighing and shaking his head.

'Can't you turn those notifications off?' I snap. 'I have a headache.'

'It's the builder,' he says, 'he's found another problem.'

'Big or little?' I ask, knowing we can't afford even little problems at this stage.

Mike shrugs his shoulders. 'Don't know. He'll tell me

later.'

When we arrive at the bar, we go to our separate offices. I watch the clock tick round to half past eight and call Doctor Berry's surgery.

'Doctor Berry's retired now,' the receptionist tells me, 'but we've got a locum.' I can have an appointment at 11 am.

I get through the urgent tasks on my to-do list before going to see Mike.

'I made another appointment,' I say.

He looks up and frowns. 'But I thought you were okay.'

'I'm still not right. Maybe I need a scan.'

He shakes his head. 'Have you called the new bar manager?' He needs to start ASAP.'

'Yes,' I say, 'he can start next week.'

'And the payroll? Have you done that?'

'All done.' I close the door and lean on the wall outside his office. If I can just get through March, see David's bar open and do this talk, I can take a break.

Walking eases the pain, so much that as I reach the surgery, I wonder if I really do need an appointment. But as I sit down in the waiting room the pain descends, like a heavy cloak, stabbing and jabbing into every muscle.

My appointment's in Room 2 again, but it's a different

doctor to the one I saw yesterday.

'Mrs Barrett,' she says, cheerily, 'how can I help?'

I sit down and begin to explain. 'It started a few weeks ago,' I say, 'I felt a pain in my neck.' She types as I talk. There's a lot to tell and I want to make sure she knows all the details. 'And now the pain's all over my body,' I continue.

'But where exactly?' she asks.

I move my hand around to show her the different parts. 'Everywhere.'

She stops typing and turns to me. 'You'll need to tell me where exactly,' she says, 'you have to be more specific.'

'It's everywhere,' I say, my hand doing another circuit around my body. She pushes back her chair. Her face tells me she's concerned and I'm overcome with relief. I feel my body relax. I'm getting somewhere at last.

'You were here yesterday,' she says, looking directly at me.

I nod. 'Yes.'

'And the doctor gave you something,' she says, 'for your anxiety.'

'Yes, but I haven't taken them.'

'Why not?' she says, sharply.

'I'm scared. I've never taken anything like that before.'

She shakes her head, and I feel as if I'm about to be told

off. 'Then I can't help you,' she says. 'If you won't help yourself.'

I feel my muscles stiffen and the stabbing in my back returns. 'Can I have a scan please?'

She shakes her head again. 'What for?'

'To put my mind at rest.'

She takes a deep breath, releases a long sigh and points to the door. 'Mrs Barrett,' she says, 'I have at least three other patients waiting and you've taken 15 minutes of my time already.'

I've not explained myself clearly enough, obviously. 'Is there anything you can do?' She comes out from her desk and goes to the door.

'I'm afraid not,' she says, opening the door for me.

I walk back to the Beach Road bar slowly, thinking about the remaining staff I need to hire for David's bar. I know he'll be expecting an update and I'm behind schedule.

When I get to my desk I call two people who might make good front-of-house staff and arrange to see them next week.

At one o'clock, exhausted, I go into Mike's office.

'Taking the doctor's advice,' I say, 'having a few days off.'

Mike keeps his eyes on his screen. 'You arranged the rest

of the interviews?'

'Two,' I say, 'the rest will have to wait.'

'We should have everyone hired by now,' he says, 'we're leaving it far too late.'

'I'll be better in a couple of days. I just need some rest.'

'See you at home then,' he says, not looking up.

Back at home Jean's in the kitchen. 'What are you doing back so early?' she shouts out, as I'm hanging up my coat.

'Not feeling too good,' I shout back, 'taking a couple of days off?' She comes into the hall.

'Can you afford to right now?' she says, trying to feel my forehead.

'Not really,' I say, stepping back to avoid her palm. I go upstairs. Near the middle of the stairs I fall to my knees. My limbs stretch out and my head presses against the sisal stair-runner. I hear Jean running into the hall.

'What on Earth are you doing?' she shouts.

I moan in agony. 'I can't move.'

'Well try,' she says, 'you can't stay there all day.'

I try to lift myself but it's no use, I'm stuck. 'Just leave me here for a bit,' I say, taking deep breaths.

After a few minutes, I pull myself up with a roar.

She shakes her head. 'What was that all about?'

'I think I need to go back to A&E,' I say, easing myself down each stair.

She folds her arms. 'Are you sure?'

'I'm sure. Can you drive me there? Please?'

Jean's car is smaller than ours and lowering myself into the front passenger seat is uncomfortable. She calls Mike while we're still on the drive.

'We'll let you know if it's anything serious,' she says.

'Good job you're there Mum,' Mike says through the speaker.

I close my eyes and stay silent.

Eight

When I wake it's 12.24 pm. I must have slept for 12 hours. I'm back at home, in our bed. I've been given the same diagnosis by a different doctor. My bloods are fine. She said I shouldn't be coming to A&E. She told me I needed to see my own doctor from now on.

Mike comes in with a mug of tea. 'Thought I'd see if you were awake.'

I pull myself up and reach for the mug. 'How come you're not working?'

'I should be,' he says, 'I need to see you're okay.'

'Still here,' I say, 'not sure why.'

He lies beside me, on top of the duvet, resting on his side. 'They've told you you're absolutely fine, there's nothing wrong.'

I turn over and pull the duvet over my head. 'So why do I feel like this?'

'I'll get back to work,' he says, 'Mum said she'll come over, keep an eye on you.'

A few hours later I'm wide-awake staring at the ceiling. There's a knock on the door.

Jean shouts from the landing. 'Made you some chicken soup.'

Before I answer she's opened the door, bringing soup and a copy of the County Herald. I can't face the soup.

'I'm not hungry,' I say, turning over.

'It's probably the flu,' she says, closing the door behind her.

When I know she's downstairs I sit up and reach for the paper. On page five a headline catches my eye: *Dismissed by the Doctors but I had a Terminal Illness.*

I don't read any further because, in that instant, something changes. Like the flick of a switch. I knew it. I get out of bed, throw on yesterday's clothes and call a taxi.

I watch for the taxi from the balcony. When it pulls up outside our house I run downstairs, hoping I can get out without Jean seeing me leave. As I open the front door she's coming out of the kitchen.

'Where are you off to? I thought you were ill.'

'I am,' I say, 'going to A&E. Can you tell Mike for me?'

She follows me up the drive. 'Tell him what?' she shouts.

'My taxi's here,' I shout back, without turning around, 'tell him I know what's wrong.'

When I arrive at Thornsea General I make my way to the reception desk. I recognise the woman behind the screen from the other night.

'I know what's wrong now,' I say, 'I need a bed.' I have to wait my turn, like everyone else, even though time is not on my side.

When I've had my blood pressure taken I pace up and down next to a wall filled with posters. Each one shows different diagrams and symptoms of diseases. I'm sure I have at least two of those displayed. For a change of scenery, I go into a corridor. Two cleaners are chatting about their pensions. How lucky they are, knowing they'll live long enough to get one. When they leave, I imagine what will happen when I finally see the doctor. I'll be taken to a quiet room and my diagnosis will be confirmed. I'll be told how many weeks, no, days I have left. Time is of the essence now and, while I can still hold a conversation, there are options to be discussed.

Nine

When I'm taken to a bay it's the same doctor I saw last night.

'Oh it's you again,' she says, 'what's the matter this time?' After being told yesterday I shouldn't be coming to A&E, I'm sure she'll appreciate me getting straight to the point. There's no need to go back to the beginning, describing everything in detail. I have a diagnosis now, that's all she needs to know.

'It's terminal,' I say.

'Let's take some bloods,' she says. We go through the same routine. I turn my head away while a nurse takes a sample.

When the doctor's back she's smiling. 'Nothing to worry about Mrs Barrett. Your bloods are fine.'

I put my head in my hands and sob. 'But, but, I can't be fine.'

'You're anxious,' she says, 'you need to stop worrying so much. Take a few days off.'

I lie back. 'Please let me stay here,' I beg, 'please. I need a bed.'

'We can't do that,' she says, pulling back the curtain. I curl up on the bed. Outside the bay, I hear her talking with two others. I won't need a bed for long. Surely they can wheel me to a quiet room and give me something? That's all I need.

The doctor comes back. 'You can go home now Mrs Barrett,' she says, tapping me gently on the arm.

I stay curled up. 'Please? Can I have a scan?'

The doctor takes my hands and pulls them slowly towards her. My arms are weak, against her strength.

'You shouldn't be coming here Mrs Barrett. You need to go home.'

'But I'm in pain. Everywhere.'

'Then see your own doctor,' she says, abruptly. She follows me out of the bay and into the waiting area.

In the car park I see I have a missed call from Mike. I call him back.

'Where are you? What's going on?'

'I'm at A&E again.'

'What's the matter now?'

'It's terminal,' I say, 'I don't have long left.'

His tone changes. 'Oh God, is that what they said?' I don't reply. Instead, I end the call without saying goodbye. Conversations are tiring now and I need to conserve my energy for the taxi ride home.

When I get home everyone's sitting in the kitchen, eating fish pie.

'We were worried about you,' Jean says, looking at Mike. She picks up an empty plate and turns to me. 'Will you have something?'

I stay in the doorway. 'I'm not hungry.'

Mike comes into the hall, closing the door behind him. 'What did they say?'

'They say there's nothing wrong, but I know there is.'

He takes me into the lounge and sits me on the sofa. 'Ruth, this stops now.'

'They're wrong,' I say, 'they won't give me a scan.'

He stands up. 'For God's sake woman,' he says, 'we're all getting tired of this.'

When Mike goes out Ellie comes into the lounge and sits beside me. 'Mum, are you okay?' I wipe my eyes.

'No love, I'm not,' I say, 'I don't have long left.' Mike comes back.

'What are you up to?' he says, standing over me, his arms folded.

'What?'

'Telling Ellie you don't have long left.'

'It's true,' I say, 'I don't.' I go to bed and climb under

the duvet, without getting undressed.

Mike comes into the bedroom a few minutes later.

'It's Daniel's birthday tomorrow,' he says, 'you'll have to get yourself right for that.' I sit up immediately, throw back the covers and head for the door. Mike puts his hand out and holds the door handle.

'I've not got anything for Daniel,' I say, trying to pull his hand away, 'I need to go to the shops.'

'It's okay,' he says, 'Mum's sorted everything. Just get yourself better for tomorrow. Okay?'

And the next day, Daniel's 17th birthday, I am a little better. I'm awake before the alarm goes off. When I go downstairs there's a grand piano novelty birthday cake on the kitchen island and two giant gold balloons shaped in a one and a seven. When Daniel comes downstairs I give him a big hug.

'Thanks for this mum,' he says, punching each balloon. I feel guilty for not organising my own son's birthday.

'It's all Grandma Jean's work,' I say, 'she did all this.' He opens our card and takes out ten twenty-pound notes.

He waves the cash. 'Thanks. Just what I needed.'

When Mike, Daniel and Ellie leave the house I go into the lounge and lie on the sofa. I watch TV, until Jean lets herself in, around two.

'You'd better get upstairs,' she says, 'Daniel won't want his friends seeing you like this.' I lift myself off the sofa and go upstairs, while Jean gets the vacuum. I lie on the bed for an hour, then drag myself into the en suite.

After my shower, I change into the *Boden* dress I wore on Christmas Day, dry my hair and apply some lip gloss and mascara. Everything seems to take twice as long as usual but I want to look nice for Daniel and his friends. While I can still celebrate with the family I want to make an effort. This will be the last time I get to see my son blow out his birthday candles. I want to make it special.

When I get downstairs Daniel's in the lounge, sitting at the piano. Two of his friends are sitting on the sofas, tuning guitars, while another is using the coffee table as a drum kit. Mike, Jean and Ellie are in the kitchen, picking at the remains of the birthday cake.

I stand by the cake. 'I missed his candles? I can't believe I missed his candles.'

'We didn't think you'd want to come down,' Jean says, 'with the state you're in.' Mike pulls out a stool for me.

'Why didn't you call me? I've spent ages getting ready.'

'Sorry love,' Mike says, 'we thought it best to leave you up there.' Ellie starts to reassemble the cake, pressing the keys and the lid together.

'It's okay Mum,' she says, 'we can do it again.' She goes into the lounge and comes back with Daniel and his friends. 'Put the candles back on,' she says, 'Mum's here now.'

After singing *Happy Birthday* we all move into the lounge. Daniel and his friends are rehearsing for their next gig and they want us to hear their latest song.

'You look lovely,' Jean says, when the band takes a break, 'it's good to see you making an effort.'

When his friends are leaving one of them stops by a framed picture in the hall. It's one I painted of Thornsea pier, in 1991.

'My mum did that,' Daniel says, proudly.

'It's brilliant,' his friend says, 'I didn't know you were a painter Mrs B.'

'Oh that was a long time ago,' I say, 'I don't paint anymore.'

'You should,' his friend says.

When we opened the Beach Road bar, in 1993, I asked Mike if I could put some of my landscapes in the bathrooms but he said 'No'. He said they wouldn't fit in with the sports bar image. Most of my landscapes are in the attic now.

Ten

I wake in the early hours, in the same dress I wore for Daniel's birthday. When the alarm goes off Mike goes into the en suite without saying a word. Back in the bedroom, he gets dressed, in silence. Later, I hear him chatting with Daniel and Ellie downstairs.

When the front door closes, and I know the house is empty, I go down to the kitchen. On the wall calendar, stuck on the fridge, I turn the page to March. It's still there, on the square for March 18th: *MUM'S TALK.* I should be having another rehearsal with Olivia today but I'll have to cancel. I find a thick black marker in the drawer and scribble until the words disappear. I need to make a phone call. Olivia takes my decision calmly.

'Okay Ruth,' she says, 'but why not?'

'I'm not going to be here.'

'You're going to be away?'

'No, I'm not going to be here at all,' I explain. My mind drifts forward to Saturday March 18th. Will it all be over by then?

'What do you mean?' Olivia asks.

'It's not good news,' I say, 'I've not got long left.' There's silence at her end. I trace my fingers over the calendar days, wondering how many I have left.

'I don't know what to say. I'm so sorry,' she says, 'how are you?' I wander into the hall and stand in front of the full-length mirror.

'Managing,' I say. Traces of mascara remain from last night, It makes me look better than I feel.

'If there's anything I can do, anything at all,' she says, 'don't hesitate to call me.'

'Sorry to let you down,' I say, 'and thanks for everything.'

'Can I come to see you?' she asks.

'No,' I say, staring at my reflection, 'sorry.' I don't want to see many people now, not when I'm deteriorating quickly.

After the call, I search for a new notebook. There are three in my bedside drawer, presents from Christmas. I select one with the most sombre design: purple flowers on a navy background. On the first page, I write an index:

Password and Login Codes

Bank Details

Insurance and Pensions

Service

Reception

I pull the chair from my dressing table to the wardrobe. Holding the wardrobe door I climb onto the chair. There's an ornate box on top of the wardrobe. It holds memorabilia from our wedding. My arms hurt but I'm able to pull it, slowly, towards me and lower it onto the bed. Lifting the lid, I take out our wedding album. Underneath I find a wedding booklet. On the next page in the notebook I write:

SERVICE

Reading - from our wedding:

Proverbs 31. Verse 2 - 31

Hymns - from our wedding:

Love Divine All Loves Excelling

Tell Out My Soul

There's work to sort out too. I'll ask Mike to bring some files home so I can work from bed, for as long as I can.

When Daniel comes home from college, he comes straight upstairs.

'Mum, are you there?' he says, tapping on the door.

'Yes,' I say, 'there are meals in the freezer.' At least

Daniel and Ellie are old enough to look after themselves now. They're both good kids, doing well at college and school. It's a relief and a comfort. I know they'll be independent soon, I'm just sad I won't get to see them as adults. I always imagined helping them get through their exams, dropping them off at university and celebrating graduations. I only managed to get Daniel through his GCSE exams last year. They'll have to rely on Mike and Jean now. Perhaps, if I have the energy, I can start another notebook, with home-making tips and recipes.

When Mike's home, around eight, he comes upstairs.

'How've you been today?' he asks. He ruffles his hair, releasing remnants of a day spent with builders. Specks of dust from bricks and MDF fall on the carpet.

'Not too good. How's the bar coming on?'

'Almost done.' He takes off his jacket. 'We should be ready by opening night.'

'And the budget?'

'Don't worry about that.'

'How's David?'

'Happy,' he says, 'but we need to start organising the grand opening - we were thinking the 11th.'

'My birthday?'

'Oh yes,' he says, smiling, 'so it is.'

I don't mind. It's unlikely I'll be here on my birthday.

In fact, I think, it's an excellent plan. It will give everyone something positive to focus on, instead of being upset about me.

'Of course,' I say, 'that's a great idea.'

Mike hands me an A4 notepad and pen. 'Can you start getting a guest list ready then?' he asks, going into the en suite.

When he comes out of the shower I hand him my own notebook.

'You've started already?' he says, 'well done.'

'Not yet,' I say, 'I've been working on something else.'

He stares at my notes and squints his eyes, as if he can't read them. 'What the Hell's this?'

'For the funeral,' I say, 'so you know what I want.' He throws the notebook at me and it hits the headboard, only missing my head by a few inches.

'You're talking rubbish!' he shouts.

'This is important,' I say, trying to hand the notebook back to him. 'Promise me you'll carry out my wishes.' But he puts on his dressing gown and goes downstairs.

When he comes back, half an hour later, I'm writing another list. This time, he snatches the notebook out of my hand. 'What are you up to now?' he shouts.

'Everything you need's in here,' I say, 'please take care of it.' He puts my notebook in his drawer and climbs into bed, turning his back on me.

'I thought you were getting better,' he says, turning off his lamp. This has all come at a very inconvenient time. I hate letting him down like this.

Eleven

At 6.30 am I'm sitting on the bottom stair in the hall, in my heavy winter coat, staring at the letter box. I've been up since four.

When I hear Mike coming down the stairs I get to my feet and hold out the car keys. 'Will you take me into town?'

He shakes his head. 'At this time?' He takes the keys and puts them back on the hook. He goes into the kitchen and I follow.

'I need a lift into town please,' I say. He's at the coffee machine.

'Where do you want to go now?' he asks, wearily.

'To Dobers,' I say, 'get something for Daniel and Ellie.' We always go to Dobers for special jewellery. We got our wedding rings from there. Perhaps for Ellie, a new charm bracelet. For Daniel, the expensive watch we've talked about for his 21st. I'm not going to see his 21st now, not even his 18th. I go into the hall, take the keys off the hook and bring them to Mike.

He sighs. 'They don't need anything.' He puts the keys in his pocket. 'Go back to bed. We're not going anywhere.'

While he's pouring milk into his coffee I reach into his pocket and take the keys. I run to the front door and pull the lock back.

'I'll drive myself then!' I shout. I open the front door and head for the car. He runs out onto the drive and tries to grab the keys just as I reach the car.

'Ruth, please!' he shouts. 'I don't need this right now.' I pull my hand away.

'But I need to get them something.'

'I'm seeing the building inspector this morning,' he says, 'you're going to have to wait.'

I click open the car door and get in the driver's seat. As I'm trying to put the keys in the ignition he snatches them out of my hand.

'Come back in the house,' he says, 'we can talk about it inside.'

I get out of the car. A few daffodils are emerging from the flower beds at the edges of the drive, a sure sign that Spring is on its way. I don't expect I'll be here to see the tulips open.

Mike's at the door. I could walk to Dobers. It might

take a while but I could. But I want him to come too, to help me choose these last gifts for our children, together.

'Ruth!' hc shouts. 'Come back inside! Now!'

I look down at my feet. My legs are hurting. 'Okay,' I say, 'but will you take me to Dobers later? Please?'

When I'm in the hall he leads me into the lounge and sits me in the middle of the sofa.

'Don't you dare move,' he says. He goes upstairs and within minutes he's back with Daniel and Ellie.

Ellie's voice is wavering as she sits by me. 'Mum, are you okay?'

'No I'm not,' I say, 'but Dad's taking me to Dobers.'

Daniel sits on the other side. He holds my hand. I lace my fingers through his, my knuckles aching.

Ellie looks up at Mike, her eyes pink. 'Is she going to be okay Dad?'

I try to reassure them. 'Everything's going to be okay,' I say, 'I'll be free of pain soon.'

Daniel shakes his head. 'What do you mean Mum?'

'Your Dad and Grandma Jean will still be here for you.'

'Okay,' Mike says, pulling me to my feet, 'let's go.'

Daniel follows us outside. 'Will she be okay?'

'I'll call as soon as I can,' Mike says, leading me to the car. I sit in the passenger seat and we listen to the local news. There's a yellow weather warning for this area. On the other side of the road, waves push against the railings, splashing over onto the promenade. Everything's slowly coming together. When the time comes at least I'll know all tasks have been crossed off my list. As we pull out of the drive, Mike indicates right.

'But town's that way,' I say, pointing to the left.' I'm not taking you to town,' he says.

I turn the radio off. 'So where are we going?'

'The hospital,' he says, turning it back on.

Twelve

The doctor I saw at A&E has sent me home. He told me there's nothing they can do for me. I get out of bed and open the curtains. It's still light. The tide's out. I want to go to the beach, to breathe in the sea air, one last time. I find Mike in the kitchen. He looks surprised when he sees me.

'Let's go to the beach,' I say, putting on my jacket.

His face lights up. 'So you believe the doctors now?'

'No,' I say, 'they're wrong.' I take his hand and pull him into the hall.

Across the road, we go down the steps to the beach. There are a few people out. A man with a black labrador and a young couple with a pram.

'I've left all instructions about what to do when I'm gone,' I say, as we reach the water's edge.

Mike pulls his hand away and shakes his head. 'You've been told,' he says, 'there's nothing wrong.' He turns back towards home, his strides getting longer and faster. I have to run to catch up.

'I'm really sorry,' I say, 'leaving you with all this work.' His pace quickens and I'm a few paces behind him again. 'If I'd have known,' I say, catching up again, 'I would have started hiring the team for David's bar earlier.'

We reach the crossing.

'There's nothing wrong with you,' he says, 'just listen to the doctors.'

'Will you tell David I'm sorry for letting you all down?' I knew we should have started hiring for the new bar before Christmas. And now they're going to be having a grand opening with not enough staff. And it will all be my fault.

When we reach home he stops at the top of our drive.

'You can let yourself in,' he says, 'I've things to do.' I go upstairs, stopping every few steps to rest. There must be something I can do to get relief from the pain. Someone who can help me. If they're not going to take me into hospital it must be because there's no point. I've left it too late. Doctors don't waste resources on treatments that aren't going to work. But there is one place I can go. Somewhere I haven't tried yet. I find the number on my phone and press Call.

A kind voice replies. 'Hello, St Kevin's.'

Thirteen

'I'm asking for myself,' I say, 'to come in.'

The kind woman's voice continues. 'One moment, let me take some details.'

I sit on the stairs, relieved to have a solution. We have tins in our bars for St Kevin's. When I agreed to collect for the hospice I didn't expect to need it so soon.

'I won't be needing it for long,' I say, 'just a couple of days.'

'We'll need to contact your doctor,' the woman says, 'we'll be in touch.' I climb into bed and curl up, pulling the duvet to my neck. I imagine my room will be beautiful at St Kevin's. The bed will have soft cotton sheets, just like here at home. There'll be floral wallpaper, or pale blue Toile de Jouy, like in our downstairs loo. And they'll play relaxing music. Most of all they'll be kind, just like the nice woman I've just spoken to.

When I wake, Mike's in the bedroom. His face red, his breathing fast. I wonder if he's been out running. 'What the Hell are you up to?'

I pull myself up. 'What d'you mean?'

'The surgery's called,' he says, between deep breaths, 'they've had a message from the hospice.'

'That was quick,' I say, yawning. But in these situations, there's not much time to lose. 'Do they have a room for me?'

'Get up,' he says, pulling the duvet to the bottom of the bed, 'we need to get going.'

While I was asleep there must have been conversations between the hospice, Doctor Berry's and Mike. I imagine the woman I spoke to would have called the surgery and told them they needed to act quickly. The results from my blood tests have been checked again and errors discovered. It can happen. You read about it all the time. I'm sure everyone's incredibly sorry but thank goodness the mistakes have been spotted.

When we drive past the sign for the hospice I tap on the dashboard. 'You've gone past,' I say, 'it's down there.'

'I know where I'm going,' he says, 'it's this way.'

At Thornsea General Mike pushes in front of me. 'It's my wife. You need to admit her.'

There aren't many people in the waiting area tonight

and I'm pacing up and down, by the wall with the posters. Movement seems to keep the pain at bay. A woman in an anorak and carrying a small rucksack approaches us.

'Ruth,' she says, softly, 'will you come with me?'

We leave Mike and she leads me down a corridor into a small room where we sit on grey plastic chairs.

'I'm a social worker,' she says, 'I'm here to see how we can help you.'

Finally, help has arrived and I'm being listened to. It's taken a while, but I'm going to be taken seriously.

'Thank so much,' I say, 'I need a bed.'

She shakes her head. 'Your doctor says you're suffering from anxiety.'

'I just need to be out of this pain,' I say, 'can you give me something?'

There's a knock at the door. Two women and a man are in the corridor. The social worker steps outside and the four of them start whispering.

The social worker comes back in the room. 'I'm going now Ruth,' she says, 'but these people will help you.'

'Am I staying here?' I ask. But she's gone.

One of the women sits in the chair opposite while the others stand in the doorway. Mike must be wondering what's going on. I wish he were here with me.

'We're going to get you assessed,' the woman says.

'Will they give me some pain relief?' I ask. 'I need pain relief.'

She looks at her two colleagues. They shrug their shoulders. 'You can come voluntarily,' she says, 'or we can make you.'

'You decide,' I say, 'I just want to be out of pain.'

'We can give you something for that,' the man says.

A porter comes with a wheelchair. It's a long way to the ward, up several floors in the lift and along bright corridors. When we get to the ward a nurse shows me my bed. It's in the corner, by the window. There are three other beds, occupied by women who smile and nod to me. When I get into bed, the nurse gives me a large tablet.

'Will this take the pain away?' I say, as she gives me a cup of water.

'It should help,' she says.

I put the tablet on my tongue and gulp it down. 'Can I get a scan please?'

'No,' she says, 'you don't need a scan.'

I study the three other women in the ward and wonder if we're all here with the same condition.

The woman in the bed opposite waves. 'What you in here for?' she asks.

'It's terminal,' I say, 'I won't be here for long.'

Mike comes into the ward and I'm relieved to see him.

He sits in the chair next to my bed.

'Are they going to give me a scan?' I ask. 'To see what it is?'

'I don't think so.'

'They said I'm going somewhere else. Is it the hospice?'

'No,' he says, 'but you'll be looked after.'

Within an hour I'm taken outside to a minibus. Two young men, who look in their mid-twenties, wearing T-shirts showing off their strong arms, help me into the back. One drives and the other rides in the passenger seat. It's dark outside and I can see we're going past South Beach. Just before we reach the dual carriageway we turn into a floodlit car park and stop in front of a two-storey building. All the lights are on upstairs. When I get out Mike's waiting for me.

'They said I can come in with you,' he says, 'until you're settled in.'

'That's nice,' I say, with the two men at my side.

At the top of the stairs, a nurse opens the doors. One of the men hands her a large brown envelope. They leave us and go back downstairs, while Mike and I go through into a lounge. There's a TV on the wall with the sound turned down showing the late evening news.

'Are you going to tell David about the budget?' I ask. 'He needs to know.'

'It's all sorted,' Mike says, 'I've told him.'

'And?'

'Don't worry,' he says, 'I'm looking after all that now.'

Ten minutes later, a nurse comes in.

'Is this the hospice?' I ask when she sits down with us.

She chuckles. 'No, it's an assessment ward. C'mon, I'll show you where you're sleeping.'

Mike gets up and hugs me. 'I'll head back now. I'll come back tomorrow, bring you some things.'

'Thanks,' I say, 'sorry about all this.'

I watch as another nurse escorts him off the ward. I feel so bad for letting him down, at such a busy time. I follow the nurse down the corridor and she leads me to a large doorway.

'It's the first bay on the left,' she says.

My eyes adjust to the darkness. 'I don't have my own room?' I say, realising I'm at the top of a long dormitory.

'Not here,' she says, turning back towards the lounge.

In my bay, I have three shelves, a low bed with cotton sheets and a woollen blanket. The nurse brings me some blue cotton pyjamas.

'You can have these,' she says, 'till your husband brings you some clothes from home.'

All through the night the curtain to my bay opens and closes, disturbing my sleep. At first, I think it's another patient. I'm afraid, so I hide my head under the covers. After the fifth time, I shout out hoping they'll go away. On the sixth time, I'm sitting up, waiting for them. When the curtain's pulled back it's the nurse who gave me the pyjamas. I smile at her, but she just looks at me, then closes the curtain. I look around my small bay. The grey curtain and pale green walls make everything look dark and dreary. This isn't how I expected to spend my final days. Alone in this dormitory.

Fourteen

In the morning my throat feels tight and my jaw aches. I try to make a noise but there's nothing, just the faint sound of air. My voice must have gone but I'm not surprised, it was only a matter of time. There's a small holdall on the shelves. Inside Mike's packed two pairs of pyjamas, my dressing gown, underwear, socks, slippers, soap, a face cloth, a towel, a toothbrush, toothpaste and lip balm. I check my watch: 11.45 am.

Twenty minutes later the curtain opens again.

'Coming for lunch?' a nurse asks. I turn over, pretending to be asleep. I hear her footsteps going into the corridor.

When I think the dormitory is empty I slide my feet into my sheepskin slippers and go to the window. It's small and narrow, with thick metal bars on the outside. At the very top there's an opening, about half a centimetre, too high for me to reach. There's another two-storey building on the other side of the car park. That one looks more modern than the one I'm in. In the distance, I can see the hills. When I see Mike again I'll ask him to take me up there for a drive, I hope I have time for one last drive in the country.

While I'm at the window, I hear someone behind me. A young woman is smiling and I smile back. She's thin, with long wavy pink hair.

'Hello,' she says, 'I'm Sophie, what's your name?' I touch my throat and shake my head. 'You've lost your voice?' she says. I nod. She goes into another bay and comes back with a giant purple pencil and a white envelope. 'Can you write?' There's a small table at the top of the dormitory, by the bathroom. I take the pencil and envelope. She follows me to the table. 'What's your name?'

RUTH, I write.

'How old are you?'

46

'Do you have children?'

YES

'Are you coming for something to eat?'

NO

'I can get you something and bring it back?'

NO THANKS

'Can you try?' she says. I shake my head. 'There's soup,'

she says, 'I'll see if one of the nurses can put it in a cup.' She leaves the dormitory and comes back with a nurse carrying a mug with a straw.

The nurse hands me the mug. 'I've watered it down,' she says, 'you should be able to drink it.'

I take the mug. The soup is lukewarm but comforting. The pain in my jaw feels a little less intense than before.

At five o'clock, I'm sitting on my bed. Sophie pulls back the heavy grey curtain.

'It's teatime,' she says, 'are you coming?' I nod. I don't have an appetite but seeing as she's come for me it would be rude to refuse.

In the dining area, Sophie takes me to a stainless-steel trolley where we collect our trays and cutlery.

'Take these over there,' she says, pointing to a food trolley, 'you can choose what you want.'

At the hot food trolley I point to the containers and a nurse serves me rice and chilli con carne. I sit next to Sophie at the long table with the other patients.

At each wall, I notice there's a nurse, arms behind their backs, eyes staring at a fixed point on the opposite wall. I tap Sophie's arm and point to each of the four nurses.

'They're watching us,' she says.

'What for?' I whisper.

'You're talking!' she says. I smile. My voice is still here, faint and weak, but for how much longer, I don't know. 'We're being watched all the time,' she says, 'one of them will be watching you now.'

'Who's watching me?' I say, looking around.

'You have to look closely to find yours,' she says.

I watch all four but I've no idea who's watching me. It's reassuring. It makes sense that I need to be watched constantly. I must be declining so quickly, they'll need to look out for signs of my demise. That must be why someone is peering into my bay all day and night. Things are becoming a little clearer with every hour. This must be where the doctors assess how quickly we're all declining.

After dinner, I go back to the dormitory and lie on my bed, exhausted. Listening to the other patients' conversations is tiring. On the other side of my curtain, I hear women chatting.

'That one's terminal,' I hear one say.

The curtain to my bay opens. This time, the nurse speaks.

'Meds times,' she says, cheerily. I sit up, waiting for her to give me my medication. C'mon then?' she says, impatiently, 'you have to go to the clinic yourself.'

I get up slowly, my limbs aching. I'm the last one to join the queue. Each patient takes their turn going in.

The clinic is a brightly lit room with a sink, two fridges, three stainless steel trolleys, one pad-locked cupboard, a weighing scale and a height chart. I'm given three tablets and a cup of water. After I gulp them down I'm measured and weighed.

'I think I'm losing weight,' I say, as I step off the scales.

'Yes, that can happen,' the nurse says, tapping into her *iPad.* When a person is in decline they're going to lose weight. The continuing pain, the losing weight, the incredible tiredness - it's all to be expected at this stage.

When I leave the clinic I go back to the dormitory and to the window at the bottom. Through the thick bars I watch people go to their cars and drive off. It's stuffy and stale in here. I press my face close to the window hoping to catch some air from the outside. Nothing reaches my lungs. If I was at home I could be on our balcony right now looking out towards the sea. I turn around and see a nurse behind me.

'Can I go outside?' I ask. 'I need some fresh air.'

'Not until you've seen the doctor.'

'When will that be?'

'Later this week,' she says.

I expect the doctor will know whether fresh air is a good idea or not, given the state of my health. Fresh air might be too much for my lungs to take now.

A piercing whistle blasts from the ceiling. The nurse runs out of the dormitory. I follow her, as quickly as I can, to see what's going on. If this is a fire alarm I'm not staying in here. When I get into the corridor I see two nurses in the doorway to the shower room.

One of them shouts to me. 'Get back in the dormitory please.'

'Was that the fire alarm?'

'Nothing to worry about!' she shouts back. 'Just get back to the dormitory.'

I go back to the window. The shrilling whistle lingers in my ears. Sophie comes in.

'What was that?' I ask her.

'Someone being attacked,' she says, 'happens all the time.'

'They say I'm seeing the doctor soon,' I say, 'to see if I can have fresh air.'

She shakes her head. 'You mean the psychiatrist?'

'No the doctor,' I say, 'they'll know if my lungs can take it. You know, with the state I'm in?'

'You'll be seeing a psychiatrist,' she says. A psychiatrist? Like *Frasier Crane* on the TV? Mike and I used to love watching that when we lived in the flat. *Doctor Frasier Crane* was always a good listener and gave good advice. Things are gradually making sense about why I'm here.

When you're coming to terms with something like this, you need someone like *Frasier Crane* to talk to. Someone who's a good listener, someone to help you process what's happened and help you prepare for what's coming. I lie on my bed and imagine myself talking to the psychiatrist, stretched on a chaise longue or a soft leather couch.

Fifteen

I'm having breakfast with Sophie, four days later, when a nurse rests his hand on my shoulder.

'You've got your meeting with the doctor now,' he says, 'and your husband's here.' I finish my coffee and follow him into the corridor. I know why Mike's here. This will be where I'm told how much time I have left. We'll probably be in a small quiet office, just Mike, me and a doctor.

It's a large room with long tables arranged around the sides. Mike smiles when he sees me and I cross the room to sit with him. A minute later a woman comes in and switches on a projector, illuminating a large square on a white wall. She sits at a table and opens the laptop.

'I think the doctor's running late,' the nurse says.

We wait for five minutes until the door swings open and a small woman enters, shaking a damp umbrella. She's about my age, I guess, mid-forties, slim, with short, spiky, jet-black hair. She throws a black leather briefcase on the table and folds a long, navy mac over a chair. I have a similar one at home, in beige. I wonder if we got it from the same place.

'Traffic's terrible,' she sighs, sitting next to the nurse, 'how long is Dr P off?' The nurse shrugs his shoulders. 'Do you have any notes for me?'

The nurse passes her a folder. We wait in silence as she reads.

In the five days I've been here I've been poked and prodded by so many doctors and nurses, more than I've seen before. I've had pads stuck to my chest and vials of blood taken from my arm. But no scan, though I ask for one every day. Perhaps this doctor will agree I can have one or tell me the results of all the tests I've had.

She looks up, over frameless glasses. 'I understand you run bars,' she says.

'Yes, that's right.' I say, quietly.

'Can you speak up please?' she says.

The nurse leans towards her and mumbles.

'Yes, that's right,' Mike says.

'It would help this meeting if you could speak a little louder please,' she says.

I clear my throat. 'I'll try,' I say, louder.

'That's better,' she says, 'and your husband's here?' She gestures towards Mike. I nod. 'So you have a happy life at home.'

I look at Mike and he nods in agreement. 'Yes,' he says, 'we have a very happy life, don't we?' He smiles as he reaches for my hand.

'Yes,' I say, smiling at him. We wait as she returns to her notes.

'So I'm sure you'd rather be back at home,' she says, 'with your family.' I must admit, spending my final days in a dormitory isn't how I imagined things would end. Perhaps going home is the best option for me now.

'Perhaps that's best,' I say. The doctor grins. I look at Mike for some assistance but he just smiles and shrugs his shoulders 'If you want me to go home,' I say, 'I will.'

'Splendid,' she says.

'But are you sending me for a scan first?' I ask. 'I need a scan to know where this pain's coming from.'

She throws her head back and laughs. 'There has to be a good reason to send you for a scan,' she says, 'and right now, we don't have one.'

There are two minutes of silence while she reads her notes. The nurse smiles at us. The woman at the laptop waits.

Eventually, the doctor takes off her glasses and rubs the bridge of her nose.

'I think it's a case of Munchausen syndrome' she says

to the nurse. The nurse nods.

'It's not,' I say, protesting, 'I'm in pain. Why would I lie about being in pain?' I stand up and pull my hand away from Mike's.

'Sit down love,' he says, 'don't cause a scene.'

'Listen to your husband,' the doctor says, 'he's trying to help you.' I sit down and Mike rubs my back. Although it's gentle, his touch still hurts. I arch my back inwards, away from his hand.

'Tell her,' I plead with Mike, 'tell her I'm not lying.'

'I'll double her medication,' the doctor says, abruptly. She looks over her glasses again. 'I was going to send you home, but perhaps it's better to send you to a treatment ward.'

'Did you hear that?' Mike says. 'They're sending you for some treatment, that's got to be good news.'

'So I'm not going to die at home now?'

'Speak up please,' the doctor shouts.

'I'd rather spend my last days at home,' I say, 'with my family.'

The doctor takes a long deep breath through her nose. I watch her nostrils flare out and in.

'I'm afraid you don't have a choice,' she says.

I look at Mike. 'Can you take me home now please?'

'I'm sorry love,' he says, 'I can't.'

'But I want to die at home.'

'You're not going to die,' he says, 'you have to trust us.'

The doctor stands up, making the chair legs scrape against the floor.

'Ruth,' she says sternly, 'I can assure you, you are not dying.'

'And the pain?'

'There's no pain either,' she says.

I sense her frustration. 'So what's the medication for?' I ask.

'There'll be a room ready for you tonight,' she says, 'you can get your things ready now.'

'Is there fresh air there?' I ask. 'I'm sure I'd feel better if I could get some fresh air.'

She laughs again. 'Yes,' she says. She gathers her belongings and leaves the room.

The nurse walks with us to the end of the corridor until we come to a locked door.

'I'll come and visit as soon as I can,' Mike says, 'but we're behind with the bar. We need to catch up if we're going to open on time.'

'It's okay,' I say. I feel guilty for leaving him with so much work. This really has come at a very inconvenient time.

'By the way,' he says, finding his car keys, 'have you

been to the café here?'

I shake my head. 'I'm not allowed out.'

'The contract's coming up for renewal,' he says, 'we should consider it.'

The nurse unlocks the door. 'I think Ruth needs some rest now.'

Mike steps into the corridor. 'I'll come back tomorrow,' he says, 'bring some more clothes.'

I go back to the dormitory and put my few belongings in the holdall. I wait in my bay, lying on my bed, until a nurse comes to take me to the treatment ward.

As I'm leaving the ward I see Sophie at the table, reading a magazine.

'I'm off now,' I say, going over.

She closes her magazine. 'They're letting you go home?'

'Not home,' I say, 'treatment ward. Whatever that means.'

Sophie smiles. 'It's that what the psychiatrist said?'

The doctor I saw was nothing like *Frasier Crane*. 'No,' I say, 'I haven't seen a psychiatrist yet.'

She looks puzzled. 'I might see you over there myself.'

When we get outside I stop to fill my lungs with the cold night air. I don't know when I'll have a chance to breathe in anything this fresh again. We walk across the car park to the modern building I've been watching from the window. We step into a huge foyer and I see a café, a shop and a long reception desk. It reminds me of an airport.

When we reach my ward the nurse presses a doorbell. We wait for a minute until another nurse unlocks the door. He hands his colleague a large brown envelope then leaves us. This is Seagull Ward. I know because there's a painting of a seagull underneath large blue letters.

'Come with me,' the nurse says, his face expressionless. He has a shaved head and a protruding stomach. I try to look into his eyes, but he's looking at my holdall. 'We'll have to take a look at all this,' he says. I follow him down a dark corridor. In a small room he points to my bag. 'If you can put it on here.' I empty the contents onto a table. He holds up each item of my toiletries and underwear, laying them out carefully on the table. 'You can pack it away now,' he says, when my bag's empty. He watches as I put everything back as quickly as I can. I follow him along another brightly lit corridor. We go through a large lounge with leather chairs and a TV. At the far end there are three dining tables. Four women sit on chairs around the edge, staring into space. One of them, a young girl about Ellie's age, has a deep red mark in the middle of her forehead. We leave the lounge and continue along another corridor until the nurse stops at a door. He swipes a small white plastic card and I go in. In the bedroom there are some shelves, a TV, behind a glass screen, a bed and a lamp. To the left, there's a wet room with a toilet, a sink and a shower.' You'll need to sign these papers.' He hands me an envelope and a pen. I sit on the bed and take out the papers, stapled together. There are a lot of words to read. Too many for me to process. My mind is slower than usual so I skip the long paragraphs and sign on the dotted line.

After he's left I close the door and change into clean pyjamas. The plastic duvet cover and bottom sheet are slippery. The duvet slips out of the cover whenever I move. I miss my cotton sheets from home. When I see Mike next I'll ask him to bring some new bedding. If I'm going to die here, at least let me die in nice bedding. Stretching out my hand, between the wall and the bed base, my fingers go under the mattress and I feel something thin, cold and hard. I switch on the bedside lamp to see what I'm holding. A razor blade.

Still holding the blade between my fingers I find my slippers and go back to the Nurses office. The one who showed me my room comes to the door.

'I found this under my bed,' I say, holding out the blade. He takes it from me and inspects it, nodding his head. There's another nurse sitting at a desk, reading a large monitor.

'Thc other one must have left something behind,' he chuckles to his colleague. He turns back to me. 'Is that all then?'

'No,' I say.

He sighs. 'What else do you want?'

'Can I get some water please?' He grabs a key from a hook on the wall. Next to the Nurses office, there's another door. He unlocks it and switches on the light.

'Help yourself,' he says, making a gesture towards a water container. I gulp two cups and fill a plastic cup again.

When I go back to my room it's in darkness. I climb under the duvet, using the light from the small window in the door. As I'm drifting off the LED lights in the ceiling flash on. I have to shield my eyes. After a few seconds, I sit up, worried there's someone in my room. The blinds in the door are open and someone's peering in from the corridor.

'Just checking you're okay,' the voice says.

'Yes, thanks,' I reply.

'Just checking you're okay,' the voice says again.

'Yes, thanks.'

'Are you okay in there?' the voice repeats, louder this

time.

I get out of bed and open the door. It's the nurse who was at the desk in the office before.

'I'm fine thanks,' I say, 'just trying to get to sleep.'

'Smashin,' she says, 'I'll check later.'

I get back into bed and the light goes off.

I wake in the night and the room is fully lit. My eyes sting, adjusting to the brightness. I search around the room, trying to find an off switch, but there's only one, for the bedside lamp. Giving up, I climb back into bed, burying my face into the pillow to hide my eyes from the light.

In my dream I'm on a cruise ship. My cabin is bare except for a single bed with a round porthole looking out onto a stormy sea. There's a knock on the door and when I go to answer it the ship's captain is in the corridor. I show him my room and say it's not what I booked. He just shrugs his shoulders and walks away. I run after him holding a razor blade between my fingers. When I catch up with him I tap him on the shoulder and show him the blade. He takes it from me, laughing.

Sixteen

I've been on Seagull Ward for a couple of days and I've still not had any treatment. Although no one's told me exactly what kind of treatment I'm going to get. Life on this ward is much the same as the other one, except the nurses have stopped weighing me. They must have enough information now. But if they know how long I have left, why aren't they telling me?

When I go into the lounge, for breakfast, some women are already waiting at the serving hatch. As I join the queue, the shutter rolls up and a nurse waits, ready to serve us. I feel a tap on my shoulder and turn around. It's Sophie.

'When did you get here?' I say, happy to see her.

'Last night,' she says, 'save me a place at your table.'

After breakfast, we find two chairs by the TV. On the door, to the left of the cabinet, there's a handwritten sign: *Art Session at 11.*

A woman, wearing a bright yellow jumper, about my

age, joins us. 'I recognise you,' she says, pointing to Sophie.

'Think I remember you too,' Sophie says.

She points to me. 'Not seen you before though.'

'I'm Ruth.'

'Jenny,' she says, 'you been here before?'

I shake my head. 'My first time.'

'Second time for me,' she says. 'Voluntary, didn't feel safe by myself.'

'Voluntary?' I ask. 'What's that?'

'It means she wasn't sectioned,' Sophie says.

A nurse comes over and switches on the TV. We watch a programme about buying and selling houses. Watching the TV makes me drowsy. I can't concentrate on anything for too long. I pick up a newspaper and read two short articles. Three days ago I struggled to read one.

The nurse comes back a few minutes later. 'Ready for clinic Ruth?' She takes me to a room where I have my blood pressure and oxygen levels checked.

'How long do I have left?' I ask, as she's inputting the measurements.

She grins. 'You're fine Ruth,' she says, 'there's nothing wrong.'

When I go back to the lounge Sophie and Jenny aren't there. The outside door to the garden is open. I haven't been in the garden yet but I don't go out before checking I'm allowed. I knock at the Nurses office door and wait.

'What is it?' the nurse asks, casually.

'Am I allowed outside?'

He chuckles. 'Of course.'

It's a nice garden, with a wooden pergola, benches, flowerbeds and a circular path around the edge. On the right, next to the lounge, there's a long window. I step on the soil to get a better look. Through the vertical blinds I see a small room with two armchairs on either side of a low table. There's a box of tissues, two glass tumblers and a table lamp. It's cozy in there, in the soft yellow light. That must be where the doctors and patients have their chats.

When I step back onto the path, I spot Sophie and Jenny under the wooden gazebo in the middle of the garden. I join them and we watch a woman walking around the path, stopping occasionally to inspect the daffodils still in bud.

'There's an art session on later,' Jenny says, 'are you coming?'

At 11am we're sitting by the TV, waiting for the art session to begin. A woman, I assume is the art tutor, unlocks the door.

'We're making Easter cards today,' the tutor says, as we

take our seats around the table. There's a large cardboard box, full of cards with outlines of Easter eggs, flowers, bunnies and chicks. I choose a blank card and draw a vase of daffodils. While the others are still chatting, I start colouring in. I wonder who will send these cards. I know I won't be here at Easter.

The tutor looks over my shoulder. 'Have you drawn that yourself?' she asks.

I nod. 'I loved art when I was younger,' I say. I try to remember the last time I did anything, it must have been long before we opened the Beach Road bar.

'You should take it up again,' the tutor says, 'you have a real talent.'

At lunchtime, I sit with Jenny and Sophie.

'The psychiatrist's here,' Jenny says, pointing to a tall man in a brown suit chatting with one of the nurses. 'Ready for him?'

'I think so,' I say. 'Never had a therapy session before.' The other two look at each other and grin. 'What did I say? I ask, puzzled.

Sophie rolls her eyes. 'You don't get therapy in here.'

'Oh,' I say, disappointed.

'Are you voluntary?' Jenny asks.

'I think so,' I say, 'I wanted a bed so I must be.'

A nurse walks towards us. 'No Ruth,' he says, 'you're

not voluntary. I shrug my shoulders. 'What does that mean?' I ask, turning to Jenny.

'It means you'll have to ask for a pass,' she says, 'so you can go out.'

When it's my turn to see the psychiatrist, a nurse takes me to a room off the corridor. When he opens the door it's not the small room with the table lamp. There are no soft chairs or low tables. It's another large room, like the one last week. There are tables around the edge and a woman at a laptop. The doctor is already here. I feel under-dressed, in my slippers, when everyone else looks smart. I must ask Mike to bring in some of my work clothes. The nurse, who brought me, sits next to the doctor. I sit opposite them, on my own.

'So Ruth,' he asks, 'do you know why you're here?'

'I'm in severe pain,' I say, 'and I haven't long left.'

He smiles. 'Not exactly. How have you been this week?'

'Been getting really bad headaches,' I say, 'and feeling shaky.'

'That can happen,' he says, 'your nurse should have explained the side effects.' The nurse smiles at me and shrugs his shoulders.

'When can I go home?'

'Not just yet,' he says, smiling.

'It's just if I've not long left,' I say, 'I'd like to be home, with my family.'

He smiles again and scribbles some notes. 'I can't let you go home just yet.'

We sit in silence for a couple of minutes.

'Can you tell me why this happened to me?'

He leans back in his chair. 'We don't know,' he says, 'but it's unusual to have someone your age presenting for the first time.'

'Presenting?'

He leans forward. 'We'd usually see someone with your symptoms from a much younger age,' he says.

'So this is a younger person's disease?' I say. 'That's causing all this pain?'

He smiles. I'm exhausted already. I want Mike to be here. If he was here he might be able to ask more questions for me. I rest my head on the table.

'Wake up,' the psychiatrist says, 'you need to pay attention.' I lift my head, hoping this meeting will be over soon. 'I'd like to send you for a brain scan,' he says, 'with your agreement.' It must have reached my brain, whatever is causing this pain. And if it's reached my brain, surely my speech will be affected soon.

'I'll have it,' I say, without hesitation.

'Good answer,' he says, 'it's good to see you want to

work with us. Co-operate.'

I remember what Sophie said at lunchtime. 'So can I get a pass please?'

'That all depends on what it's for.'

'Am I allowed to go to the cafe?'

'Seeing as you're being compliant,' he says, 'I think we can allow that.'

After the meeting the nurse takes me back to the lounge. 'How was that?'

'When do I get some treatment?' I ask.

'You're getting it now.'

'Oh. I see,' I say.

Jenny and Sophie are in the lounge but I don't stay to chat. I go straight to my room and lie down. The meeting has been tiring.

Mike comes to visit in the afternoon. We meet in a small visitors' room.

'I'm getting a brain scan,' I say.

He nods. 'Yes, they've told me.'

'They must know it's something serious,' I say, 'if they think I need a brain scan. Have they told you how long I've got?'

'There's nothing wrong with you,' Mike says, 'you just have to believe it.' This is difficult for Mike, he's not taking this very well at all.

'Have you told people about me?' I ask. 'Do they know where I am?'

'I've told them you're at your mum's,' he says, 'I've said you're looking after her.

I tilt my head. 'Why?'

'I've said she's had a hip operation,' he says. It would be better if Mike could face up to the truth. At least then people will be able to support him through this.

'Mike,' I say, 'I'm not at Mum's, I'm here and Mum's absolutely fine. Isn't she?'

'Yeah,' he says. The tiredness hits me again. I close my eyes and rest my head on the table. Mike rubs my arm.

'And Mum and Dad? What have you told them?'

'They know you're here,' he says, 'they send their love.'

When he leaves, I go back to bed and doze, but it's not long before I'm shaken by the shrill of the alarm. This is the third time it's gone off since I've been on Seagull Ward. Each time it blasts I count to three and then it comes; the thunder of heavy boots running down corridors. This time they're heading towards my room. I open my door. In the doorway, across from my room, a woman is screaming, held down on the floor by two nurses.

'Get off!' she shouts. 'You're hurting me.'

Another nurse comes down the corridor. 'Don't stay

out here,' she shouts to me, 'get back in your room.'

'What's going on?' I ask. 'Will she be okay?'

'Nothing for you to worry about,' the nurse shouts, 'nothing to see here.'

I don't go back in my room. Instead, I go into the lounge. Jenny's there, sitting at a table.

'Noise wake you?' she says.

'It's mayhem down there,' I say, 'needed to get out of the way.'

'Should be in PICU that one,' she says.

'PICU?'

'Intensive Care,' she says. 'She needs moving out. It's not fair.'

Two of the nurses come back into the lounge. 'Control has been restored,' one says, as they go back into the office. Jenny and I go into the garden and find an empty bench.

'Any news about you going home?' she asks.

No,' I say, 'what about you?'

She leans in so a nurse, standing nearby, can't hear us. 'Can't make up their mind about me,' she says. 'They say I'm ready, then I'm not.'

It starts to rain and we go back into the lounge. We listen to conversations between the other patients. Some of them seem to know each other, chatting about things they've done on the outside. A nurse comes over and tidies up the magazines on the coffee table.

'What date is it today?' I ask.

The nurse looks at the newspaper in her hand. 'March 10th,' she says.

'It's my birthday tomorrow,' I say to Jenny.

Jenny rubs her hands and smiles. 'Let's have a party.'

Seventeen

Today's a big day for me: turning 47, having a brain scan and being able to make my first visit to the café, with my pass.

The café is bright, colourful and noisy. There's a good selection on the menu board behind the counter: delicious-sounding cakes and fresh sandwiches. I order an espresso and a pain-au-chocolate. The nurse who's brought me sits at the table behind. I have a copy of Coastal Monthly and I take my time reading short articles, savouring the coffee and pastry.

After an hour, it's time for me to go back.

'Enjoy that?' the nurse asks, unlocking the door to the ward. She's one of the friendlier ones here. I think she's a student, she doesn't look that much older than Sophie.

'Yes thanks,' I say, 'I'm still worried though.'

She stops at the office. 'What about?'

'The scan this afternoon,' I say, 'will they tell me? When they find something?'

'Maybe, maybe not,' she says, cheerily, 'try not to worry.' But I can't help it. How else can I explain the headaches, whole-body pain, weird dreams and restless legs?

After lunch, another nurse drives me to Thornsea General. This one's not so chatty, which is a shame because I need someone to take my mind off the scan.

'Will I be in there long?' I ask him, when we reach the hospital.

'Don't think so,' he says. We walk down three corridors to get to the CT clinic. In the waiting area, I'm too nervous to sit so I pace up and down by the windows.

As the nurse said, the scan's over quickly. The nurse operating the machine doesn't say much either. I search his face to find clues about the results, but he just smiles.

When we get back to Seagull Ward there's no one in the lounge. I sit by the TV and read a few articles in the paper. As I get up to leave, I notice another patient, coming towards me. It's the woman from the room opposite mine. We haven't spoken since I've been here. She looks a little younger than me but she's a few inches taller and probably a few pounds heavier.

'Hello,' I say, trying to be friendly. She mumbles something, too quiet for me to hear properly. Her eyes are locked on mine and she's giving me a fierce stare. I wonder if she's mistaken mc for someone else, someone she's really not happy with.

She steps towards me. 'And I told 'em they shouldn't have said that,' she says, her eyes fixed on me. 'Throwing me in there like that. Grabbing me. Didn't want to go in.' I need to pass her if I'm to get to the corridor but she's getting closer, blocking my way. I look around but there's no one about except for two nurses in the office, with their backs to the window. Her speech is louder and faster as she gets closer. 'Could have done anything to me.' I take a small step to the right, hoping one of the nurses might turn around and see us. 'Told him not to touch me. Didn't want him touching me.' At last, one of the nurses comes out, looks straight at me, and goes out towards the corridor. The woman comes close enough for me to smell her breath. Her eyes are fixed on mine. 'You ignoring me?'

I keep my voice low but try to keep it friendly. 'No, I'm not ignoring you.'

She steps closer towards me. 'They tried to ignore me.'

I take another step back. I'm trapped between her and an armchair. 'I won't ig-'. She swings her arm forward and the flat of her palm lands on my cheek. 'Ahhhhhh!' I scream. I fall back, landing on the wooden arm of the chair. I roll onto the seat and slide onto the floor, my legs twisting beneath me. 'Help someone quick!' I shout. 'I've been hit!' With my head in my hands and my eyes shut tight, I hear her running. Within seconds there's a hand on my shoulder.

'Are you okay Ruth?' I lift my head. It's the nurse I saw coming out of the office and going into the corridor before. The woman's gone.

'Where is she?' I say, looking around.

'Who?' the nurse asks.

I try to get up but I fall back. 'The woman who hit me.'

The nurse puts her hands out with her palms towards me. 'Who? Who hit you?'

'The woman,' I say, sobbing, 'she's in the room opposite me, you saw us here before.' I try to get up but fall back again. The nurse helps me to my feet and leads me to a chair at a dining table.

Another nurse brings me a cup of sugary tea. 'No one was here,' the nurse says, putting the tea down, 'you're getting yourself upset.'

'But she was,' I say, 'it was so quick.' I sip my tea. My back feels bruised and my cheek stings.

In my room, I inspect my cheek. It's bright pink. I try to

look at my back. It feels tender when I press it but there's only a small mirror on the bathroom wall. I lie on my bed and drift into sleep.

In my dream I'm in a zoo. There's a tiger running towards me and when I turn to run away I realise I'm in the enclosure too. I try climbing over the fence but it's too high. There are people watching from the other side of the fence, just staring at me. I wake up sweating and have to peel my face off the plastic pillowcase.

One of the nurses comes to my room to tell me Mike's here. When we get into the corridor I see him, talking to two nurses. We go into the room with soft lighting and armchairs. He's brought birthday cards and three gift bags.

'Happy Birthday love,' he says, kissing me on my sore cheek. In the first gift bag I have silk pyjamas and new sheepskin slippers. I run the soft silk through my fingers and feel the softness of the lining. 'From Daniel and Ellie,' he says, as I take out a matching silk dressing gown from another bag.

'Tell them thanks,' I say.

He points to a smaller gift bag. 'That's from Mum.'

I peer into the bag. 'Soaps and a mug. Lovely.' I take out a box of scented lily of the valley soaps. The mug is bright yellow with a picture of a sunrise and the words

Brighter Days Are Ahead on the inside.

I turn my face to the wall. 'Is my cheek still red?'

'Not really,' he says, 'what've you done now?'

I stand up, turn around and lift my jumper. 'Can you see a bruise?'

'No,' he says, giving it a quick look, 'there's nothing there.'

I push down the waistband of my jeans. 'There. Can you see anything there?'

'Yes,' he says, 'there's a bit of a bruise.'

'Did they tell you what happened?'

'What happened?' He's looking at his phone.

'I got attacked, By another patient.'

He shakes his head. 'The nurses said they found you crouched on the floor,' he says, 'you'd fallen backwards.'

'After I was hit.' I say, 'did they tell you that?'

'There was no-one around when it happened,' he says, 'it was just an accident.'

I put my hand on my back and press where it feels tender. 'No. It wasn't an accident.'

'Let's not make any trouble,' he says, 'you'll be home soon.' I look up at the ceiling. Perhaps I did dream it or imagined it. I have been having very strange dreams lately. Perhaps I could have fallen into the chair. He puts his phone back in his pocket and scrunches the used envelopes into a tight ball. 'You know it's the opening night for David's bar tonight,' he says, 'so I can't stay long.'

'That's okay,' I say, remembering, 'have a lovely time.'

A nurse walks us back to the locked door at the end of the corridor.

'Hope it all goes well tonight,' I say, when Mike kisses me the cheek.

He reaches for my hand and strokes my thumb. 'Yeah,' he says, 'shame you can't be there.' He's been amazing these past few weeks, having to get the new bar ready pretty much all by himself. It's good of him to come and see me today, when he's got so much on.

'Tell David and Cara I'm sorry,' I say, 'for missing their party.'

After dinner, Sophie and Jenny tell me to stay in my seat at the dining table - they have a surprise. When they come back, Sophie's carrying a large cake box and Jenny's balancing a tower of small presents on a huge envelope.

'Let's sing *Happy Birthday* to Ruth!' Sophie shouts, putting the cake box on the table.

Even a few of the nurses join in singing *Happy Birthday* to me.

'Where did you get all this?' I say, unwrapping a new toothbrush.

'Some of us donated things,' Jenny says, 'and we got the rest from the shop.'

There's a bottle of strawberry-scented bubble foam, a bar of tea-tree soap, a roll-on deodorant and a pink hair scrunchie. Inside the card, I count nine signatures.

'Thank you so much,' I say, and for a moment I forget about my sore cheek, my bruised back and this morning's scan.

When I go for breakfast the next day, I see the room across from mine is empty. Jenny's coming along the corridor and stops when she reaches my door.

'She's gone,' she says, looking into the empty room.

'Gone home?' I ask.

'No. Intensive Care probably.'

I feel guilty for telling the nurses about the woman. 'Was it because of me?'

'No,' Jenny says, 'she shouldn't have been here anyway.'

Eighteen

I have to wait another six days before I know the result of the brain scan. Every day, since my birthday, I've been asking a nurse when I'll get the results.

'Try not to worry about it,' each one has said. Every time.

When I'm called to meet the psychiatrist, after breakfast, I change from my slippers into my leather ankle boots, and from my pyjamas into my smart denim jeans and jumper. Mike hasn't packed any of my work suits and this is the smartest outfit I can find, for the occasion.

'Is Mike here?' I ask the nurse as we're going into the room.

He shakes his head. 'No,'

'Didn't he want to come?' I ask. The nurse shrugs his shoulders. Now the Liverpool bar is open Mike's going to be busier than ever. I shouldn't be surprised he doesn't want to be here for my results. When I enter the room, the psychiatrist is already in his chair. He smiles when

I sit down. The lighting's different today, softer. The secretary's here too but there's no laptop, no projector. I know it's bad news. Why else would they have dimmed the lights like this?

The psychiatrist smiles. 'How are we today?'

'I've been worried all week,' I say, taking a seat.

He passes a white envelope to the nurse. 'I have your results,' he says, 'you can read it yourself.' When the nurse hands me the envelope my hands start to tremble. I try to lift the seal but my fingers are moist with sweat. 'Take your time,' he says, 'no rush.' I wait a few moments and take a breath. I just wish I could do this in private, without these three watching me. I feel like I used to on Christmas morning when I was a child, opening presents in front of Mum and Dad. Everyone in the room: the psychiatrist, the nurse, the secretary; they're all waiting. I take out the letter and put it face down on the table. 'You won't know if you don't look,' the psychiatrist says, still smiling.

I count to three in my head and turn it over quickly. I read the first few lines then see the three words halfway down the page that tell me what I've been waiting to know.

Nineteen

W*ithin Normal Range.*

I look at the expectant faces. 'What does this mean?'

'It means they didn't find anything on your brain scan,' the psychiatrist says.

My arms stretch out and I lower my head on the table. In this moment, in this silence, something changes: a tiny spark, a small chink of light, a faint sense of hope. When I lift my head the room is just as it was before, the light still dimmed, but there's something different too.

'Does this mean I'm not dying?' I ask, hopefully.

'You never were,' he says.

The pain I've been carrying all these weeks eases a little in that instant. 'Can I go home now?'

'We can think about it now,' he says.

I put the letter back in the envelope. 'Will it happen again? I don't want to feel pain like that again.'

He stands and pushes his chair in. 'There's definitely a

risk,' he says, 'now you've had it once.'

'Do you know where the pain came from?' I ask. He smiles and shakes his head. I get up and shuffle towards the door. Before I reach for the handle I stop and turn back to him.

'These tablets,' I ask, 'how long do I need to take them for?'

He zips up his briefcase. 'Probably for the rest of your life,' he says, smiling.

I find Jenny in the lounge watching TV.

'I got the results of my scan, I got the all clear,' I say. 'They might let me go home.'

'Brilliant,' she says, 'amazing.'

'What about you?' I ask.

'Soon,' she says, 'but not yet. Have to be certain it's safe for me.'

I sit down in the chair next to her. 'Do you want to go home?'

'I get afraid sometimes, when I'm on my own.'

I imagine being back at home with my family and wonder how long it will be before we can all be together again around the kitchen island.

The psychiatrist's given me another pass to the café. This timc I can go by myself, without a nurse. I'm given a signed ticket stating the time I must report back to the ward. I have an entire hour, all to myself.

For this hour, I tell myself, I'm just an ordinary person, with the same freedoms as anybody else. When the hour's over I walk back to my locked ward and hand back my pass. It won't be long before I can go to a café anytime I want, for as long as I want.

The next evening Mike brings Daniel and Ellie in for the first time since I've been here.

I hug them both. 'I've missed you two.'

Daniel gives me a packet of jelly babies. 'We're missing your cooking Mum.'

Ellie's brought me a bar of *Godiva* chocolate. 'When are you coming home Mum?' she asks. 'I want you back at home.'

'Soon,' I say, reaching for her hand, 'not long now.'

Seeing my children tonight has made me realise how much I've missed them. I go to bed with something I didn't think I had this morning: a future.

Twenty

On my last morning on Seagull Ward, I take my duvet and pillows from their slippery plastic covers and drop them onto the hard mattress. The nurse, watching from the corridor, comes into my room.

'Let's get you out of here,' he says, 'we need to get it ready for the next one.'

'I won't miss these sheets,' I say, handing him the bedding.

'Then you won't be in a rush to come back.

I drop two copies of Coastal Monthly into the waste basket. 'I hope I don't come back here.'

You're lucky you got a bed,' he says. 'You know how much it costs to keep you here?'

'A lot?'

'Thousands a week,' he says, 'sure some of 'em come here for a holiday.'

'A holiday? Really?'

'When they need a break,' he says, 'you know how it is.'

I think of Jenny, what she said about sometimes being afraid to be on her own. 'Not really.'

Onc final check around the room and I close the door, handing the nurse my plastic card.

I take my luggage to the lounge. There's no one else here. Some women are in the craft room, the rest in the garden, or their rooms. I sit in the high-backed leather chair, the one I fell against on my birthday. Two nurses come in and stop by the office.

'First shift on here,' one says, 'usually do forensics.'

'One or two here should be in forensics,' the other replies. They both laugh.

I pick up a magazine from the coffee table and read an article on *What Your Next Career Move Should Be* when a nurse comes over.

'Ready for your discharge meeting?' he asks, waving some forms. I follow him to the corridor. In a small room we sit on soft chairs, a low table between us. He hands me the forms, signatures are required, before I can leave. 'We're not recommending it,' he says, 'but if you can sign this to confirm you're discharging yourself.'

'Not recommending?'

He nods. 'You've asked to be discharged haven't you? That's what you told the doctor.'

'Have I?' I can't remember. 'Did I?'

'That's what it says on here,' he says, pointing to a paragraph on the form. I'm not going to argue with him now. I just want to get home, sleep in my own bed and eat some good home-cooked food. I sign and date the forms and hand them back. 'We don't like keeping you in here longer than you need to be,' he says, 'and we need the beds.'

For a moment I wonder if I should tell them I need to stay. 'But you think I'm well enough to go home?'

'You'll have to see the Crisis Team,' he says, 'they'll keep an eye on you - on the outside.' He hands over a large white paper bag. 'Your medication. Should last you four weeks.'

I look inside. There are four large boxes which I put in my holdall. When he opens the door, Mike's in the corridor.

'Ready to go home?' Mike says, taking my suitcase.

He reaches for my hand and strokes my thumb. 'Not quite,' I say, 'there's something I need to do before I go.'

I take the gift bag Jean gave me on my birthday and an unopened tube of toothpaste. I go into the dining area but Jenny and Sophie aren't there. I leave the gift bag and the toothpaste on a table and go out into the garden where I find them sitting underneath the gazebo.

'Come inside,' I say, 'I've left some gifts for you.'

'Oooh, presents,' Sophie says, 'c'mon Jenny let's see what we've got.'

In the dining area, Jenny takes one of the wrapped soaps and sniffs the paper.

'Lily of the valley,' she says, 'I love soaps. Thanks so much.'

I give Sophie the ***Brighter Days Are Ahead*** mug.

She examines the mug. 'Let's hope so.'

'Take care, you two.' I put my arms out to hug Jenny. Sophie steps back

'I don't do hugs,' she says, smiling.

I take one last look around and turn towards the door. 'You never know,' I say, turning back, 'we might meet up on the outside.'

Mike's in the corridor, talking to the nurse who found me after I was hit by the other patient.

'Thanks for everything you've done for her,' he says, 'we can't thank you enough.'

'It's been a pleasure,' the nurse says, 'take care of yourself Ruth.'

When the outer door to the ward is closed, Mike and I continue along the corridor until we reach the entrance foyer. As we're passing the café Mike grabs my arm and takes me over to the counter.

'Did you come here much?' he asks, looking at the

menu board on the back wall.

'A couple of times,' I say, 'when I got a pass.'

'The contract's coming up for renewal,' he says, 'what do you think?'

'About what?'

'About us expanding into hospital cafés. I've mentioned it to David.'

It's not something I've considered before now. 'Haven't we got enough on our plate already?'

'Diversifying would be good for us,' he says, grinning. 'And you've got insider knowledge now.'

When we get in the car there's a bunch of pink roses in the back. 'They're beautiful! That's so thoughtful,' I say, getting in the passenger seat.

'They're for Mum,' Mike says, turning on the radio, 'a thank you for the last few weeks.'

'Of course,' I say, 'she must have been a big help.'

It's late March and a beautiful sunny day. There are signs of Spring in the flowerbeds around the car park.

'Just need to swing by the golf club first,' Mike says as we're waiting at the junction, 'before we go home.'

We turn right and drive up the coast road towards the Golf Club. There are a few golfers out on the greens today. As we approach the entrance I notice a small group of people by the road.

'What are they doing?' I say, trying to read their placards.

'Protesting again,' he says, 'bloody nuisance.'

I wind down the window to get a better view. 'What are they protesting about?'

'The new link road,' he says, 'they're wasting their time.' As we pass, he puts his head out of his window. 'Go and do some real work!' he shouts at them. 'Lazy dossers!'

A woman with long strawberry blonde hair, tied with a green polka dot scarf, shouts back. 'We need the woodland! You'll miss it when it's gone!'

'Scroungers, the lot of them,' he says, as we drive away.

'Maybe she has a point,' I say, 'we need the woodland.' I wind up my window and watch the protesters recede in my wing mirror.

'We need good transport links,' he says, 'that's what we need.'

When we get home, there's an aroma of onions and red wine coming from the kitchen. I've eaten so many pies and chips these past few weeks I'll be happy not to have any more for at least a year. There's a string of bunting across the kitchen wall spelling out *WELCOME HOME.*

'Lovely to have you home,' Jean says, hugging me.

'What's cooking?' I say, 'Smells delicious.'

'I've made Mike his favourite,' she says, 'beef stew and dumplings. He deserves a treat.'

When Daniel and Ellie come home the three of us go across the road to the beach.

'You're definitely home for good now?' Ellie says, linking her arm in mine.

'Yes,' I say, 'home for good.'

'And you're not going to get ill again?'

'I hope not,' I say. But I really don't know if I'm home for good or if I'll get the pains again.

I stay up till 7.30 pm when I feel a heavy tiredness envelope me. When I get to our bedroom I open the balcony doors and step out. I've missed that familiar sight, the lights twinkling along the pier stretching into the darkness. I watch the cars going past and breathe in and out, slowly.

When I climb into bed I lift the white seersucker cover and slide in. The silk pillowcase and heavy cotton sheets feel luxurious on my skin. I open my bedside drawer and find a long, white unopened box; a Christmas present from Mum. I spritz the Heavenly Relaxing Sleep Mist on the pillow and breathe in the lavender and jasmine fragrance. I close my eyes and drift off into a deep sleep.

In my dream I'm being led up some steps from a

dungeon. I emerge into a brightly lit court and a judge in a wig is sat opposite me. A barrister is in a blue gown and there's a woman at a laptop next to him. When I look down I'm in my pyjamas.

I'm woken up by Mike coming to bed.

'There's something I can't stop thinking about,' I say, when he climbs in next to me. Something's been bothering me since I heard the two nurses talking outside the office yesterday.

'You need to stop worrying,' he says, 'that's why you got ill in the first place. Remember?'

'You'll tell me the truth?'

He sighs. 'What d'you need to know?'

'Do I have a criminal record?'

He moves his hand down my right leg and tickles around my ankle. 'Oh no.' He laughs. 'Where's your tag?'

I pull my leg away. 'Not funny,' I say, 'I'm serious.'

He puts his hand on my waist. 'Of course you don't. Why d'you think that?'

'Something I heard today,' I say, 'two nurses on the ward.'

He strokes my shoulder. 'Don't let it bother you.'

'And how they wouldn't let me have fresh air,' I say

'how I had to get a pass to go to the café. Was it punishment?'

'Not at all,' he says, 'to keep you safe.'

I turn over. 'Was it?'

'Forget about all that now,' he says, 'let's focus on the future.'

Twenty-One

In the morning I still have questions. Mike and I are in bed. I've been awake for an hour waiting for him to open his eyes. When he does, I'm sitting up.

'Was I sectioned?' I ask him.

He sighs and turns over on his back. 'That's what they told me.'

'Why?'

'You needed to go into hospital.'

'Jenny told me she was voluntary,' I say, 'I think she could go out by herself.'

'Does it matter?' he says, 'you're home now. Why worry?'

When the alarm goes off, I ask him again. 'Did they tell you how I got ill?'

'No,' he says, 'it doesn't matter, you're better now.'

'They didn't believe me,' I say, 'they didn't believe I was in pain.'

'Ruth,' he says, angrily, 'let it go. This isn't doing you

any good.'

'I felt like a criminal in there.'

'They were just trying to keep you safe,' he says, 'that's all.'

When he leaves for work I go across the road to the bus stop. The Number 48 takes me to Thornsea General where I have an appointment with the Crisis Team. A tall man, with a purple folder, meets me at the office and leads me to a small room off a corridor. We sit opposite each other on hard plastic chairs. There's nothing to focus on in this room, just bare cream walls and a door with a small window. With nothing else to look at I study his purple folder, wondering what it contains about me.

'So you're taking your medication?' he asks.

'Yes.'

He makes a note. 'And how are you feeling today?'

'I'm okay,' I say, 'but I have some questions.'

He looks at his watch. 'What type of questions?'

'How did it happen?'

He looks towards the window in the door. 'How did what happen?'

'I need to know how I got ill,' I say, 'so it doesn't happen again.'

He shrugs his shoulders and shifts in his chair. 'That's impossible to say.'

'Will there be an investigation?' I ask, looking at his file and wondering what's in my notes.

He sighs. 'About what?'

'About why I got ill?'

'Don't think so,' he says.

He looks at his watch again. 'That's not what I'm here for,' he says, 'I just check you're okay. That's all.' He stands and opens the door. I follow him into the corridor.

'Will I see you again?' I ask.

'No,' he says, 'we'll send someone out, a community nurse.'

On the bus home, I count all the doctors and nurses I've seen in the last five weeks. I've asked each one similar questions but none of them have been able to answer. Hopefully, the community nurse will.

In the evening Mike takes me out for dinner to the Italian on Railway Street. He tells me about the new bar in Liverpool and how well it's doing.

'So David's happy with everything?' I ask.

'He's delighted,' he says, 'he's invited us over for dinner again.'

'And what did you tell him? About why I was away.'

'The same as everyone else,' he says, 'you were looking after your mum, after her hip operation.'

When I go to the bathroom I *Google* 'Hip Operations' and 'Recovery'. When I get back to our table Mike's sole and my risotto have been served.

'I'm ready to come back to work,' I say, 'I need to start pulling my weight again.'

'Are you sure?' he says, pouring me some wine.

'There must be loads that needs doing,' I say. 'the longer I leave it, the worse it will be.'

'Are you well enough?' he says, filling his glass. 'I'm not sure coming back so soon is a good idea.'

When we're walking home together, I wrap my arm around Mike's.

'I've been thinking about our anniversary,' he says. Organising holidays and special occasions is something I usually do. And it's not for months yet.

'How about a night at a country hotel?' I suggest.

Mike nods. 'Sounds perfect to me.'

'With a *Michelin* star restaurant and a copper rolled top bath.'

'Leave it with me,' he says.

When we get to our drive he stops and reaches for my hand.

'There's something I need to tell you,' he says. He looks

down at the gravel, shifting his weight between each foot. It's freezing cold and I want to get inside. 'There's been a few changes at work, 'whilc you've been away.'

I smile. 'That's fine.'

'I hired someone,' he says, 'we couldn't wait till you got better.'

'You hired a temp?' I say. 'That's fine. I knew you couldn't do it all by yourself.' I release my hand from his and head for the front door.

'Sort of,' he says, following behind.

I take my coat and shoes off in the hall. 'Well I'm back now, we can let them go.'

'Let's not rush things eh?' he says, locking the front door.

I'm not going to get into an argument with him about when we get rid of a temp. Mike's never liked spending money on staff. It won't be long before he's telling me to give them their notice. He's warning me, before I get back to the office. It's just a temp, that's all.

When we get into bed I rest my head on Mike's chest. 'Should we tell David I was in the Unit?'

'No,' he says, 'that would be a bad idea.'

'But we're business partners,' I say, 'isn't it best he knows?'

'I mean it Ruth, he mustn't find out.'

'And the budget,' I say, 'did you tell him about the budget?'

'You don't need to worry about that anymore,' he says, 'it's all fine.'

Twenty-Two

On the last Friday in March, I want to make the most of a free day before getting back to work. I set off along the seafront, in the direction of the town. At the top of the pier, I buy a coffee and a croissant from the little van. I carry on to the boating lake then turn back, towards home.

Across from our house, I stop near the seafront railings to read the noticeboard. The leaflet for the Leader at the Microphone event is still there. As I'm reading the other notices I hear someone calling my name. I turn to see Sophie jogging towards me.

'Ruth,' she says, catching her breath as she stops, 'I thought it was you.'

It's lovely to see her. 'What a surprise, how have you been?' She's still very thin but has more colour in her cheeks than when we were in the Unit. 'What are you doing up here?'

'I live up here now,' she says, taking a purse out and

counting five 50-pence pieces. 'I live on Marsham Crescent.'

I point across the road. 'That's our house over there,' I say, 'the one with the cerulean blue door.'

'All that's yours?' she says. I nod. 'You must be well off.'

I turn back to the noticeboard. 'We missed the Leader at the Microphone event,' I say, 'I almost spoke at that.'

She points to the leaflet with an abstract painting. 'Look at that. There's a free art exhibition in the Town Hall,' she says, 'you should go. Take your paintings.'

I take a closer look and note the times it's open. 'Thanks,' I say, 'I might take a look.'

The Number 48 slows as it approaches.

'This is mine,' she says.

'Going to the General?' I ask.

'Crisis Team,' she replies. I almost invite her to our house for a meal but stop myself. It's best to check these things with Mike.

'Take care of yourself,' I say. I want to hug her but she's already stepping onto the bus. I wait at the kerb and she waves from the top deck.

When the bus is out of view I take the stone steps down to the sand. There are a few people on the beach: a man throwing a ball to a dog, a woman pushing a double buggy. The sea's a long way out today. I walk to the water's edge where I unzip my boots and slip off my socks. I pull my jeans to my calves and let the icy water wash over my feet, closing my eyes. Taking deep breaths I feel the sea air fill my lungs and listen to the seagulls. I swing from side to side, my arms outstretched. Who cares who might be watching? I'm alive, not aching or in pain, and feeling so much better. Home, family and the business are all that really matters now. I'm never taking any of this: the sand, the sea, the air; any of this for granted. But, more than this, I'm not taking my family, my marriage, and my work for granted, ever again. I came so close to losing all of it. Brushing off the wet sand I put my damp feet into my boots and smile as I make my way back towards the stone steps. There's still a couple of hours before anyone will be home and I don't feel like going back just yet. I remember the art exhibition poster and walk to the Town Hall.

When I get there, a sign at the entrance indicates the way to the art exhibition. At the bottom of a long corridor I find an elderly man sitting at a table, reading a tattered paperback.

'Welcome,' he says, taking a bookmark and placing it

carefully between two pages. He hands me a folded paper leaflet. 'You'll find descriptions and the artists in this.'

The pieces on the walls are a mixture of oil, pencil, watercolours, portraits, still life and landscapes. In the middle of the room a table holds four glazed ceramic pieces and a fabric collage. A few of the pieces have red stickers on but most are still available to buy. The last piece, nearest to him, is a portrait of a young boy in oils.

'The young boy in oils,' I say, 'the way they've caught the light from the lamp.'

'It's my grandson,' he says, 'but it's not for sale.'

'I used to paint a lot, when I was younger,' I say, putting the leaflet back on the table.

He pushes the leaflet towards me. 'Then you should join our art club.'

'Oh, I don't think so,' I say, 'I don't have time for that now.'

'You should always make time for your art,' he says. I put the leaflet in my bag. 'We're on Railway Street,' he says, 'next to The Swann. It's the one with the bright blue door.'

'I don't think I can,' I say, apologetically.

He looks at me with a pleading gaze. 'You'd be very welcome to join us.'

'Sorry,' I say, 'I've no time right now.' I'll have so much

to catch up on when I get back to work on Monday and, with David's bar open now, I'm going to be busier than I ever was before.

When I get home Mike's in the kitchen. Daniel and Ellie are upstairs.

'Who were you talking to at the bus stop?' Mike asks, as soon as he notices me.

'Oh that was Sophie,' I say, opening the fridge, 'we were in the Unit together.'

'What's she doing up here?'

'She's moved up here,' I say, turning to him, 'Marsham Crescent.' He lowers his eyebrows and stares at me. I turn back to the fridge and check to see what needs to be used up tonight for dinner. A head of broccoli, some parsnips and a few carrots.

'Hope you didn't tell her where you live,' he says.

'I did actually,' I say, 'I showed her our house.' I search for the colander and find it in the dishwasher.

'As long as she doesn't bother us,' he says. I put the broccoli in the colander and rinse it under the cold tap.

'She won't be any bother,' I say, 'she's a good kid.'

Twenty-Three

It's been a while since I've put on a smart suit and walked to the Beach Road bar with Mike.

'What did you tell the staff?' I say, as we're setting off from home.

'I told you already,' he says, 'you were looking after your mum, after her hip operation.'

'And they believed you?'

'Why wouldn't they?' he says.

In my office I open my laptop. There aren't many emails. I try to log in to the staff rota account. I'm locked out.

Mike pops his head around the door. 'How you doing?'

'Did you change my log-in?'

He nods. 'When you were admitted.'

'I need to get back in.'

'Don't worry about it,' he says, 'plenty time for all that.'

Before I can ask anything else the door's closed and he's gone. I swing my chair around and examine the noticeboard on the wall behind me. It looks unusually tidy. All the sticky notes and printed-out emails have been removed, revealing ncat green felt.

I go in to see Mike. He's at his desk, his leather swivel chair visible from the doorway. When I get further in, I notice the furniture's been rearranged. A woman sits on a tan leather swivel chair with an *Apple Macbook* on a new desk at the other end of the office, opposite Mike's desk. Mike stands up and comes over to me.

'Ruth,' he says, 'let me introduce you to Mary.'

The woman stands and puts her hand out to me. I walk over and shake her hand.

'Ruth,' I say, smiling, 'lovely to meet you.'

'Welcome back,' she says. Mary is tall with long straight dark hair. Slim, with a tiny rosebud mouth and a perfect button nose. I guess she's in her mid-thirties. She's wearing a red pencil skirt, a black cashmere jumper and a pearl choker necklace. There's nowhere for me to sit except the long black leather couch, now moved from the wall to beneath the window. I sit in the middle, keeping my eyes fixed on the filing cabinet opposite. I wait, like a bored child, brought into work by their parents.

'So what are you doing for us Mary?' I ask.

Mary looks at Mike, looks at me, then looks at Mike.

'Mary's looking after staff and accounts,' Mike says.

I look at Mary. 'My job?' She gives me a weak smile.

'For now,' Mike says, looking at his screen.

I stand. 'Can't stay here all day,' I say, 'loads to do.'

When I get to my office I switch off the laptop and send Mike a text: *Going Home.*

There's no need to avoid the staff. As far as they're aware I've been at my parents, looking after Mum. I go into the bathroom, re-apply my lip balm, brush my hair and spritz perfume over my jacket. I go down to the pool room, on the first floor. There are a couple of customers in already. Chrissie, the bar manager, is filling the fridge with mixers.

'Welcome back,' she says, smiling, 'how's your mum?

I smile. 'Very well, thanks.'

Downstairs, in the kitchen, Sam, our chef and Chrissie's boyfriend, is at the sink.

'Hi Sam. Just saying hello.'

He turns around and smiles. 'Hi Ruth, How's your mum?'

'Wonderful, thanks.'

I lean on the wall in the car park, relieved I've got my first day back out of the way. Chrissie and Sam talk to everyone in our bars. If I can convince them all's well there should be no awkward questions from anyone else.

At home I call Mike. 'Is that the temp?'

'Sort of,' he says.

'Where did you find her?'

'Speak later,' he says.

'How long's she here for?'

'I can't talk right now,' he says, quietly.

'See you at home,' I say, 'you can tell me then.'

After dinner, Mike and I go into the lounge while Daniel and Ellie go to their rooms. He picks up the remote and flicks through the TV channels.

'This temp,' I say, 'what's her name again?'

He continues staring at the TV. 'You mean Mary.'

'We need to end her contract.'

'Not yet,' he says, eyes still fixed on the TV.

He finds the Sports Channel where three ex-footballers discuss the next game.

I wait for the adverts. 'Is it worth me coming in tomorrow?' I ask.

'Better than moping about here,' he says. He turns to me. 'Thought you wanted to come back.'

'But what am I doing?'

He says nothing but gets up and goes into the kitchen. When he comes back he has a glass of beer and a bowl of crisps.

At half-time I press my heel into his thigh. 'So what am I doing?'

He moves a couple of inches away from me along the sofa. 'What do you mean?'

'At work? What am I doing?'

He drains the beer from the glass and stands up. 'Let me think about it,' he says.

After the match I press my heel into his thigh again. He gets up.

'You still haven't told me,' I say.

'I have an idea,' he says, picking up his glass. He goes out into the kitchen and comes back with another glass of beer and a bowl of pistachios. He offers me the bowl.

'No thanks,' I say. 'What's your idea?'

He sits down and reaches for my hand.

'How about Director of Customer Experience?' he says. 'How does that sound?'

I shrug my shoulders. 'Explain.'

'Well,' he says, 'I've been talking to Mum and Mary and we think we need to get closer to the customer. Understand them a bit better.'

Twenty-Four

Though it's raining it's a pleasant walk to the bar on my second day back. Mike's gone in before me, saying he had something urgent to take care of. I'm protected by my yellow waterproof jacket and navy bucket hat. I'm wearing the staff uniform: cream t-shirt, black trousers, cream apron and a whistle on a lanyard. Nobody sees me come in and I go up to see Mike.

'What do you think?' I say, standing in the middle of his office, by the bench.

'Suits you,' he says, 'what do you think Mary?'

Today Mary is wearing a slim-fitting black pinafore dress over a white blouse with black sheer tights and red heels.

'Lovely.' She swivels her chair around and I can't see her face.

'You look great,' Mike says.

'Have you told the staff what I'm doing?'

'Sure,' he says, 'Director of Customer Experience.'

'For now,' I say, 'remember?' Mary swivels her chair around to face us.

'Take your laptop too,' Mike says, 'if you want a break, staff will think you're still working.'

'But I am working.'

'Of course you are,' he says, 'just if you need a break. That's all.' I go over to Mary. Perhaps I was a little unfriendly to her yesterday, when we were first introduced. She's helping us out, just until I get back on my feet. I should have been more welcoming.

'Happy to help you while you're here,' I say, 'answer any questions.'

'Thanks,' she says, 'but Mike's already filled me in.' I turn to Mike but he's stood at his window looking outside.

I cross the landing to the bathroom. Through the open window, I hear shouts of 'Service!' coming from the kitchen below. I spend two minutes looking in the full-length mirror. A Director going back to the floor, like in the TV series. I admit, I was a little reluctant when he first explained it. Now I realise this is actually a good idea. Coming back to work full-time, after being ill, was asking too much. This way I can ease myself back in and nobody needs to be any the wiser.

I go downstairs to the bar. When Chrissie sees me in a

staff uniform she looks puzzled.

'What's going on Ruth?' she says, shaking her head.

'Didn't you get the message?' I say. 'I'm Director of Customer Experience now.'

'But the uniform?'

'To get closer to the customers,' I explain, straightening the bar towels, 'no good being stuck upstairs.'

Between eleven and two, I take food orders, moving between the kitchen, booths and the bar. Some regular customers say how good it is to see me back. A few ask me about Mum and her hip operation.

'It's marvellous what they can do now,' one says, 'I got excellent care.'

'Is she having physio now?' another says. 'That really helped me.'

I smile, happy to listen, relieved there are no awkward questions I can't answer.

When I'm tired I grab the laptop from under the counter and take it to an empty booth. I have research to do, on our new colleague. I log into my *LinkedIn* account. There are a few people with her name on there, but not many who've worked in hospitality. I do find a match, although there's no photograph. If I'm right she was an operations manager for a chain of restaurants in London.

On our way home, I link my arm through Mike's. 'Where did you find Mary?'

He lets out a loud laugh. 'On a dating app.'

I pull my arm away and give him a gentle slap. 'Be serious.'

'She's great isn't she?'

'What's she doing in Thornsea?' I ask. 'She was in London wasn't she?'

He stops. 'How do you know that?'

'I *Googled* her.'

We carry on, in silence, until we reach our drive.

'You've still not told me about her,' I say, as he's putting the key in the lock.

'What do you want to know?'

'Everything,' I say, 'if she's sharing an office with you.'

In the hall he takes off his fleece jacket and boots.

'I think she split from her husband,' he says, 'she's come back to her parents.'

That's all I need to know, for now.

Jean's in the kitchen and I can smell the wonderful aroma of cottage pie.

'Have you met Mary?' I ask her. She rinses the potato masher under the tap. '

Isn't she great?' she says, 'a real find, very good at her

job.'

Mike smiles. 'We're lucky to have her. And David likes her.'

'David's met her as well?' I say.

'Of course,' Jean says, 'he's our business partner. He needs to know who he's working with.'

I go upstairs and take off my trousers. I have a red mark where the waistband has been digging in. I take a shower and change into my silk pyjamas. I lie on the bed and roll over into the foetal position. I don't want to be serving customers downstairs, knowing Mary and Mike are upstairs, sharing an office. I must suggest something Mike will approve of. Whatever I decide, I won't be wearing this uniform again.

Downstairs, Jean's taking the cottage pie out of the oven and Mike's getting the dinner plates.

'I'd like to try something different tomorrow,' I say, 'if that's okay with you two.'

'As long as you don't interfere with Mary's work,' Mike says.

'I won't,' I say, 'I think you'll be impressed.'

Twenty-Five

In the morning I get a hair appointment at the new place that's opened in Railway Street. The hairdresser suggests adding some darker tones. While I'm waiting to get my hair washed I swipe through smart work-wear outfits and order two trouser suits and a pair of black patent heels. At the beauty salon, a few doors down, I have my nails shaped, painted a deep emerald green and my eyebrows tinted. And in the chemists, I spend at least an hour searching for the perfect shade of foundation and lipstick.

When I get to the bar, after lunch, I go straight to the kitchen where I find Sam, filling the freezer with tubs of luxury vanilla ice cream.

'Everything okay Ruth?' he asks, closing the freezer door.

'This place could do with some tidying up,' I say, pointing to the shelves.

'They're not usually this bad,' he says, 'been a bit manic

lately.'

I open the doors of a metal cupboard and two colanders fall towards me. I step to the side to avoid them. They clang as they tumble across the tiled floor, one stopping at his feet, the other by the sink. I wait, in silence. Sam looks at me, takes a deep breath and picks them up.

'You'll have to wash those now,' I say.

He turns and drops them into the empty sink. 'We're a bit short-staffed at the minute,' he says, taking some empty boxes from the shelves.

'Staffing's nothing to do with me anymore,' I say, 'that's Mary's department.' He mumbles something under his breath but I don't catch it. 'What was that?' I snap, turning to him.

'Nothing, it doesn't matter.'

I turn to leave. 'I'll come and check again soon. See if anything's improved.'

Chrissie's next on my list. I find her in the bar.

'Who cleaned the floor last night?' I ask, abruptly.

She looks up, with a startled expression. 'Err, I think I mopped it. Yeah I did.'

I gesture for her to follow me. 'Take a look at this,' I say. We walk over to a corner by the front window. There's a ball of dust in the corner and a couple of old chips trodden into the floor.

She looks at the chips, then at me. 'Sorry Ruth.'

'Go and fetch a brush and mop please?' I say. 'And don't leave it like this again.' I help her move the stools, then watch as she brushes and mops the floor again.

'Okay now? she asks, when she's returned the mop to the cleaning cupboard.

'I'll be checking tomorrow,' I say, going back to the kitchen.

Gary, the pot washer, is the final one to get the new treatment. I search for an item to show him.

'What's wrong with this?' I say, holding out a dinner plate.

'Looks okay to me,' he says, shrugging his shoulders.

Sam, washing lettuce leaves at the sink, turns around to watch us. Gary's mouth curls into a smirk and Sam covers his mouth.

'Turn it over,' I say, 'and take a look.'

'There's a small chip in the base? Is that what you mean?'

'Any damaged crockery goes in there,' I say, pointing to a cardboard box on the bottom shelf.

'Sorry Ruth. It's so small, I didn't notice.'

'If you could pay a bit more attention from now on. That will be appreciated.'

I leave the kitchen, satisfied I've made an impact. I go

upstairs to my office and *Google* '*Difficult Conversations With Staff*'. Three hours later, I'm finishing an article I've found in *Management Today* on managing under-performance. There are some great tips I can suggest to Mike and Jean which, I know, will impress them. I take out my notebook to copy some of the text.

There's a knock on my door. It's Mary.

'Can I have a word?' she says, standing in the doorway. It's the first time we've been alone together. It's a good opportunity to find out more about her. Specifically, what are her long-term plans and how long is she planning to stay with us? If she's looking for her next career move I'm willing to give her a good reference.

'Of course,' I say, 'any help I can give, just ask.'

'There've been some complaints,' she says, sitting down.

I find a blank page in my notebook. 'Let me take some details. 'I'll investigate.' I'm pleased to have a problem to resolve.

She inspects her perfect nails. I wonder if I should have had a French manicure like hers. 'They're about you.'

I put my pen down. 'Me?'

'Three members of staff have come to see me.'

'Oh,' I say.

'I think you need to apologise,' she says, 'they're not

happy.'

'What? Why?'

She gets up and goes to the door. 'Nice hair by the way.'

I shut down my laptop and close the lid. I sneak downstairs, careful I don't meet any of the staff on my way out. There's probably a thread on the staff *WhatsApp* chat about this already. I've never had any staff complaints before. And to Mary of all people. I send Mike a text: *Going Home.*

I head for Railway Street. Didn't the elderly man at the art exhibition say that's where the Art Club was? I find it next to the Swann Pub. When I open the bright blue door the elderly man is sitting on a stool at a high table. There are a couple of other people here, heads down, paintbrushes in hand. A tall woman in dungarees and a headscarf is at the sink, washing brushes.

'Welcome,' the elderly man says, 'are you joining us?'

'I came to the art exhibition,' I say, hoping he recognises me, 'in the Town Hall.' The woman at the sink turns and smiles. She looks familiar but I'm not sure where I've seen her before. As she comes closer, I read the badge on her dungarees: *Save our Woodland.*

'Welcome,' she says, wiping her hands, 'I'm Milly.'

'Hi,' I say, 'I'm Ruth.'

'And I'm Henry,' the elderly man says, 'Milly's father.'

'You're just in time for our watercolour workshop,' Milly says, 'take a seat.'

Henry passes me a clipboard. 'Put your details on here. It's £3 a session.' I find three pound coins in my purse and add my name to the list.

As the layers of colour build the picture of the boating lake I'm a million miles from work.

When we take a break, Henry goes over to a box of vinyl records on a shelf at the back. There's an old record player next to them, like the one I got for Christmas when I was 16. It's still in my bedroom at Mum and Dad's.

'What are we having today Dad?' Milly asks, lifting the cover from the turntable.

Henry holds up the album cover for us all to read it: *American Classics by Leroy Anderson conducted by Leonard Slatkin and the BBC Concert Orchestra.*

We carry on painting. The embarrassment of this morning is diluted among the paints, chatter and music.

'This reminds me of the time I went to Taos Pueblo,' Milly says.

I've never heard of it. 'Where's that?' I ask, putting my brush down.

Milly tells us all about the time she went travelling around New Mexico, after art school. 'That was my favourite place out of the whole trip.' For the past five years Mike and I have gone to the same golf resort in Marbella. Mike loves it there and, I admit, we are spoiled. But Taos Pueblo? It sounds so exotic, so exciting.

I walk back along Beach Road, my painting tucked safely under my arm. I smile at passers-by and say Hello to strangers. I have some apologising to do and it's better I get it over soon, while I'm in a good mood.

When I reach the bar I head straight to the kitchen. There are boxes out, covering the floor and Sam's holding a half-full bin bag.

'Sorry it's not all sorted,' he says, 'if you can give me a couple more days.'

'Don't worry about it,' I say, 'you're doing a great job.'

He puts the bin bag down. 'Oh,' he says, 'okay, thanks.'

'Sorry for before. I went a bit too far.'

'No worries,' he says, smiling.

I leave the kitchen and find Chrissie and Gary in the bar. Like Sam, they accept my apologies graciously.

At home Mike's at his laptop in the kitchen.

'I believe Mary had to have a word with you,' he says, not looking up.

'It's alright,' I say, 'I've already apologised. I went too far before.' I stand behind him and wrap my arms around his shoulders, kissing his neck.

He turns towards me. 'You've had your hair done.'

I move away so he can see it properly. 'You like it?'

'It suits you,' he says.

I wrap my arms around him again.

'Can't I just have my old job back?' I kiss his neck again. 'Please?'

He gets down from his high stool, releasing my hold. 'Not yet,' he says, 'especially not now. Not after upsetting the staff.'

'But I've apologised,' I say.

'And we've been invited to David and Cara's,' he says, 'tomorrow night.'

'Should we tell them I was ill?' I ask, getting a glass of water.

'No,' he says, 'I don't want them to know.'

Twenty-Six

As Mike and I are driving to David and Cara's house I feel a knot in my stomach.

I check my makeup in the passenger mirror. 'What if he finds out about me being ill?'

'Why would he?' Mike says. 'Don't worry?'

David and Cara meet us outside the lift in the car park.

'Ruth,' David says, 'how lovely to see you again.'

I smile. 'You too David,' I say, 'so sorry I missed your opening night.'

'It couldn't be helped,' David says, 'how's your mum?'

'Great thanks,' I say, looking at Mike, 'she's recovering well.'

We take the lift to the hall and David leads us into the lounge.

'Where did she have it done?' he asks.

In that moment I freeze. No one's asked me that question yet and I have no reply prepared.

'Erm, erm,' I stutter, looking at Mike, hoping he'll

assist.

'Over in Elsford,' Mike says.

'Yes,' I say, catching my breath, 'in Elsford.'

'Elsford?' David asks.

'That's where I'm from,' I say, 'originally.'

It's Cara who comes to my rescue. 'Why don't I take Ruth out to the stables?'

'I'd love to,' I say, nodding to Cara, gratefully.

When we return to the dining room, David and Mike are seated and chatting about football. Starters is garlic mushrooms on toast.

'So I hear you have a new role Ruth,' David says. 'Congratulations.'

Before I can reply Mike interrupts. 'Yes. Director of Customer Experience.'

'That's right,' I say, turning to Mike, raising my eyebrows.

'And Mary seems very capable,' Cara says, 'I like her.'

'Me too,' David says, 'it's good you're expanding your team.'

Mike reaches for my hand under the table and gives it a gentle squeeze.

'And Ruth will be looking at new projects for us too?'

'Sounds interesting,' David says, 'tell me more.'

'The Thornsea Unit,' Mike says, 'we're going to put in a bid to run the visitor café.' I look at Mike who smiles back at me and squeezes my hand, tighter this time.

David wipes his mouth on a napkin. 'Could be very lucrative, keep me updated about that.'

I stay mostly quiet for the rest of the evening and wait until we're in the car, alone.

'So where did that come from?' I ask, as we're exiting the gates.

'What?' Mike says.

'The Thornsea Unit café? What was all that about?'

Mike pats my leg. 'The café. We're going to put a tender in. To run it.'

Twenty-Seven

The Thornsea Business Association Awards Dinner takes place every year on the first Thursday in April. In 2015 we won the Best Hospitality award. Tonight it's at the Railway Hotel. I'm wearing my green taffeta cocktail dress. I haven't been able to fit into this since my 40th.

In the foyer, Mike, Jean and I study the table plan. We're sitting with two councillors who, Mike tells me, are on the licensing committee. Also on our table is Thornsea's star striker, Bruno Araujo. According to Mike, Bruno's the reason we managed to avoid relegation last season.

'Make sure you sit next to Bruno,' Mike tells me, reaching into the inside of his tuxedo. He hands me a 50% money-off voucher. 'Let him have this.'

As we're having our picture taken, for Coastal Monthly, I notice Mary on the other side of the Ballroom. When she sees me she waves.

I nudge Mike, 'Mary's here.'

'I know,' he says, unsurprised.

I try to get a glimpse of who she's come with. A partner? At least she's not on our table.

After the soup Mike leans in and whispers. 'How you getting on with Bruno?'

'Fine,' I say, hoping Bruno hasn't heard him.

Mike whispers into my ear again. 'Now's a good time to give him the voucher.'

I reach into my clutch bag and rest the voucher against Bruno's wine glass. 'Just a little something from us,' I say, as he picks it up.

He puts the voucher in his pocket. 'Thanks,' he says, 'I'll donate it to our new project.' He tells me he's starting a project to get men talking and supporting each other.

In between the main course and dessert Bruno continues. 'We're starting a talking café, where fans can chat or get advice before matches.'

'Sounds great,' I say.

'Maybe you could advertise them in your bar?'

'I'll speak to Mike,' I say, knowing he'll say no.

I go outside for fresh air. When I come back I see Olivia. She hugs me.

'Ruth! How are you?' she says. 'You look great!'

I remember the last time we spoke. 'I think I've got

some explaining to do.'

She puts me at ease. 'Don't worry about it, just glad you're well again.'

'I'm sorry I missed your event,' I say, 'heard it went well.'

'A complete success,' she says, 'apart from you not being there of course.'

Back at our table Mary's chatting with Mike and Jean. She's sitting in my seat, leaning back against my bolero jacket. I wait behind them, watching as they laugh together. When she gets up she comes over, still laughing.

'Settling back in okay?' she says, sipping the last of her champagne.

'I'm trying,' I say.

'It must be difficult for you,' she says, 'you're bound to make a few mistakes - after what you've been through.' I smile but don't reply. I need to have a word with Mike, but not here.

When we arrive home Ellie and Daniel meet us in the hall.

'You're late back,' Ellie says.

Mike loosens his cummerbund. 'Everything okay?'

'There was banging on the door,' Daniel says, 'about an

hour ago.'

I sit on the bottom stair massaging my toes. 'Who was it?'

'Don't know,' Ellie says, 'they went before we could see.'

'Probably the wind catching the door knocker,' Mike says, pushing the bar across the door.

In bed Mike pulls me towards him, but I pull away.

'What did you tell Mary?' I ask. 'About why I was off work?'

'The same as everyone else,' he says.

I turn away from him. 'You sure?'

'Of course,' he says, rubbing my back.

Twenty-Eight

In my dream, I'm on a fairground ride. Red and blue lights flash in the tunnel as the carriages gather speed, creating a deafening noise. I'm rocking violently from side to side.

'Ruth! Ruth!' Mike's shaking me. 'Wake up!' The lights from my dream fill our room and there's a thunderous noise above.

'What the hell's going on?' I say, sitting up.

Mike opens the curtains. 'It's on the beach.'

We stand on the balcony. By the bus stop, there are three police cars and an ambulance. The seafront railings are wrapped in blue and white tape, behind a row of orange cones.

Wide awake, with overcoats over our pyjamas, we go outside into the cold night. Across the road, there's a large white tent by the stone steps. A police officer comes over.

'Can I help?' she shouts.

'We live across the road!' Mike shouts back.

The officer gestures at us to move away. 'If you could go back home please,' she shouts, 'no one's allowed down there.'

'We own the Sports Bar,' Mike shouts. He points across the road. 'We can open early.'

It's 7 am before anyone comes into the bar. The first is a woman, carrying a dictaphone and a laptop bag. I guess she's in her late twenties. She has beautiful long black curly hair and brown eyes. Then a man with shoulder-length grey hair, carrying a large shoulder bag. I recognise him straightaway. He's the photographer from the Awards Dinner last night. They both ask for flat white coffees.

'Do you know what's happened on the beach?' I ask the man, offering him the payment terminal.

'They've found a body,' he says, 'a young woman.' It must be ten years since a body was last found on the beach. An accidental drowning, two teenage boys, in a dinghy late at night.

'Do they know who it is yet?' I ask.

'Not formally,' the woman says, 'but it's probably the girl who's gone missing.'

'I didn't know anyone was missing.'

'Sophie Carlton,' the man says. He takes his coffee and they go to a booth at the back. I follow.

'Excuse me,' I say, when they're seated, 'did you say Sophie Carlton?'

The woman looks at the man, then at me. 'The police put a message out yesterday,' she says, 'she didn't turn up to a hospital appointment.' There's an explosion in my stomach and my legs are shaking. I lean on their table to steady myself.

'Are you okay?' the man asks, concerned.

'I know Sophie,' I say, 'I was talking to her last week.'

The woman reaches into her bag and takes out a wallet. 'You know her?'

'We were in hospital together,' I say.

The woman puts a business card in front of me:

Rebecca Dodd

Reporter

County Herald

'We're with the paper,' she says, 'would you be willing to say a few words?'

I step back. I've said too much already. 'Sorry,' I say, 'I can't.'

'No worries.' She gives me a sympathetic smile. 'I understand.'

Back behind the bar, I make myself a mug of tea, adding

a generous capful of whiskey. It must have been Sophie at our door last night.

Before they leave the woman comes over. 'Sorry you had to hear it from me,' she says, 'I didn't know you were friends.'

'Are you sure it's her?' I ask, hoping there's been a mistake.

She offers me her card again. 'Will you take my details, in case you change your mind?'

'No,' I say, my hands behind my back, 'sorry.'

'No worries,' she says, 'I understand.'

When Chrissie starts her shift, I go up to Mike's office. He's at his desk, staring at his laptop screen. He doesn't look up as I go in.

'They think it's Sophie.' I say, going over to the window.

'Sophie? Who's Sophie?'

'We were in the Unit together,' I say, 'you saw us talking at the bus stop last week.'

'Oh,' he says.

From the window, I watch two police officers waiting to cross the road. 'Should I tell the police?'

'Tell them what?'

'Tell them I knew her.'

'What good will that do?' he says. 'Why would they

want to know?' I turn back to the window. Below, the two officers are at the door to the bar.

'The banging on our door last night,' I say, 'do you think it was Sophie?'

'No,' Mike says, 'probably the wind.'

'I think it was her,' I say, 'she knew our house.'

He sighs. 'Don't think about it.' I turn from the window and head for the door.

'I'm going to tell the police,' I say, crossing the office, 'it might help.'

Mike gets up quickly and stands between me and the door. 'Don't get involved.' He puts his hand up, to stop me reaching the handle.

'I need the bathroom,' I say.

He puts his hand down and moves out of the way. I get onto the landing and go downstairs.

From the doorway, at the back of the bar, I watch the two officers talking to Chrissie. I watch for half a minute before turning around and going back to my office.

An hour later, while I'm reading the County Herald online, there's a knock at my door. It's Chrissie.

'There's someone asking for you, downstairs.'

I'm trying to look calm but my heart's racing. 'The police?'

'No,' Chrissie says, 'from the County Herald.'

'Oh her,' I say, my shoulders relaxing. 'She's trying to sell us advertising. Tell her I'm not available.'

Twenty-Nine

The following day I sleep until noon. There's a new post on the police's *Facebook* page, Sophie's body has been formally identified. This was an unfortunate and tragic event, it states, and there are no suspicious circumstances. Sophie's family have asked for their privacy to be respected at this time.

I open the balcony doors, it's just the usual traffic along the seafront now. The police cars and media have moved on. A double-decker bus stops across the road. When it moves away, a woman is standing at the kerb. She shuffles towards the seafront railings; a bunch of flowers in one hand and a giant brown teddy under her arm.

Perhaps I'm being intrusive, but I want to pay my respects to Sophie too. I throw on the same clothes from yesterday and go across the road. When I get near, the woman is leaning on the railings, with her back to me. I make a loud deliberate cough and she turns, dropping the teddy on the pavement. I recognise Sophie's features in her face. I guess she's a few years younger than me, but she looks frail and tired. Her light blonde hair, streaked with grey, is pinned back with tortoiseshell clips.

'Sophie's mum?'

She nods, picking up the teddy, holding it tight to her chest. 'I wanted to bring this for her,' she says, 'she loved teddies.'

'I live across the road,' I say, pointing to our house. We stand together at the railings, looking at the patch of sand where the white tent stood yesterday. 'I was in the Unit with her,' I say, 'only talking to her last Friday.'

'Thornsea Unit?'

I nod, remembering the day we met in the dormitory. 'She was one of the first people to talk to me.' The woman starts to sob, her shoulders shaking as she takes rapid breaths, squeezing the teddy even tighter.

'We found a note in her flat,' she says, 'they'd told her she might have to go back.'

'And she didn't want to?'

'She hated it in there, she said she'd never go back.'

She rests the teddy by the railings. It flops to one side. She tries again and again to make it sit up, each time it flops over.

'I've got some string at home,' I say, 'wait there.'

Back in our kitchen I find some string. I rip a page out

of a notebook and write my name and telephone number.

Back at the railings we secure the teddy and flowers.

'I hope he's going to be okay,' Sophie's mum says, 'I'd hate anyone to pinch him.'

I give her the ripped page with my details. 'I'll keep an eye on him, don't worry about that.'

'Ruth. I think she mentioned you.' She puts out her hand, 'I'm Terese.'

'If I can help in any way,' I say, 'anything at all.' We turn and lean against the railings.

'I tried to get her the help she needed, but it was hard.' She starts sobbing again. I put my arm around Terese's shoulders.

'Will you let me know about the funeral please?' I say. 'I'd like to be there.'

'Of course,' she says, 'of course.'

I leave Terese, with the teddy and the flowers, and carry on to the bar. When I reach the car park I make a call. My daughter doesn't pick up so I leave her a message:

'Just your mum here, telling you how much I love you.'

In the bar, I make myself a coffee and take it to a booth at the back. From here I can keep an eye on the door in case the reporter from the County Herald comes back. I can hide myself in the corner and sneak out the back if I need to.

Jean comes in half an hour later. I think about deploying my escape plan, but I'm too late. She spots me and comes over, holding a copy of Coastal Monthly.

'Remember I was chatting to the photographer at the Awards Dinner?' she says, putting the magazine down.

I suspect she's been making plans again. 'Yes?'

She grins. 'Well you, me and Ellie are going to be local celebrities,' she says, 'they're doing a feature on us.' I get down from the booth, taking the magazine with me. I don't say a word but head upstairs, Jean following behind. When we get to my office I leave the door open and she comes in. I close the door and slam the magazine on my desk.

'What do you think you're doing?!' I shout. 'Making decisions without me!'

She picks up the magazine. 'For goodness sake Ruth, what's up now?'

I pace up and down, feeling my cheeks getting hotter. 'But we never discussed this.'

'Calm down,' she says, 'you're overreacting.'

I push past her, open the door, cross the landing and go into the bathroom. In the mirror, I examine my reddened face, streaming with tears.

Jean comes in, a few minutes later. 'Have you calmed down now?'

I go to the sink and splash my face with cold water. 'I should have been consulted,' I say, patting my skin with a towel. She sits in the armchair by the window.

'We talked about it when you weren't here,' she says, 'you've been off. Remember?' I want to scream, but I don't. Instead, I go back to my office and go to the wall calendar behind my desk. All the weeks in March are crossed out, in red. I hear Jean going down the corridor to Mike's office. I go back to the bathroom and look in the mirror. Mike will be annoyed with me. I take a deep breath and prepare my apology.

When I get to Mike's office she's sitting on the leather bench talking with Mike and Mary about me.

'I shouldn't have done that,' I say, interrupting their conversation, 'sorry.'

Jean looks at Mike. 'You did overreact a bit.'

'I'm upset about Sophie, that's all.'

Mike gets up and hugs me. 'We know it's upsetting,' he says, 'but no need to take it out on Mum. What's she ever done to upset you?'

'I'm sorry,' I say, again.

'You need something to work on,' he says, 'a project.' He goes over to Mary's desk and picks up a yellow file. 'For the café,' he says, handing it to me.

I open the file. 'What's this?'

'The café in the Unit,' he says, 'we could run it.'

'You're serious? You want us to run the visitor café? In the Unit?'

He nods. 'And you know it best.' I take a moment to consider his proposal. If I win it might mean I might get my old job back. And if I get my old job we won't need Mary anymore. I open the file and leaf through the first few pages.

'Okay,' I say, heading for the door, 'I'll do it.'

Back in my office I put the file on a shelf and my head on the desk.

Thirty

That night I go to bed early, taking the café file with me. Mary's already scribbled notes in some sections. When Mike comes to bed I'm balancing my laptop on a pillow.

'Working late?' he says, smiling. 'You're keen.'

'Making up for lost time. And I want us to win this.'

He climbs in next to me. 'I was worried you'd be upset.'

'About what?'

'About Mary taking on your old role,' he says, turning off his lamp.

I close the laptop lid and slide it under the bed. 'She's just helping out,' I say, 'I know that.'

'Good, glad you understand.'

I move closer and rest my head on his chest. 'I know it's not for long.'

'And it's not just us anymore,' he says, 'David needs to know we're on top of things.'

In my dream I'm in Times Square, New York, on

a bicycle. Floating past all the brightly lit advertising billboards. Travelling at 100 miles an hour, the colours blending, filling the sky. Then I slow down, almost to a stop, where I hover hundreds of feet above the ground, inspecting each pixel.

In the morning I hear Jean and Mike talking on the landing, outside the bedroom.

'How's she been?' Jean asks.

'Okay, I think.' Mike replies.

'Still annoyed with me?' Their conversation stops and they go upstairs.

When I step onto the landing, I hear them, in the top lounge.

'She's still unstable,' Jean says, 'I mean what was all that about yesterday - about a photoshoot for God's sake?' I sit on the stair, listening, as still as I can.

'She does get upset more easily,' Mike says.

'Should we get back in touch with the Unit?' Jean says, 'Maybe she should go back in.'

'Let's keep an eye on things,' Mike says, 'see how she gets on.'

I grab the handrail to pull myself up.

When I reach the doorway Jean looks at me and smiles.

'We thought you were asleep.' The two of them are sitting close together on the sofa.

I sit opposite, holding a cushion on my lap. 'You woke me. I heard you talking.'

'I'm not sure you should be back at work,' she says, 'you're clearly still unwell.' I look at Mike, but he says nothing.

I put the cushion against the arm of the sofa and lie down, pulling a faux fur throw over my legs. 'I'm fine,'

She continues, 'You do seem to be getting worked up about the smallest of things.'

'Sorry,' I say, adjusting my arms to get comfortable.

'It's not doing you any good,' she says, 'you'll end up there again if you carry on.'

Mike gets up. I don't want to be left alone with Jean while she's like this. I kick off the throw and follow Mike downstairs.

In the kitchen, he opens the fridge and takes out the remains of a cheesecake.

'Are you going to let her speak to me like that?'

'Like what?' He cuts a slice of cheesecake for himself. 'She has a point. You're not helping yourself.'

'I apologised,' I say, 'why is she carrying on?'

'She's worried,' he says, 'putting the cheesecake back in the fridge.

I won't get upset. I must stay calm. I go into the downstairs loo and check my reflection. My eyes are pink, glistening. I need to take a walk, by myself.

I head across the road to the railings. The teddy is still there, with the flowers. There's another bunch today. I lean forward, to smell some red roses, when a large floral wreath is placed on the pavement next to my feet. I look down and read the card: *With our deepest sympathy, from all at The County Herald x.*

As I turn around, my boot catches on a stone. I'm only saved from falling forward by the person beside me.

'Thanks,' I say, lifting my head. 'Oh, it's you.'

The woman from The County Herald is holding my arm. 'You okay?'

I pull away. 'Fine. Good job you were there.'

'You're from the bar. You knew Sophie?'

I'm still shaken from my near fall and lean against the railings. 'Yeah, we were in the Unit together.'

She puts out her hand. 'Rebecca.'

I remember her name, from the card I wouldn't take. 'Ruth,' I say, shaking her hand,

'I'm investigating the Unit.'

'Investigating? Why?'

'Let's get a coffee,' she says, 'I'll tell you.'

She has a kind face. And it's only the County Herald.

Not exactly a national tabloid. And I'm not ready to go back home yet to face Jean and Mike.

'As long as you don't print anything,' I say.

She nods. 'Strictly off the record.' We set off towards the pier. 'I've spoken to some people already.'

'Patients?'

'Not many patients, families mostly.'

When we get to the little van at the top of the pier she buys me a black coffee. We sit on the bench nearby.

'What have they told you?'

'They don't think their relatives got good care,' she says. My phone buzzes. It's a text from Terese with the details of Sophie's funeral.

'I don't want this in the paper,' I say, putting my phone back in my pocket. 'If my family found out.'

'Of course.'

I take a deep breath. 'I was assaulted by another patient. The staff denied it.'

'You're not the first to tell me something like that,' she says.

'You won't print that will you?'

'No. Not without your permission.'

She stands and offers me her business card again. This time I take it.

'Let's keep in touch,' she says. 'You know where I am.

Thirty-One

I'm at Thornsea Crematorium. One of Sophie's brothers is finishing a beautiful poem he's written for her. There are so many young people here. I wonder if Sophie knew she had all these friends.

Afterwards I wait outside, away from the other mourners. When she spots me, Terese comes over and I hug her.

'Beautiful service,' I say, 'you did her proud.'

'Thanks so much for coming,' she says. Her hair is straight today. The tortoiseshell hair clips replaced by thick black ones.

'If there's anything I can do to help,' I say, 'anything at all.'

Two young girls come over to hug Terese. They tell her how sad and shocked they are about Sophie. When they've gone she turns to me.

'I have to clear out her flat by next week,' she says, 'I don't have a car. I don't know what I'm going to do.'

'I can help,' I say, 'no problem.'

Two days later I'm turning into Marsham Crescent. Terese has told me to look for Orchard House. I know the building well. It's where Alison and I stayed on our holiday in Thornsea, when it was the Orchard Guesthouse. I've not been in this street since Mike worked here. As I get out of the car, I see Terese coming along the pavement, pulling a large shopping trolley.

'Can you do a few trips to the tip?' she asks, when she stops at the gate. 'I won't fit much in here.'

Sophie's flat is on the ground floor. I remember this was the lounge bar. The huge oak fireplace is still here but it's been boarded up and replaced with an electric heater. Sophie's flat is tidier than I expected. The bed's made and the kitchen counters are clear.

'I made a start yesterday,' Terese says. On the small kitchen table there's a sewing machine, holding a long piece of black silk.

'She could sew?' I say, impressed. 'I didn't know.'

'I taught her. She made a lot of her own things.'

We open drawers, emptying clothes into bin liners. The shopping trolley is for things Terese wants to keep but it's soon two-thirds full. I hold up a framed photo of the two of them together, hugging and smiling into the camera. It can't have been taken too long ago.

'Are you keeping this?' I ask.

'Go on,' she says, 'but once this trolley's full that's it. I don't have a lot of room at home.'

Terese puts a mug into her bin bag.

'Can I have that?' I say, reaching for the familiar yellow mug. She looks puzzled but hands it to me anyway. 'I remember giving her this,' I say. I put the yellow ***Brighter Days Are Ahead*** mug in my bag. It's a little stained on the inside but I'm pleased to see Sophie must have used it, at least once.

We've been here for four hours, and there's still loads to do, but I've been sitting on the floor too long and I need to stretch my legs.

'C'mon,' I say, 'let me buy you lunch.'

We go around the corner to the Swann. Terese isn't hungry but I order lasagne with chips.

'There's a reporter from the County Herald,' I say, 'she wants to speak to me about the Unit.'

'Rebecca Dodd?'

'You know her?'

'She put a note through Sophie's letterbox,' she says, 'asking me to contact her.' Terese picks at an open bag of cheese and onion crisps and sips her shandy. 'It's got a bad reputation.'

I look at my watch. I've still got work to do on the café project.

We walk back to the flat and survey what's left of Sophie's possessions.

'I'll call some charity shops,' Terese says, 'they might take some things.'

After three trips to the tip we're left with two suitcases and the shopping trolley. I give Terese a lift home and we take Sophie's things to her old bedroom. Terese sits on the bed and squeezes a pillow into her chest.

'Just have to get through the inquest now,' she says.

I go back to my office and work until seven, finishing off the first stage of the café bid.

At home Mike's in the lounge watching a match. There's a bottle of Rioja and a jar of olives on the coffee table.

'How's the café project coming on?' he asks, as I sit down.

'First stage completed. I've sent it back, two days before the deadline.'

He smiles and taps me on the leg, twice. 'Well done.'

I take some olives from the bowl. 'I was with Sophie's mum today,' I say, 'helping her clear out the flat. The

Orchard Guesthouse is flats now.'

'And that was such a nice street years ago,' he says.

The second half of the match starts and I curl myself into the corner of the sofa. My mind's not on the game but on the Unit. When the match is over, and Mike's happy with the result, I continue.

'She was telling me about the Unit,' I say, 'how it's got a bad reputation.'

'They looked after you well.'

I push my foot into his thigh. 'I was assaulted. Remember?'

'You've just sent them a bid to run their café,' he says, 'don't go looking for trouble now.'

I shake my head. 'I'm not.'

'David says well done on putting the bid in,' he says, showing me a *WhatsApp* message on his phone. I get up from the sofa and go upstairs to our bedroom. On the balcony, I look over to the railings and the teddy. I have my first appointment with a community nurse in the morning. She's called Jess and she's from the Early Intervention Service. I'm hoping she can give me some answers.

Thirty-Two

Jess is 10 minutes late. When I open the front door she's admiring the tulips. She has bleached blonde, chin-length wavy hair and wears bright red lipstick, faded jeans and a dark green parker.

'I love this garden,' she says, putting out her hand to shake mine.

'My mother-in-law's work. I've not had much time for gardening.'

When she steps into the hall she looks around and smiles. 'This is lovely. Love your wallpaper.'

'I'll show you the views from the second floor,' I say, going upstairs.

When she gets to the bay window, in the top lounge, I can see she's impressed by the view. We stand side by side.

'What a lovely place you have here,' she says.

'I really missed this,' I say, 'when...well...you know...,' my words trailing off.

She sits on the sofa and I sit on the one opposite. I'm

curious to know what the Early Intervention Service is.

'It's for people who've experienced psychosis.'

I pull a face and shake my head. There must be some mistake. No one ever mentioned psychosis. 'I didn't have that.'

She takes out a folder and reads a form. 'That's what it says in my notes.'

'No one told me that.'

'You were hallucinating? Or hearing voices? Imagining things that weren't real.'

'I was in a lot of pain. So bad, I thought I was dying.'

'But you weren't were you?'

'I wasn't dying, no.' I shake my head. 'The pain was very real though. It made me think I was dying. I just wanted to be out of pain.' Jess clicks her pen and scribbles something in her notes.

I go downstairs to the kitchen and, while the kettle's boiling, I *Google* 'Psychosis'. When I return to the lounge Jess is standing at the window again.

'Help yourself to the biscuits,' I say, putting the tray on the coffee table.

'No, thanks,' she says, 'I'm trying to be good.' I pour coffee from the cafetiere. Jess pours a black tea.

'But you seem much better now,' she says, sitting down.

'I am thanks.'

She clicks her pen and scribbles again. 'No hearing voices?'

'I never heard voices. I was in a lot of pain.'

The doorbell rings and I go downstairs. It's a parcel for Daniel. Probably equipment for his band. When I go back upstairs I'm curious to know more about my diagnosis.

'This psychosis?' I ask. 'How would I have got it?'

She smiles. 'It's not something you can catch,' she says, 'it just happened.'

I remember the time Daniel broke his leg, when he was 15, and the consultant showed us a diagram and explained the physiotherapy he needed.

We sip our drinks in silence.

'And you're aware of the weight gain?' she says.

'Nobody mentioned weight gain.'

'Side effect of the medication,' she says, 'don't worry too much, just something to be aware of.' I'm regretting bringing out the fancy biscuits now.

'I try to go for a walk most days,' I say.

Jess puts her folder and pen back in her bag and reaches for her coat. 'I think we're done,' she says. We walk to the top of our drive.

'Did you hear about Sophie Carlton?' I ask.

She finds her keys in her bag. 'I heard about it,' she says, 'awful.'

'I've been thinking about her a lot. She didn't want to go back to the Unit.'

'Best not dwell on these things,' she says, turning towards her car, 'focus on the future.'

After our meeting I go up to the bedroom and open my bedside drawer. I take out Rebecca's article, about Sophie. I must have read it at least 20 times before today. When I go onto the landing Ellie's downstairs, hanging up her coat.

'Hi Mum,' she says, 'everything okay?'

'Fine, darling' I say, 'here, come and give me a hug.'

When Mike comes home I don't wait for him to take his coat off before I tell him what Jess told me earlier.

'I saw a community nurse today,' I say, greeting him in the hall, 'she said I had psychosis.'

'That's what they told me,' he says, casually. He takes his boots off and kicks them against the wall.

'Why didn't they tell me when I was in there?'

'Would it have made any difference?'

I follow him into the kitchen. 'She said I was hallucinating.'

'You were,' he says, opening the fridge door.

'Not about the pain. Do you think I'll get it again?'

'How should I know?'

'I need to know why it happened,' I say, leaning on the island.

He takes out a jar of olives. 'Why?'

'In case it happens again.'

'Let's not think about that,' he says, putting the jar back, 'we're focusing on the future, remember?'

Thirty-Three

I call Doctor Berry's surgery the following Tuesday.

'Can you describe your symptoms?' she asks.

'Oh I don't have any symptoms,' I say, 'I just need to talk to a doctor.'

At six o'clock I get a call from the surgery. 'Mrs Barrett,' the voice says, 'I'm Doctor Rupi. How can I help?'

'I'm trying to find out what happened to me,' I say, 'why I was admitted to Thornsea Unit.'

'It says on my notes mental illness,' he says, 'psychosis.'

'I'm trying to find out about the pain.'

'As I say Mrs Barrett, psychosis.'

'Do you think it will happen again?'

'That's impossible to know,' he says, 'but since you've had it once there is a possibility.'

'I was in a lot of pain,' I say, 'can you tell me why I was in pain?'

'As I've told you Mrs Barrett: mental illness, psychosis.'

I hold out the phone in front of me. I feel like throwing

it against the wall, but I don't. Instead, I look at the calendar on the fridge. I'll have to order another calendar soon, for the start of the new academic year.

'You're still taking your medication?' he asks.

'Yes,' I reply.

'And you know about the weight gain?'

'Yes,' I say, 'and I have really bad dreams too.'

'That might not be linked,' he says.

'Thanks,' I say politely and end our call.

Thirty-Four

On the morning of our photo shoot for Coastal Monthly, Jean, Ellie and I have been at the Beach Road bar since 5 am. The makeup artist and hairdresser have been and gone. I'm dressed in a powder blue trouser suit and feeling fabulous after my early morning makeover. Our photographer is the one who was with Rebecca, after Sophie's body was found. When he catches my eye he gives me a knowing nod and I smile.

'You ladies look great,' he says, as we stand in front of the red neon Barrett's Sports Bar sign behind the bar.

'We do, don't we?' Jean says. I must admit this photo shoot has been a lot of fun.

In between the photo shoot and a Directors' meeting at 9 am, I have 40 minutes to myself. As it's a beautiful Spring morning I take a walk along the promenade. I regret not changing into more comfortable footwear before setting off. When I reach the pier, my phone rings: it's Terese.

'We're trying to get a bench installed,' she says, 'opposite your house.'

'What a lovely idea,' I say, stepping out of my heels for a moment.

'We have to get permission from the Council. Can we count on your support?'

'Of course, you can.' I wriggle my toes before squeezing them back into my shoes for the walk back.

I arrive outside Mike's office dead on 9 am. There's a *Do Not Disturb* sign on the door. I can hear him and Jean talking. I wait outside and listen.

'All I'm saying,' Jean says, 'is it wise to still have her as a Director?'

'You want her to resign?' Mike asks.

'What if she ends up ill again?'

'I don't think she'll agree Mum. It'll be difficult if she won't agree.'

'I can't help thinking about our Lizzie,' Jean says, 'she went into hospital and never came out.' I push the door open. 'Oh hi love,' Jean says, 'we were just waiting for you.'

I sit next to Mike and stare at Jean. She shifts in her chair, looking down. Mike reaches across the table and strokes my hand.

'First item,' he says, 'approval of the last meeting's

minutes.' We all nod our agreement.

'Second item: Thornsea Unit café tender. Mike looks at me. 'Ruth, can you update us?'

'First stage done,' I say, 'just waiting to see if we've got through to the next stage.'

Jean smiles. 'Well done Ruth.'

Before we finish the meeting Mike has an Any Other Business item.

'Not strictly business related,' he says, 'but I've had a tip-off from a councillor. Someone's applied to have a bench installed across the road from our house.'

'Terese,' I say, 'Sophie's mum.'

'Can you object?' Jean says, with a heavy sigh. 'These benches can attract the wrong sort.'

I shake my head. Are my husband and mother-in-law really going to object to a bench? For a friend of mine?

'I'm thinking of you love,' Mike says, 'you don't want to be reminded every time you look out of the window?'

'Are we done?' Jean says, standing up.

'There is something,' I say.

Jean rolls her eyes and sits down again. 'Well make it quick.'

'It's about my role here,' I say, 'and how long Mary's staying.' Jean closes her eyes.

'When we know you're properly better love,' Mike says,

reaching for my hand, 'let's not rush things.'

It's a tradition, after each Directors' meeting, for the three of us to go out for lunch. After this one, we go to the Golf Club. We sit at a table by the bay window, overlooking the greens. While Mike's in the Gents I have a chance to talk to Jean, alone.

'I heard you mentioning Lizzie earlier,' I say, 'will you tell me what happened to her?'

'I think I'll have the salmon today,' Jean says, closing her menu.

'Before I came into the meeting,' I say, 'you were telling Mike about Lizzie. You think that's going to happen to me?'

'I don't want to talk about it Ruth,' she says, looking out of the window again. Mike comes back.

'I was asking your mum about Lizzie,' I say.

Jean coughs. 'I don't talk about Lizzie. You both know that.'

'Ruth. Stop it,' Mike says, angrily, 'you're upsetting Mum.'

For the rest of the time we're at lunch Jean and Mike talk about other golf club members. I stay silent.

Thirty-Five

On the morning of our 25th Wedding Anniversary, there's a card and 24 red roses on the kitchen island. Mike's at the coffee machine.

He turns to me and smiles. 'Espresso, for the lady?'

'Happy anniversary,' I say, handing him the painting I made at Art Club.

He takes out the watercolour. 'You did this?'

'An original,' I say, 'might be worth something one day.'

He puts it back in its envelope. 'I've got a meeting this morning,' he says, 'and you've remembered we're away tonight?'

'Can't wait,' I say, kissing him on the lips.

I don't do any work that morning. Instead, I take a bath and spend a long time at my dressing table. When he comes home, after lunch, he throws our bags in the boot while I get into the passenger seat. While he's checking the tyres I find an old parking ticket on the dashboard.

'From when you picked me up from the Unit,' I say, as he's getting in the car.

'You've made such a lot of progress since then,' he says, squeezing my hand, 'I'm proud of you.'

'So can I have my old job back, please?'

'Let's not rush things,' he says, 'while you're doing so well.'

The hotel is two hours' drive away. We stop at a motorway service station and, when he comes back from the shop, he's bought a CD.

'*Lady Gaga*?' I say. 'Didn't know you liked her.'

He smiles. 'Trying to widen my musical knowledge. Be down with the kids.' The only gigs we've gone to since the kids were born have been Daniel and his band.

'We should go to some concerts,' I say, 'what do you think?'

'Yeah,' he says, 'Mary goes to lots. I'll ask her.'

I look out of my window. 'Not with Mary, just you and me.'

He turns up the stereo and taps his fingers on the steering wheel.

We leave the motorway and turn down a country lane. After seeing a sign for The Borough Hotel we turn into a tree-lined drive. At the bottom we discover a large golden-coloured building, with turrets and archways.

The hotel manager, at the reception desk, greets us with a wide smile. He beckons for a bell boy who returns pushing a luggage trolley. Mike's booked the Honeymoon Suite for the night. We follow the bell boy across the gravel path to a converted stable block. Our room is huge and, on the other side of the French windows, we have our own enclosed garden.

'Happy Anniversary,' Mike says, when the bell boy has gone. He looks very pleased with himself, surveying the room. 'Will this do?'

'Wow!' I go over to the roll-top copper bath. 'Can't wait to try that out.'

He picks up a brochure. 'And there's a spa here too.'

I look through it, reading about the treatments. 'We can get a couple's massage. We've never had one of those before.' I wonder if I've remembered to pack a swimsuit? I unzip a front pocket and feel inside. No swimsuit there but there is something. An envelope? It's the paperwork from when I left the Unit. 'From the last time I used this,' I say, handing Mike the stapled papers.

He takes them over to the bin and rips them into eight pieces. 'You don't need this anymore.'

I take the menu from the bedside table and read out the ingredients from the eight-course tasting experience: 'Chrysanthemum, sea buckthorn, anise hyssop, barbecued beetroot, rosehip, shrimp, samphire, sweet cicely, woodruff, oxalis. Shall we have this tonight? In the restaurant?'

'Let's order it for room service,' he says, 'then we can relax a bit.'

He takes the bottle of *Billecart - Salmon Brut* from the ice bucket. I open the French doors and he fires the champagne cork into the hedge at the back of our private garden. I bring two crystal champagne flutes and the bubbles spill over as he pours.

'C'mon Mrs Barrett,' he says, 'let's celebrate our long and happy marriage.'

The following day, we have breakfast in the hotel restaurant. It's an old hall, with tall stained glass windows, rich floral rugs, oak panels and chandeliers.

'Have you thought any more about Mary?' I ask, tucking into my scrambled egg.

He wipes his mouth on a napkin. 'Not while I've been with you,' he says, grinning.

I kick him gently under the table. 'About her job,' I say, 'there's no need for her to stay with us now.'

He reaches for my hand. 'But everything's just perfect right now. Why change it?'

'Do you think I'm well enough now? I just want to go back to how things were.'

'But you can relax a bit more now we have Mary.' he says. 'Don't you like having more time to yourself?'

I watch him while he finishes his breakfast. I guess things are good right now and not having to worry about staff issues or the accounts has been a pleasant break. But, I do need to get back to being in charge of those things. Like I was before.

We drive straight from the hotel to our second bar, next to Thornsea football club. There's been a midweek match and Mike wants to see how busy it's been. Bruno Araujo scored a hat trick but we were still beaten 4:3. When we get to the bar Mike goes straight to the kitchen while I take a seat at the window. The bar manager brings me a coffee. A middle-aged man, sitting next to me, finishes his breakfast and leaves. When I get up to leave I notice he's left his newspaper. I pick it up and put it in my bag to read later.

Outside, Mike reaches for my hand and smiles.

'Everything okay?' I ask.

'Everything's great,' he says, 'business is great, we're great. Couldn't be happier.'

I stop to kiss him. 'Thanks for a lovely night last night.'

'I wish I hadn't any meetings this afternoon,' he says, kissing me back, 'so wc could carry on.'

I whisper in his ear. 'We can this evening. If you don't stay at the bar too late.'

The traffic's heavy on the way back and we get stuck at some traffic lights. I take the copy of the County Herald from my bag. It's still folded over showing a full-page advert for Thornsea Conservatories.

It's the headline I notice first:

FAMILY DEMAND ANSWERS AFTER SISTER'S DEATH

By Rebecca Dodd

And the photograph second.

Thirty-Six

It's Jenny. She's standing in front of a tree, eyes bright and wide, mouth smiling. She looks so alive, so well. I close the paper and put it in my bag. I can't read it, not here with Mike.

'Are you coming into the bar?' he says, as we get near the seafront.

'No,' I say, 'can you take me home?'

Mike drops me off at home and I run upstairs to our bedroom. In the en suite, I take out the paper and read the rest of the article. Jenny's sister, Suzanna, is trying to find out what led to her death. According to the report, she believes Jenny was allowed to leave the Unit too early. I feel lightheaded and sick at the same time. Lowering myself onto the floor, I lay in the space between the shower and sink. I pull the bathmat towards me, lowering my head onto it. Why Jenny? What was so awful you felt you had to do this? I close my eyes and fall asleep.

I wake to knocking at the door.

'Ruth, Ruth are you in there?' Mike's shouting. 'Ruth, love, are you okay in there?' His voice is getting louder.

I'm okay,' I say, lifting myself up.

He bangs on the door. 'Are you coming out?'

'Coming!' I shout back.

He opens the door. 'What are you doing down there?' He helps me to my feet.

'I fell asleep,' I say, getting up.

He picks the paper off the floor. 'What's all this?'

'One of the women I was in the Unit with.'

He shakes his head. 'Another one?' I sit on the bed while he reads. 'Mum's upstairs,' he says, 'come and say hello.'

When I get to the top lounge Jean's standing looking out of the window.

'Where did you go?' she says, turning around. 'We were worried about you.'

Mike hands her the newspaper. 'One of the women she was in hospital with.'

She shakes her head, 'How sad, but you won't have known her very well, would you?

'Jenny,' I say, 'we were friends.' Jean holds out the paper. Mike takes it from her and goes out towards the landing. I follow him downstairs, with Jean behind me. 'But I was reading it. I want it back.' When we get to the utility room he lifts the yellow bin lid. 'Please Mike, please don't throw it out. I need it. It's about Jenny.'

Jean moves herself between me and Mike. 'C'mon Ruth, this isn't doing you any good.'

I beg him to give it to me. 'Mike please.'

'Don't let her have it Mike,' she says, 'it'll only upset her more.' He puts the paper in the yellow recycling bin and pushes past me. Jean gives me one of her *Behave Yourself* looks and follows Mike into the kitchen. I open the lid of the yellow bin, take out the paper and hide it under my jumper.

When it's safely in my bedside drawer, upstairs, I find Jean in the kitchen.

'Will you tell me what happened to Lizzie?' I ask, again.

Mike comes in from the garden.

'Tell her Mike,' she says, 'I won't talk about my sister.'

'Stop it Ruth,' Mike says.

'Was she in Thornsea Home - where I was?'

'They demolished the Home,' Mike says, 'to build the Unit.'

'It's the same,' I say.

'It's not,' Mike says, 'they don't treat people like they used to.'

Mike gets a phone call and goes into the lounge.

'You're making things worse for yourself,' Jean says, 'getting upset about things you shouldn't.'

I don't say anything while Mike's out of the room. I wait until he's back with us before I reply. 'I'm just curious that's all.'

'Too curious for your own good,' Mike says, sitting next to his mum.

I go back to the bedroom and take the paper from the drawer. Jenny's sister, Suzanna, is urging the Unit to investigate. She doesn't want what happened to Jenny to happen again. I want to get in touch with Suzanna, offer my condolences. It's the least I can do. I call Rebecca and arrange to meet.

Thirty-Seven

Two days later, I meet Rebecca by the coffee van at the top of the pier. We sit at the nearby bench.

'Like I said on the phone,' I say, 'when I read about Jenny, I had to get in touch.'

She takes a dictaphone out of her bag. 'It's great you're willing to speak now. Do you mind if I record this?'

'Actually, I was hoping you could just tell me more about what happened to Jenny, that's all.' She puts the dictaphone away and looks disappointed. 'I'd like to see her sister,' I say, 'just to tell her how sorry I am.'

'I'll pass on your number,' she says, 'if you want me to.' I nod. 'Did you hear about Sophie's inquest?' I haven't. 'The coroner said they weren't at fault. They couldn't have done anything to prevent it.' I get a text from Mike asking me where I am. I text back: *Gone for a swim.* 'I don't want to pressure you,' Rebecca says, 'but if you were to reconsider doing an interview for the paper.'

'I'm sorry,' I say.

'But you were in there. It would be great to have a first-hand account.'

I shake my head. 'I've wasted your time.'

She looks at her watch. 'Never mind, you know where I am, if you do want to talk.'

'Do you know about Jenny's funeral?' I ask.

'This Friday,' she says, 'I'll text you the details.'

I walk back to my office and, at my desk, read some more articles about managing staff.

A few minutes later Mike pops his head around the door. 'Everything okay?'

'Fine,' I say.

'Where have you been?'

'Nowhere, just needed to clear my head.'

'Good,' he says, 'and you've remembered it's Mum's party on Friday?'

Thirty-Eight

Jenny's funeral starts at one o'clock. I've told Mike I'll be late to Jean's birthday party. I've told him I have an appointment at Thornsea General with Jess.

The funeral is in a Catholic Church half an hour's drive away. There aren't many people here, about thirty. I haven't been in a Catholic church for years. When I was little Mum used to take me to watch weddings on Saturdays. It was one of her favourite hobbies, that and going to bring-and-buy sales. We'd sit in the back pews watching young couples exchange vows. It was the music I loved the most. I learned the names of the pieces from the wedding booklets: *Handel's Arrival of the Queen of Sheba, Purcell's Trumpet Tune, Bach's Ave Maria and Mendelssohn's Wedding March.*

The priest says a few kind words about Jenny, though I doubt he knew her well. Suzanna gives a moving eulogy. Jenny didn't have any children. Her husband, Richard, died of a heart attack in 2016 and Jenny struggled with the grief. But the main thing, Suzanna wants everyone to know, is that Jenny was a much-loved sister, auntie and friend.

'At least Jenny and Richard will be reunited now,' Suzanna says at the end, breaking down in tears.

As I'm leaving the church I spot Rebecca with Terese.

'Coming for a drink?' Terese asks, as we hug. I hesitate for a moment and think about what I'm going to tell Mike if he asks. I'll tell him my hospital appointment was delayed.

'Of course,' I reply.

When Suzanna comes over Rebecca introduces us.

'You were in the Unit with Jenny?' Suzanna says, shaking my hand.

'Yes,' I say. 'If there's anything I can do to help.'

Suzanna's shoulders shake and she sniffs and wipes her eyes. She sits at our table and a young woman brings her a glass of sherry.

'You know Rebecca's investigating?' Suzanna says.

I feel awkward. 'Yes.'

'Have you let her interview you?'

I look at Rebecca who smiles at me. 'No,' I say, 'it's a bit complicated for me.' I want to tell all of them about the bid I've sent in, to run the café. I want to tell all of them that Mike and Jean won't be happy if I'm in the paper talking about the Unit in a bad way. But, instead, I say nothing and finish my cold tea.

'I understand,' Suzanna says, 'you have to do what's right for you.'

I check my phone. Mike's sent me two texts in the last 30 minutes asking where I am. I say my goodbyes and head for Jean's house.

On the drive back I'm thinking of Rebecca and her investigation. I'm thinking of Sophie and Jenny and wondering if they would have said yes to being interviewed for the County Herald.

As soon as I arrive at Jean's party I go to find Mike. I've met most of the people at the party before. Mike's with Mary, chatting with two of Jean's neighbours.

'We thought he'd exchanged you for a younger model,' the man says, pointing to Mary.

I grab Mike's hand and lift it to show them our wedding rings. 'We're still very much together.' I look at Mary. She gives me a friendly smile then looks at the floor. I make an excuse about needing a drink and go into the garage, where I mix a lime and soda at the makeshift bar. Mike follows me in.

'Where've you been?' he says, abruptly. 'I called the hospital. They told me you didn't have an appointment this afternoon.'

I take a sip of my drink. 'You were checking up on me?'

'I was worried,' he says, 'your phone was switched off.'

'I was fine.'

'Anything could have happened to you. I've been worried sick.'

I look around. There's no one else here. 'I've been at a funeral,' I whisper, 'is that okay?' Another guest comes in. Mike grabs my hand and leads me into the garden. He stops at the tree, right at the bottom, by the fence.

'Whose funeral?'

'Jenny's,' I say, 'I wanted to pay my respects.'

'The woman in the paper?' I nod. 'For God's sake,' he says, shaking his head. He drains his glass of red wine and goes back up the garden leaving me beside the tree.

It's a pleasant evening and I'm happy to stay in the garden. There's an empty bench by Jean's greenhouse, the perfect spot to people-watch and stay away from Mike for a while. Simon, Mike's cousin waves to me from the patio. He and Mike are about the same age. We used to see him a lot when we first got married. Is he still teaching? I wonder. I'm sure he used to be Head of Science at a high school.

'Long time no see,' he says, sitting next to me.

'Haven't seen you in ages,' I say.

'How's your mum?' he asks. 'Heard she'd been in hospital?' I wait a few seconds to consider my response.

'Actually, it was me. I was the one in hospital.'

Oh,' he says, sympathetically, 'everything okay now?'

I smile. 'I hope so.' We watch the small groups of guests by the house. Jean's laughing with Mary and Mike. Mary sees me and waves.

'Who's that with Auntie Jean and Mike?'

'Mary,' I say, 'she works for us now.'

Mike comes to the top of the garden, ushering people inside.

'Everyone in for the cutting of the cake.' He spots the two of us on the bench. 'Hey, you two, cake time.'

Simon and I stay at the back of the lounge. Mike, Jean, Daniel and Ellie are in the middle, in front of the cake. It's a four-tier chocolate tower with a silver 75 on top. Jean blows out the candle and everyone sings *Happy Birthday*.

'What can we say about this remarkable woman?' Mike says, putting his arm around his mum. 'Most supportive mother, auntie, sister, neighbour and friend.'

'And businesswoman,' Daniel chips in. There's a ripple of laughter.

'Thanks Daniel.' Mike puts his arm around Jean. 'Mum's always been there for me. I don't know where I'd be without her.'

Now it's Jeans turn to speak. She squeezes herself between Mike and Daniel, holding their hands.

'How lucky am I?' she says. 'Having such a wonderful son and grandchildren? When Mike's dad died, and he was only eight, I wondered how we'd cope.' She puts her arms around Mike's waist. 'But we have and you've been a wonderful son.'

'Three cheers for Grandma Jean,' Ellie shouts, 'Hip! hip!' I walk into the garage to get another lime and soda. Simon follows me.

'You still working?' I ask.

'Pretty much retired now,' he says, 'discovered there's more to life than work.'

I remember Simon has talked about his Auntie Lizzie before. I take the opportunity to see if he'll tell me more about her.

'I want to know about Lizzie,' I say, 'about what happened to her.'

'Why not speak to my mum?' he says. 'She'll tell you.'

'She won't be upset with me?'

'No,' he says, 'not if you get her another brandy.'

Simon goes towards the house, probably going to find his wife Kate. I smile, thinking how nice it's been, chatting to him. I decide we should invite him and Kate for dinner one night. I watch Simon and Mike pass each other by the doors to the lounge. They chat for a while. Simon goes in and Mike walks down the garden towards me.

'You and Simon been having a cosy chat?' he says, sitting beside me. He's holding a glass with, perhaps, one mouthful of red wine remaining. I can smell the wine on his breath as he leans in.

I lean back. 'Well, I wouldn't call it cosy, exactly.'

'I was watching you two,' he says. He drains his glass. 'You know he and Kate have split up?'

'No, I didn't,' I say, disappointed.

'He's just told me then,' he says, 'only last month.' I shake my head. There's always some couple separating these days.

'We should invite him over for something to eat. Cheer him up.'

'I don't think so,' he says. He gets up and goes back into the house. I suspect he's going to find Mary.

I find Simon's mum, Mike's Auntie Anne, sitting in an armchair in the front lounge. I know Jean's in the conservatory, which means I should be safe asking her about Lizzie.

'I've got you another brandy,' I say, handing her a double *Courvoisier.*'

'Thanks Ruth,' she says, taking the glass, 'how are you? How's your mum? Jean said she had a hip operation.'

'I'm fine, she's fine, thanks,' I say, sitting on the floor

by her feet. 'I was talking to Simon about Lizzie. He said you could tell me more.'

Anne tells me her eldest sister, Lizzie, was born in 1932. Their father was a signalman on the railway and their mother worked in her parents' shop, selling wool and knitting paraphernalia. Lizzie was a quiet child who enjoyed playing with her dolls in the back room of the shop. When she was 19, she got pregnant by a man who had come on holiday to Thornsea. Her parents accepted the situation and helped Lizzie when the baby was born. But Lizzie struggled to bond with her daughter. On several occasions, Lizzie's mother had to look after the child when Lizzie refused. When the baby was six weeks old Lizzie tried to leave her baby on a bus, only being stopped by the conductor who happened to know the family.

After the bus incident, Lizzie refused to leave the house and continued to struggle as a new mother. Her parents sought help from the family doctor. Within a few weeks, she was admitted to Thornsea Home and the baby was adopted by a couple from London.

Lizzie was allowed to come home and worked in the wool shop but went back to Thornsea Home several times. She never married or had another boyfriend. When she was 40, in 1972, she had her most severe breakdown. She went into Thornsea Home and never came out.

'Did you go to visit?' I ask.

'It was horrible,' Anne says, 'all these women just wandering round with nothing to do.'

'How did Jean take it?'

'Not well,' she says, 'only visited her a couple of times. She hated going to see her, it upset her too much. When our Lizzie died, Jean hadn't seen her for years.'

Simon comes in to find his mum. I leave the front lounge and find Mike, in mid-conversation with another couple, in the conservatory. When he sees me he grabs my hand. I can tell he's had a lot to drink.

'We're opening a place in Manchester with David Fitzroy,' he tells the couple, slurring his words.

'Wow.' the man says, excitedly, 'David Fitzroy, amazing.'

I'm driving us home. Mike's slouched in the passenger seat, eyes half closed. Daniel and Ellie are asleep in the back.

'Is that David's plan?' I ask. 'Manchester next?'

'Yes,' he says, 'that's bar number two.'

'And then is that it? No more bars after that?'

'That's up to David.'

'Do I get a say?'

'Not really,' he says, 'why? What's the matter?'

I'm thinking of the chat I had with Simon earlier. Maybe we are working too hard 'Nothing. Maybe we're doing too much.'

'Nonsense,' Mike says, slurring his words again, 'you're talking nonsense.'

Thirty-Nine

On Monday morning, I get a call from Terese.

'About this bench,' she says, 'I've had a response from the council. I can't have it installed. They've had an objection.'

I try to sound surprised, but I have a hunch who might have objected. 'Really? That's terrible.'

She sounds upset. 'Is it one of your neighbours?'

'I might be able to help,' I say, 'leave it with me.' I go into Mike's office without knocking. Mary's sitting at her desk and he's standing by the filing cabinet. I sit on the leather settee and wait to be noticed.

'Everything okay darling?' he says, keeping his back to me.

'Not really,' I say. Mary looks over at Mike, her lips developing into a faint smile. 'This bench for Sophie, there's been an objection.'

He turns around and looks at Mary. 'That's a shame. They don't always get approved.' He looks at me and smiles.

'Was it you?' I say, giving him a hard stare. Mary takes a bag of almonds from her drawer and begins to eat them slowly, her eyes fixed on Mike.

'If there's a bench across the road,' he says, 'it'll be a permanent reminder.'

'So it was you. You objected to Sophie's bench.'

He puts the folder down and sits beside me, taking my hand. 'Do you really want to be reminded? All the time? About what happened?'

I release my hand. 'It's to remember Sophie.'

'Exactly.'

In my office I *Google* memorial benches on the council website. I call Terese.

'It was my husband,' I say, 'he's the one who objected.'

Terese sounds despondent. 'Is there anything you can do? I just want somewhere to go and remember her.'

I follow the links on the website. 'You can appeal, ask them to reconsider.'

'How?'

I continue reading. 'I'll write a letter of support for you. I'll try to get him to change his mind.' I have no idea how.

I don't mention Sophie's bench for the rest of the day. I wait until Mike and I are on our own, clearing up after dinner.

'Will you have a rethink about the bench?' I ask him. 'I've told Sophie's mum she can appeal.'

He slams the dishwasher door shut. 'This is getting ridiculous Ruth!' he shouts. He pulls the boiling water hose from its cradle and sprays it around the sink.

I match the volume of his voice. 'What is?'

'You,' he says, 'getting involved in other people's battles. Leave their families alone. Let them grieve in peace.' He puts the hose back, shaking his head.

'I'm just trying to help a friend.'

He points his finger at me. 'She's not a friend. You're interfering.'

In our bedroom I open the balcony doors. The teddy's still there, at the railings. Is he right? Am I really just interfering? Involving myself in other people's grief? I take the newspaper articles out of my drawer and sit on the bed.

After ten minutes, Mike comes in and sits beside me. He puts his arm around my waist.

'You don't have time for all this,' he says, softly. He takes the sheets of newsprint from my hands. 'You need to forget about these two now, it's upsetting you too much.'

I try to get the sheets back but he pulls his arm away. He goes to the waste basket, scrunches them into a ball and drops them in.

'Don't do that to my friends,' I say, rescuing the sheets. I straighten out the paper and put them back in my drawer.

'You've got two children to look after and a business to run,' he says, opening the bedroom door, 'you don't have time for all this.'

He goes downstairs and I lie on the bed, staring at the ceiling. I've told Terese I'll help her get this bench approved and I'm not going to let her down. He's not going to win this one. I open my phone and check the football fixtures for the evening. There's a match on tonight, he's probably watching it now. I'm praying his team wins. At halftime, when his team are 3:0 up, I go downstairs to the lounge.

'How are they doing?' I ask, sitting by him.

He looks up and smiles. 'They've been brilliant. Just need to keep this up.'

I take his hand. 'Will you have a rethink about the bench please? For Terese?'

He rubs his eyes and cheeks. 'Does it really mean that much to you?'

'Yes,' I say, 'it does.'

'Okay then,' he says, 'I'll withdraw the objection.'

'Thanks,' I say, kissing him on the cheek.

'Then will you stop getting involved?'

'I'll try,' I say.

Forty

I'm in Manchester, with Mike and David, walking towards an empty fish and chip shop with a *For Sale* sign. It's on a corner, in between a late-night convenience store and an old pub. There are four whited-out windows on each side of the front door, secured with a heavy chain and padlock. A young man, in a navy suit and brown leather shoes, strides confidently towards us.

'Shall we go in?' he says, shaking Mike's hand. 'Let's see what you think of this.' He unlocks the doors and we step inside. There are booths along one side and a bar along the other.

'What happened?' I ask.

'Bankruptcy,' the agent says.

I tap Mike on the arm. 'Bankruptcy doesn't sound good.'

'They might have gone bankrupt,' Mike says, going behind the counter, 'doesn't mean we will.'

David starts measuring the windows. 'Badly managed

probably.'

'Obviously it needs a bit of a refresh,' the agent says, running his finger along a dusty table. While Mike, David and the agent go through to the kitchen, I stay at the front. Terese calls.

'Wonderful news!' she says. 'The appeal worked. We've got permission for the bench.'

'That's great,' I say, pleased I've been able to get a good result for her.

'Thanks for helping. Whatever you did - it worked.'

When the three of them come back David's smiling and Mike's looking pleased.

'I think this could be the one,' David says, 'what d'you think Ruth?'

I shrug my shoulders. 'I'm not too sure, it could be risky.'

Mike gives me a harsh stare. 'Ignore her David, she hasn't got our vision.'

We say goodbye to David in the car park. As we watch him driving away, Mike takes my hand.

'That wasn't helpful,' he says.

'What did I say?

'If you can't say anything positive in front of David, don't say anything at all.'

'But-?' I protest.

'I mean it,' he says, 'or I'll bring Mary next time.'

'But it could be risky,' I say, 'maybe we're taking on too much.'

As we're driving back home, on the motorway, Mike's reeling off all the advantages of opening a bar in Manchester.

'But it's going to be a lot of work,' I say.

He sighs. 'We thrive on hard work.'

'Do we?' What if that's why I got ill?' I fix my eyes on an isolated farmhouse standing defiantly at the side of the motorway. I imagine the family who might live in that farmhouse and what their lives are like.

'How about us moving?' he says, after we've been driving in silence for at least ten minutes.

'And go where?'

'Nearer to David and Cara.'

'What about the children? They've got their exams this year. We couldn't move yet.'

'Not yet, no,' he says, 'but they'll be off making their own life soon,'

'And you're mum?'

'She can come with us.' I push the button on my seat to recline and close my eyes. I don't want to leave Thornsea. I don't want to leave our home. I just want to go back to how things used to be, before we even started this business venture with David. Before I got ill.

Jean's sitting at the kitchen island when we get home, her hands wrapped around a mug of tea.

'So what was it like?' she asks.

'We really liked it,' Mike says, 'don't think Ruth's so keen.'

I open the fridge and take out carrots and leeks. 'I'm worried we're taking too much on,' I say, putting the vegetables in a colander, 'that's all.'

'I'm going to get changed,' Mike says, 'see if you can persuade her Mum.'

'You need to be more positive about all this,' she says. 'You know it's what he's always wanted.'

While I'm chopping the carrots, Jean comes over and stands close to me.

'And he's talking about moving now,' I say, chopping the leeks, 'I don't want to do that.'

'You need to think about him for once,' she says, 'it's not always about you.' I put the knife down and, in my head, count to ten. When Mike comes back he shows Jean the photos he took in Manchester.

'David wants to put in an offer,' he says.

I go to the sink to wash my hands. 'Do I get a say in

this?' I say, looking out of the window.

'Not really,' he says, 'if it's what David wants.' I turn around, wiping my hands on a towel.

Jean's smiling from ear to ear. 'Go for it. Your dad would be so proud of you.'

I stay calm all through dinner. When Jean leaves, and Daniel and Ellie are upstairs, I find Mike in the lounge.

'Does my opinion not count anymore?' I say, picking up old newspapers from the coffee table. I'm blocking his view of the TV. He sits up and leans to the side.

'What's the matter now?'

'Everything,' I say, deliberately standing in front of the screen, 'I'm fed up of this.' He leans back into the sofa.

'Of what? This is what we've worked for all our lives.' I take the old newspapers to the utility room. When I've stuffed them in the already full recycling bin I run upstairs and lie face down on the bed. After a few minutes, he comes in and lies next to me. 'Are you okay?' he says, rubbing my back.

I turn over. 'I'm fine, why?'

He goes towards the door. 'Okay,' he says, 'just checking.' Before he reaches the landing I sit up.

'I'm just cautious,' I say, 'that's all.' He puts his hand on the door frame.

'You're not getting ill again are you? Should I call the

Unit?'

'I'm fine,' I say, firmly, 'there's nothing wrong.'

It's another half hour before I go downstairs. He's in the lounge. I sit on the opposite side of the sofa and rest my feet on his knees.

'You're not serious about moving are you?' I say, softly.

He massages my right foot. 'Of course,' he says, turning to me, 'we'll be able to afford it. Soon.'

I pull my feet away. 'But I'm happy here.'

'And I think we should rent an apartment too,' he says, 'near the Manchester bar.'

'Can we afford that?'

'Sure,' he says, 'no problem.'

Forty-One

Terese has messaged to say Sophie's bench will be arriving on a council truck on Thursday morning. When it arrives I've already been watching from our balcony for half an hour. I watch as the van parks near the noticeboard. Two workmen lower the bench carefully onto the pavement. I watch as they fix it into the ground. The teddy's still there, tied to the railings. One of the workmen cuts its string and throws it in the back of the truck with a couple of old bouquets. I run downstairs, grab my coat and go outside. When I cross the road one of the workmen is lifting orange cones back onto the truck.

'I've come for the teddy,' I say, when I get close enough for him to hear me.

'Sorry love,' the older of the two workmen says, lifting another cone onto the truck, 'we've been instructed to remove everything. Health and safety.'

'But that teddy, it's mine. I want it back.'

He looks at the younger one who has now stopped

sweeping and is listening to us. The older one shrugs his shoulders, takes the teddy from the truck and hands it to me.

'Here,' he says, shaking his head, 'I'm not supposed to, so don't tell anyone.'

I hold the teddy close to me. His fur is damp and cold but I don't mind. 'C'mon Teddy, you can stay with me.' The two workmen look at each other and laugh. I stay by the bench and wait for the workmen to drive away.

When they've gone I read the words on the plaque out loud:

'I will find my calmer waters
And be glad that I'm alive'

I call Terese. 'The bench is here and I've rescued Teddy.'

'Thanks,' she says, 'I'll call Rebecca. She said she'll arrange a photo for us.'

Back at home I have an email from Thornsea Unit. We've passed the first stage for the café contract. Now the real work begins: outlining how we're going to attract more customers and offer a better value-for-money menu. I need to do some research.

After lunch I drive over to the Unit singing along to the radio. If I get this contract, perhaps we can give it to a manager to look after. Mike can give me my old job back, just looking after our own bars, like I used to. And we can tell Mary she's not needed anymore.

In the Unit car park I take a moment. This time, I tell myself, you're going in as a free citizen. You don't need a pass and there'll be no locked doors. I take a deep breath. 'C'mon Ruth,' I tell myself, 'you can do this.'

In the café, I order a latte and a flapjack and sit close to the counter. From here I observe the woman serving, count the number of customers and make a note of what they order. In the first 20 minutes I count three customers: two nurses and a man in a suit. I assume the man in the suit is a manager or a doctor. Later there's a group of four: two men and two women. I expect one's a patient. It's hard to tell which one though, until I look under the table and see who's wearing slippers.

I stay in the café until 4 pm. As I'm heading towards the exit I check out the magazines in the rack outside the shop. I spot a copy of this month's Coastal Monthly. I flick through it and find the feature on our business. It's a double spread across pages 12 and 13.

The women behind Barrett's Sports Bars are driving the

business forward in an exciting partnership with ex-Premier League footballer, David Fitzroy. They're looking forward to the opening of the second Fitzroy's Bar in Manchester city centre next year.

We all look fabulous: me in my powder blue suit, Jean in her cream trouser suit and Ellie in a red dress. There's even a little article about Ellie and her football. I pick up two more copies

and take them to the till.

I've been in the café so long I've forgotten where I parked the car and end up walking the full perimeter of the car park. I'm annoyed with myself for not paying more attention to where I parked, until I see a large marble stone behind a small picket fence. I step over the foot-high fence and read the inscription on the stone.

This stone commemorates

the women and men

who lived and died here as patients

of Thornsea Home from 1925 - 1994

Immediately, I think of Lizzie. When I come back, I'll bring some flowers.

On my way home I stop at the Beach Road bar. As I walk into Mike's office he and Mary are at their desks, laughing.

'Something funny?' I ask.

'It was nothing,' Mike says, coughing. Mary stops laughing too and looks at her screen.

I open the magazinc at our feature. 'Have you seen us?'

Mike takes the magazine. 'You all look great.' He gets up from his desk and takes it over to Mary. She gives it a quick glance.

'Very glamorous,' she says, handing it back to him.

I sit on the leather settee. 'And we're through to the next stage for the café.'

'Really?' he says, smiling. 'Well done.'

'You sound surprised,' I say.

'No,' he says, 'but just imagine we get it. This could be huge. What do you think Mary?'

Mary looks up. 'Huge,' she says, 'really huge.'

'And they've put the bench in,' I say, 'across the road.'

Mike raises his eyebrows. 'Let's see how long it takes before someone else tries it now?'

I shake my head. 'Tries what?'

'What your friend did,' he says.

I get up from the leather settee and go across to the door. 'They won't. Terese put some words on it. To give people some hope.'

He makes a loud snorting noise. 'And you think that might stop someone?'

'It might,' I say, closing the door behind me, 'it just

might.'

Forty-Two

I'm the first to arrive at Sophie's bench for the photo. I've washed and blow-dried Teddy. He looks immaculate, almost brand new. I carry him under my arm and hold a bouquet of yellow roses in the other hand. Terese arrives soon after with Sophie's brothers. Rebecca is next to arrive, with the photographer and, finally, Suzanna. The photographer tells us to all stand together. I edge away from the rest of the group and stand on the other side of the noticeboard.

Terese beckons to me. 'Come back here,' she calls, 'we need you in this too.'

'It's okay,' I say, waving my hand, 'I don't need to be in.'

Suzanna comes over. 'Yes you do.' She pulls me towards the bench. 'Please Ruth.'

'Okay, okay,' I say, as I let her lead me back to the group.

'That's better,' Terese says, looking to her left and right, 'we're all ready now.'

I don't stay long after the photographer's left. I don't want Suzanna, or Rebecca, to ask me about being interviewed for the paper again. When I get back to my office, Jean's sitting at my desk. In my chair.

'Been out?' she asks, getting up slowly.

'At Sophie's bench,' I say, 'getting a photo for the paper.'

She gives me a disapproving look as she squeezes past me. 'Is it a good idea?' You getting involved in all that.'

'It's what her mum wants,' I say, sitting at my desk. Jean sits at the other side of the desk watching as I start up my laptop. The awkward silence is broken when Mike comes in, two minutes later. He drops two files on my desk.

'Some more work for you,' he says.

I look at the files. 'Marketing? But you do all the marketing.'

'Thought you wanted more work to do?'

I turn the pages to find samples of promotional material going back to 1993, when we opened Beach Road.

'I just want my old job back,' I say, closing it, 'get back to how things used to be.'

'C'mon Ruth,' Jean says, 'things are changing. We're a

growing business.'

Mike picks them up. 'Or I could give these to Mary,' he says, 'if you're not capable.'

I take the files from him. 'As long as you don't interfere. As long as you let me do it my way. Let me have full control.'

'Of course,' he says, 'of course.'

I shut down my laptop and close the lid. 'I'll work from home,' I say, grabbing the files and heading for the door.

As I get closer to home I see Terese and Suzanna are still chatting by the noticeboard. At least they'll be pleased to see me again. Teddy's on the bench now, holding the yellow roses.

'He looks happy there,' I say, stroking his arm.

'I'll take him home,' Terese says, 'thanks for looking after him.'

An elderly woman in a motorised scooter comes along and stops to read the inscription. I go over and say hello.

'Not seen this bench before,' she says, stroking Teddy's arm.

'It's in memory of the young woman who died here.'

'It's lovely,' she says, 'and if it helps one more person it will be worth it.'

I smile, remembering Mike's comments. 'That's what we hope too.'

I go back to Terese and Suzanna. 'You've got a supporter there,' I say, pointing to the woman as she sets off again towards the pier.

'Just imagine loads of these benches, all over the country,' Suzanna says.

'A Sophie's bench in every seaside town,' Terese says, wiping her eyes, 'what would she make of that?'

After dinner there's a lovely sunset. I ask Mike if he wants to go for a walk. There's something bothering me and I need to tell him. We walk almost as far as the Golf Club. All the way there I hardly say a word. I just listen to him talk about the Manchester bar. When we turn back towards home I speed up and go on ahead. When I reach Sophie's bench he's at least ten metres behind. I sit and wait.

'Want to sit here?' I ask, when he catches up.

He stands in front of me, with his hands on his hips. 'No thanks.' My phone buzzes. It's Terese.

'We're having a meeting about our benches charity,' she says, 'will you join us?'

'I'll call you back,' I say, looking at Mike. I put the

phone in my pocket. 'Terese,' I say, 'she's setting up a charity.'

'Doing what?'

'Getting benches installed, like this one.'

He throws his head back and laughs. 'You'll have to tell her no,' he says, 'you won't have time now.' He turns towards the road and presses the button at the crossing. I get up. If I don't tell him what's been bothering me, I'll miss my opportunity and I'll have to wait until he's in a good mood again. The red man turns to green. Mike takes long strides across the road. I run to catch up.

'I don't like you and Mary sharing an office,' I blurt out.

He keeps up his stride. 'You're not jealous?'

'I'll move out of my office,' I say, 'I can work from home.'

When we reach the top of our drive he hands me the front door key.

'Going for a drink,' he says, 'see you later.'

When he comes home, just before midnight, I'm sitting at the kitchen island, reading Coastal Monthly. He comes over and kisses me on the cheek.

I grab his hand. 'So are you telling Mary or am I?'

He washes his hands at the sink. 'About what?'

'About her moving out of your office.' There's a long silence while he searches for a bottle of wine. I let out a long, deliberate sigh. 'Are you going to tell her, or shall I?'

'Okay,' he says, putting a bottle of Rioja in front of me, 'I'll tell her. Happy?'

Forty-Three

Ellie and I go on a shopping trip into town the following Saturday. When we get home, late afternoon, Mike's pushing my new desk against the kitchen wall.

'Welcome to your new office,' he says, smiling.

I survey my new workspace. It's a long narrow desk, in between the door to the hall and the patio doors. I have a new swivel chair in cream leather and a walnut base. And on the wall, facing my chair, a corkboard in a white frame.

'Lovely,' I say, 'thanks.'

I take my laptop from its case and place it in the centre. It's such a beautiful space I have the urge to do some work straight away.

'I've sent you the details of a new marketing consultancy I've hired,' he says. In my inbox I have three emails from Mike with the subject heading: *Marketing Ideas for You To Work On.*

'But I thought this was going to be my project.'

'You're in charge, of course,' he says, 'this just gives you a head start.'

I shake my head. 'But you said-'

'You are,' he interrupts, 'of course you are. I just don't want you taking on too much yet.'

'I'm fine,' I say.

'But we don't know that yet,' he says, 'slow and steady, eh?' I sit in the chair and adjust the height with the lever. He's moved the calendar from the fridge to the pin board.

'You've remembered it's Bruno's charity dinner tonight?' I say, reading from the calendar.

'Looking forward to it,' he says, going to the front door.

We're the first to arrive for Bruno's fundraiser. While we're at the bar Bruno comes over.

'Thanks for your support tonight,' he says, kissing me on both cheeks.

'Hope you raise lots of money,' I say, as Mike puts a glass in my hand.

He nods. 'It gives fans something to do, before the matches.'

When he leaves us Mike looks puzzled. 'What was all that about?'

'His new project,' I explain, 'for the fans to get together

before the matches. It's for mental health.'

Mike shakes his head and looks forlornly into his wine glass. 'Isn't that what we do?'

I look around to see if Jean and Mary have arrived yet. 'Well I think it's a good idea.'

'You do now,' he says, 'wait until our takings are down.'

'But if it's good for the fans,' I say, 'isn't that good for us too?'

He looks glum. 'Not if they're spending money elsewhere.' He looks happier when Mary comes in with Jean.

I bump into Mary on my way to the bar when the meal is over.

'Having a nice time?' I ask, hoping my tone sounds friendly.

'Yes thanks,' she says, cheerily, 'are you?'

I don't want to ignore the fact I've got her removed from Mike's office. 'Thought you should get your own office. If you're going to be staying with us?'

'Thanks,' she says, and I wonder if she means it.

'Are you enjoying it? Working for us?'

She looks at her watch. 'Great,' she says, 'thanks.'

'Good,' I say, 'glad to hear it.'

She looks toward the door. ‘Sorry Ruth,’ she says, ‘need some fresh air.’ I head back to our table and grab Mike’s hand as I sit down.

He turns to me. 'Having a nice time?'

‘Lovely,’ I say, ‘you?’

‘Lovely,’ he says, turning his head towards the exit.

Forty-Four

I have another meeting with Jess the following Monday morning. It's a sunny day and I watch for her car from our balcony. I meet her at the top of the drive and lead her through to the back garden. We sit in the shade, under the sun umbrella.

'How have you been?' she asks, taking out her folder. 'You're looking well.'

She asks me if I'm still taking my medication. I nod. She asks me if I'm getting enough exercise and eating well. I nod.

'I still don't know why it happened though,' I say, 'why I felt in so much pain.'

She shakes her head. 'But you're not in pain now are you?'

'No,' I say, 'no I'm not.'

'So that's all good then.' She starts to cough, almost choking. I rush inside to get her a glass of water. When she's drunk the whole glass, in two gulps, I go back into the kitchen to refill it. This time I add some ice cubes.

'Did you see the piece in the paper?' I ask, handing her the glass. 'About Jenny Fisher?'

She takes a sip of the water. 'Who?'

'Jenny Fisher. It was in the Herald. Her sister said she was allowed to leave the Unit before she was ready.'

She puts her glass down. 'Oh yes, I remember now. Don't worry. It will all come out in the inquest.'

'So do you think the Unit was to blame?'

She shrugs her shoulders. 'It's difficult, everyone's just trying their best.' She finishes her water and puts her file in her bag. 'I'm glad to see you doing so well.' She takes out a small thin book, a diary I assume, from her bag. She finds a page and writes a note before stabbing the page, deliberately, with the tip of her pen. 'I've enjoyed meeting you,' she says. 'I hope you stay well.'

'Will I be seeing you again?' I ask, when we reach the front door.

She checks her reflection in the hall mirror. 'I'll let you know. We're having a reorganisation. I might be moving. This might be the last time I see you.'

I hope she can detect the disappointment in my voice. 'Will I have to see someone new?'

She turns and nods. 'I'm sure they'll be lovely.' I'm not sure I can face having to get to know someone new again and having to explain what happened. We walk to the top of the drive where she clicks her key fob. The indicators on a blue *Vauxhall Zafira* flash twice. 'But if you ever feel you need to,' she says, 'you can always call the office.'

'If you're moving on,' I say, 'perhaps I should too.'

She stops at her car door and turns back to me. 'Nothing's definite yet.'

After lunch I sit at my new desk and read the emails between Mike and the marketing agency. Our contact there has suggested we do some profiles of our staff, for the website. That sounds like a fun project. I write the names of all our staff in a list. Sam is passionate about his cooking and, since I upset him, I owe him a big favour.

At the Beach Road bar I go up to my old office. It's a force of habit but I remember, just in time, it isn't mine anymore. I knock and Mary opens the door, holding a spray bottle in one hand and a microfibre cloth in the other.

'Settling in okay?' I ask her, trying to sound friendly.

'Needs a good clean first,' she says. She sprays the top of the filing cabinet and rubs it vigorously. A sweet smell of orange fills the space between us. She stops cleaning and turns towards me, holding the trigger of the spray bottle like a loaded gun. 'Anything else?'

I take another look around the room. 'No, thanks.' I go downstairs to the kitchen. Sam's nowhere to be seen, but Chrissie should be in.

'Is Sam in today?' I ask, when I find her restocking the fridges.

She shakes her head. 'No,' she says, then whispers, 'he's not well.'

I go around to her side of the bar. 'Everything okay?'

'Not really,' she says, 'it's hit him bad this time.'

'What?'

'Calls it his Black Dog,' she says, 'I've not seen him this bad before.'

I look around the bar. There's no one else close enough to hear us. 'Can I come and see him? I might be able to help.'

'I don't think so,' she says, 'he'll not want to see management.'

'Not as management, as a friend.'

She shakes her head. 'I'm not sure,' she says, 'he's not very talkative right now.'

'Well the offer's there,' I say, 'just get in touch.' I leave Chrissie and go upstairs to see Mike.

'Well Mary's moved out now,' he says, not looking up from his screen, 'just like you asked.'

'I know,' I say, 'thanks.'

'Anything else? It's just I'm a bit busy.'

I lean on his desk. 'Sam's not well. Sounds like depression.'

'What's he got to be depressed about?' he says, still looking at his screen.

I sit on the leather settee. 'I saw Jess again today. Think I'll ask to be discharged.'

He looks up and tilts his head. 'Is that wise?'

'I think so,' I say, 'she's going somewhere else anyway.'

My phone buzzes. It's a text from Chrissie: *I've talked to Sam. He says you can come round.*

'Yes!' Mike cheers, clapping his hands.

I look up from my phone. 'What is it?'

'We've got an apartment in Manchester.'

'What do you mean?'

'We're renting it, Isn't that great?'

Forty-Five

I'm not familiar with this part of Thornsea but the sat nav tells me I'm going the right way. When it announces *Your destination is on the left*, I stop at a small semi-detached house with a neat garden. Chrissie's already at the front gate.

I hand her a large food hamper I won at Bruno's charity dinner. 'Won this in a raffle,' I say, 'thought you might like it.' Chrissie takes the hamper and puts it on the path on her side of the gate.

'Sorry Ruth,' she says, 'you've had a wasted journey. He doesn't want to talk to anyone today.'

'That's okay. I understand.' I catch a glimpse of a curtain moving in the upstairs window. 'Has he seen his doctor?'

'Not yet,' she says. She opens the wicker hamper and inspects the contents: cheese, wine, crackers, olives and pickle; before taking it to the front door.

'I'll get back then,' I say, not wanting to outstay my

welcome.

She walks back towards the gate. 'Did you know Sam has another job? Delivery driver.'

'No, I didn't.'

She takes a quick look behind her, towards the upstairs window. The curtain stays closed. 'He asked Mary for a pay rise but she said no.'

I put my hand on her arm. 'I might be able to help.'

'Could you?' She starts crying. 'I'm worried you're going to sack him.'

'Of course not,' I say, 'we wouldn't do that.'

'But if he doesn't get himself better. If he takes too much time off.'

'I'll speak to Mary,' I say, 'and Mike. I'm sure we can do something.'

I follow the sat nav directions back to the Beach Road bar. It's after five when I get there but the lights in Mary's office are still on. I knock on her door and wait. When she opens it, she has her coat on.

'Hi Ruth,' she says, 'I was just about to leave.'

'It's about Sam. Can I come in?'

She sighs. 'Okay, but make it quick.' The office looks different already. She's moved the desk to the other wall and taken my pictures down.

'You know he's not well?'

She nods. 'I know. It's causing us a lot of hassle.'

'And he's doing another job?'

'He needs to concentrate on the one he's got here,' she says, 'or he'll only have one.'

I smile. 'Chrissie says he asked for a pay rise.'

She lets out another long sigh. 'We had to refuse,' she says, 'otherwise everyone will want one.' She opens the door for me.

'He's a loyal member of staff,' I say, stepping onto the landing, 'they both are. I'm worried they might leave us.' I follow her downstairs and out into the car park. 'Can you reconsider?' I say, as we walk to her car, 'We don't want to lose him.'

She stops at her car and turns to face me. 'I thought you'd been told to stop getting involved.'

I smile and try again, hoping she'll reconsider. 'But I'm worried about him. And I'm worried about Chrissie.'

She gets into the driver's seat and winds down the passenger side window, right next to where I'm standing. She leans over and I bend down to hear her.

'I thought you'd been told to stop worrying,' she says, 'it's bad for your mental health.' She looks straight at me and smiles.

I look her in the eye. 'My mental health's fine.' She winds the window up, looks straight ahead and turns on the ignition. I watch as she drives out of the car park.

When I arrive home Mike's in the lounge, watching TV.

'Mary just called,' he says, without looking up.

'Why did you tell her?' I ask him, picking up the remote.

He grabs the remote from my hand. 'Tell her what?'

'About me.'

'I've not said a word,' he says, turning up the volume.

I stand in front of the TV, blocking his view. 'You promise?'

'Promise,' he says, leaning to the right, 'now get out of the way.' I go into the kitchen, sit at my desk and open the laptop. There's no update from the Unit about the café.

Mike comes in and opens the fridge door. 'Mary's not happy,' he says, taking out a fresh packet of smoked salmon, 'you're getting involved where you shouldn't.'

'How does she know what happened to me?'

'I've no idea,' he says, finding a knife in the drawer.

'So she does know?'

He cuts the packet open and lifts a slice. 'Maybe.'

'Who told her?' My voice louder this time. 'Was it Jean?'

He puts the slice in his mouth and the packet back in the fridge. 'Why does it matter?' he says and goes back to the lounge.

I'm still awake when Mike comes to bed. I don't say a word while he undresses and goes into the en suite. I wait until he's climbed underneath the duvet.

'How long's she going to be with us?' I ask, as soon as he's turned his lamp off.

'What's your problem with her?' he says, turning away from me. 'She's doing a great job.'

We're lying back-to-back. I shuffle forward, until there's no part of me touching him. 'But it was my job, and I want it back.'

'You're still not better,' he says, 'and she's very competent and reliable.'

I don't sleep well that night.

Forty-Six

It's a Wednesday afternoon, late September. Mike and I are on our way to Manchester to visit our new apartment. It's the first time I've seen it. Before we get to the motorway, I get a call from Rebecca.

'Thought you'd want to know about Jenny's inquest,' she says.

'Of course.'

'Not great news. The Coroner said the Unit didn't contribute to her death.'

'How's Suzanna?' I ask.

'She's upset,' she says, 'she starting a campaign. Get today's paper - it's all in there.'

When we stop for petrol I get a copy of the County Herald. There's Jenny's picture, again, eyes wide with a bright smile, in front of a tree.

'Don't tell me,' Mike says, sarcastically, 'another of your friends?'

'It's about Jenny,' I say, 'after the inquest result. Suzanna's starting a campaign.'

'For goodness sake,' he says, 'what do they want now?'

'For advocates.'

'Advocates?'

I carry on reading. 'Someone who represents the patient. Helps them understand their rights, helps them speak up.'

'Like I was for you?' he says.

'No,' I say, reading further, 'someone independent.' I fold the paper carefully, put it in my bag and take out my phone.

'What are you up to now?' he says.

'Signing her petition,' I say, 'she wants to get an advocate for every patient at the Unit.'

'Be careful.'

'Of what?'

'The café.'

I stop typing. 'You think I shouldn't sign it?'

'Let's not ruin our chances, that's all I'm saying.'

In the centre of Manchester the sat nav directs us to an underground car park. A lift takes us to the 14th floor. Inside the apartment, there's a narrow corridor with strip lighting, illuminating the floor leading to a lounge and kitchen diner.

'It's very white,' I say, admiring the glossy units.

'I like white,' Mike says, 'and chrome.' He opens a door. 'Here's the main bedroom.'

'Very nice,' I say, looking around, 'nice finishes.'

'It's all high spec.' He comes out of the main bedroom and opens the bathroom door.

'That's a lovely big bath,' I say.

He turns on the hot tap. 'Fancy a bath together?'

I go back to the lounge. 'No thanks.' I hear him turn off the tap. 'Can we afford all this?'

'Of course,' he says, coming into the lounge, 'with this new bar and, definitely when we get your café contract.'

'If we get the café contract,' I say, 'that's not certain.'

'As long as you don't go signing any petitions against them.'

We go out into the lobby and wait for the lift.

'I agree with Suzanna,' I say, 'the Unit did let Jenny down.'

'How?'

'They let her go home by herself and she wasn't ready.' The lift arrives and we step in.

'She did it herself,' he says, tidying his hair in the mirror, 'the Unit didn't.'

'She was vulnerable,' I say, 'and they should have known.'

'There's only so much these places can do.'

I shake my head. 'She went there voluntarily, for help. And they let her down.'

We leave the apartment and walk around the corner to David's new bar. Four men in hard hats and heavy work boots are chatting by the bar. One of them comes over to us, wiping dusty hands on his trousers.

'Just finishing off,' he says, 'it's looking good though.'

'Will it be ready in time?' Mike asks.

'Definitely,' he says, 'Mary keeps us on our toes.'

I watch Mike's face as he and the builder chat about how great Mary is.

When we're walking back to the car I can't help myself from saying something.

'Mary gets involved in a lot of things.'

Mike squeezes my hand. 'She's amazing, isn't she? Wish I could clone her.'

'And David's still happy with everything?'

'Yeah,' he says, 'he thinks she's great too.'

Forty-Seven

I'm at home when I receive an email to say that we're through to the second stage of the café project. I call Mike.

'But there's some bad news too,' I say, reading the details, 'they want a presentation, to their Directors.'

'I'm good at presentations,' he says, 'leave all that to me.'

I'm determined to show him, and the others, I can handle this myself. 'No,' I say, 'it's my project. I'll do it.' I only have three weeks to prepare. I'm quite relaxed doing presentations to Mike and Jean, when we have our own Directors' meetings, when it's just the three of us, and I'm sitting down. But I've never had to do anything as formal as this. I panic for a moment, before calling Olivia.

She's as cheerful as ever. 'How lovely to hear from you,' she says, 'how have you been?'

'I need your help,' I say, 'for a presentation.'

'I'm free this afternoon. We can work out a plan.'

As soon as I finish the call, Suzanna calls me. 'Did you sign our petition?'

I cross my fingers behind my back. 'Think so,' I lie.

'We really need more names,' she says, 'if you can spread the word.'

'I'll see what I can do.'

'Jenny might still be here if someone had been with her,' she says, 'when she was being discharged.'

'Good luck with it,' I say, feeling slightly guilty. I'm sure one less name won't make much difference.

I meet Olivia at the Beach Road bar after lunch. She gives me some useful tips about my presentation and, after two hours, I feel better prepared.

As we're saying our goodbyes, she raises the subject I thought I'd avoided.

'Any more thoughts about getting on stage in March?' she asks. 'We've saved you a place from this year.'

I feel a spot of rain on my cheek and brush it away. 'Give it to someone else,' I say, 'someone who really wants it.'

Olivia takes out a small umbrella and shakes it open. 'C'mon Ruth, say you'll do it.'

I shake my head again. 'No one wants to hear me speak,

especially not what I've learned from sports stars.'

She laughs. 'So what do you want to speak about?'

'I don't,' I say, laughing along with her.

'I'm not giving up on you,' she says, 'I'll get you on that stage one way or another.'

Forty-Eight

Three weeks later I have my final discharge meeting at home. I'm wearing my powder blue suit and patent leather heels, just in case the psychiatrist comes formally dressed too. But he's wearing jeans and a lumberjack shirt. This one is friendly and chatty, much more friendly than the ones I met in the Unit. There are forms to fill in. The community nurse, who comes with him, explains we all need to be certain being discharged is right for me.

'What a great house,' the psychiatrist says, as he sits on the sofa in the downstairs lounge. 'You must love it here.'

'Yes,' I say, 'I do.'

'So do you have any questions for us?' the nurse asks, sitting next to him.

'Jess told me I had psychosis?'

'Yes,' the nurse says.

'Do you know why it happened?' I ask. 'Nobody's been able to tell me?'

The nurse shrugs her shoulders. 'It could be anything.'

'I thought I'd be able to talk to someone, while I was in the Unit. Find out why it happened.'

'That wouldn't have helped,' the nurse says, 'you're in no fit state for talking when you're in there.'

I think of the chats Sophie, Jenny and I shared. 'How about now?' I ask. 'Could I talk to someone now? Would that help?'

The nurse looks at the psychiatrist. 'You mean talking therapy?'

I nod. 'If that's what you call it. Yes.'

'Probably not,' she says, 'and there's a long waiting list.'

'We don't think you'd benefit,' the psychiatrist says. I remember so much about being in the Unit. Almost every detail.

With the forms signed, I walk with them to the top of our drive.

'Do you see that bench over there?' I say, pointing across the road. 'One of the women from the Unit, Sophie Carlton, her mum had it installed, in her memory.'

The psychiatrist scans the railings along the seafront. 'That's nice.'

'The two friends I made in there,' I say, 'both of them ended their lives. Not long after they came out.'

'I'm sorry to hear that,' he says.

The nurse puts her hand on my shoulder. 'You must

focus on yourself now. Don't let things like that upset you.'

I go to bed early, keen to get a good night's sleep before the presentation for the café contract. In my dream I'm back on Seagull Ward, in a meeting with a psychiatrist. I'm wearing my powder blue suit and patent leather heels. standing at a lectern, a screen behind me. I'm reading a *PowerPoint* presentation about why I deserve one hour on my own at the café. When I look up the psychiatrist is wearing pyjamas.

Forty-Nine

Mike, Jean and I arrive at the Thornsea Unit forty minutes before our meeting with the Directors. We sign in at reception and go to the café. There's a small queue of customers waiting to be served. It's only when I'm standing at the counter, that I realise this project is a very bad idea. I've only just been fully discharged from the whole system, what on Earth am I doing getting involved with the Unit again?

'Feeling confident?' Jean asks, as I take our tray to a table.

'No,' I say, 'in fact-'.

Mike interrupts. 'She sounded great in the run-through this morning. I was impressed.'

'This must be a little goldmine,' Jean says, sitting down.

I suddenly feel very hot. 'What if we've made a terrible mist-'

Mike interrupts again. 'And we'd never have known about this, if she hadn't been admitted.'

Back at reception, half an hour later, there's a secretary waiting.

'Really sorry,' she says, 'the Directors are running late. Can we move you to 1.30?'

'Not a problem,' Mike says, cheerfully.

While the other two go back to the café, I head for the Ladies. My stomach has been bubbling ever since we stepped in the foyer. All the cubicles are empty and I go in the first one. Before I unlock my door, to come out, I hear someone come in. They go into the cubicle next to mine and slam the door shut. I hear them, gasping and sobbing. Heavy boots follow, then a loud click above. A long thin steel bar is across the top of my door. I try to open it but the door won't budge.

'What's going on?' I shout out.

A man shouts from the other side. 'Nothing to worry about. Just a precaution. We'll have you out soon. Just waiting for backup.' There are more people and voices on the other side of the door.

'She's locked herself in,' another voice says.

'I'm not going in isolation!' the woman in the next cubicle shouts. 'Not again!'

'Can you let me out please?' I shout. 'I'm here for a meeting.'

There's a knock on my cubicle door. 'You can come out

now.'

The bar at the top of my door clicks back. I push it open.

There are four nurses, each with lanyards, name badges and what look like small torches hanging from their belts. One of the nurses looks familiar.

'You okay?' he says.

'I'll be fine,' I say. I wash my hands, drying them on my trousers.

'Sorry about that,' another nurse says, 'got a really challenging patient here.'

The woman shouts out again from behind the cubicle door. 'I'm not going back. I want to go home.'

When I join Jean and Mike I try my best to look calm. Inside I'm shaking. They continue chatting about the project as I sit down. The clatter of the plates and cutlery is too loud and shrill. My head hurts, as if caught in a vice. I need to get outside. As I get up I knock my chair against the one behind me.

'Careful,' Mike says. Then, apologising to the man behind who is now standing, 'Excuse my wife. She's a little clumsy.'

'I'll see you both outside,' I say, and make my way out. Mike follows me outside. I stop by the foundation stone by the entrance.

'What the Hell are you doing?' he says, when he catches up.

'This is a bad idea,' I say, 'it'll never work.'

'What are you talking about?' He throws his hands up. 'It's practically ours.'

'Tell them we've changed our mind,' I say, 'tell them we can't do it.'

His face is red, his nose twitches like it always does when he gets really angry. 'Don't be so stupid,' he says. He turns and goes back inside.

I lean with my back against the wall taking long, deep breaths, watching people come in and out. No one notices me. When I check my watch it's 1.20pm - still no sign of them. I check again at 1.30pm, 1.45pm, 2.00pm.

At 2.30 pm Mike and Jean come out and walk straight past me. I have to jog to catch up to them.

'Where've you been?' I say, catching my breath.

Jean stops and turns to me. 'Doing your presentation,' she says, 'what did you think?' She carries on walking and I follow behind. When we get to the car she goes to the front passenger door. I get in the back.

'I'm sorry,' I say, 'I just couldn't do it.' Mike doesn't speak as we drive under the car park barrier.

'Well done son,' Jean says, 'you did great.' She looks directly at me through the passenger mirror and scowls.

At home I go straight up to our bedroom while Mike and Jean go into the kitchen. My head is pounding and I feel sick. After an hour, I go downstairs. Jean's sitting at the island, alone.

'You let yourself down today,' she says, nursing a mug of tea.

I get a clean mug from the dishwasher. 'A woman ran into the toilets. It all happened so quick. I was scared.' Mike comes in from the back garden. 'How did it go, the presentation?' I ask him. But he won't talk to me.

Jean folds her arms. 'He did very well, considering.'

'I'm sorry,' I say, 'I was too upset.' I make myself a cup of tea and sit across from Jean and Mike. The three of us sit in silence. Jean drains her cup. She puts her hand on Mike's arm.

'Maybe it's time you stepped back Ruth,' she says. 'I just don't think we can rely on you anymore.' I look at them both, hoping to find some signs of understanding in their faces. But they're not wavering. I leave my tea, half-finished, and go into the hallway. I grab my coat, head for the door and cross the road.

At Sophie's bench I read the inscription on the plaque:

I will find my calmer waters

And be glad that I'm alive

I sit down, looking towards the horizon. The water's

calm. That's what I need, I think, somewhere quiet and calm, away from here. I take the steps down to the sand and walk to the water's edge. On my way back to the steps I get a call from Olivia.

'How did it go today?' she asks.

'Not good,' I say, 'I didn't do it.'

'What happened?

'It's complicated.'

'Do you want to meet up? Talk it through?'

'Thanks,' I say, 'but I'll be okay.' I call Mum. 'Can you get my room ready?' I say, almost in tears. 'I'm coming home.'

Mike and Jean are still in the kitchen when I get in.

'I'm going to Mum and Dad's,' I say, wiping a couple of tears away, 'just for a few days.'

'It'll do you good,' Jean says.

Mike nods. 'You need some rest,' he says, 'don't want you getting ill again.'

For the next couple of days Mike and I are civil to each other. All I can hope is, when I come back from Elsford, things will be better between us, somehow.

Fifty

It's a three-hour journey by train to Elsford. While I'm waiting for a taxi outside the station, I call Mike.

'You got there okay?' he asks.

'At the station now,' I say, 'what are you up to?'

'Doing a bit of research in Manchester.'

I can hear people in the background. 'Who with?'

'David and Cara,' he says, slowly.

I can hear Mary's voice. 'Who else?'

'Mary's with us too,' he says, 'Cara invited her.'

'Oh really,' I say, 'well have a lovely time together.'

Dad's in the garden and Mum's at the front door as I'm paying the taxi driver.

'Come here love,' Mum says, wiping tears away when we hug.

Dad smiles. 'Your mum can't wait to spoil you,' he says, pulling me close.

'I've got your room ready,' Mum says, 'and your *Vimto* and *Digestives*.'

The three of us sit on white plastic garden chairs under the gazebo. Mum's made a quiche, which she serves with salad and new potatoes. Dad brings out a bottle of red wine.

'So what will you do with yourself?' he asks, refilling my glass.

'Get outside. Go for some walks.'

'That will do you good,' Mum says, 'you probably need some time just to relax.'

'You probably went back to work too soon,' Dad says.

'Maybe,' I say.

Alison comes over later. When I open the front door she's holding a huge bunch of sunflowers. 'I'm so glad to see you,' she says, handing me the bouquet. It's so good to see my best friend.

'Thanks for the Get Well card,' I say, 'and my birthday card.'

'I'm glad you're home,' she says, hugging me, 'you'll get looked after here.'

'I'm being spoiled already,' I say.

Later, when it turns colder, we leave the shelter of

the gazebo and go inside. Mum and Dad go in the back lounge while Alison and I move into the dining room.

In the piano stool, I find the small photo album I made after we went to Thornsea on holiday, in 1988. That was the summer I ended up ditching my plans to go to university. Alison, because she didn't find her future husband that week, went to university. After her degree, she gained a Master's and now she has an important job in social work.

My bedroom hasn't changed since I left home to live in Thornsea. Old copies of *Cosmopolitan* are stacked neatly on the shelves and four empty *Anais Anais* perfume bottles are on the dressing table. I find my old blue vanity case at the bottom of the wardrobe, a present for my 18th birthday from one of Dad's cousins. I take out letters, diaries and wedding booklets, placing them carefully on the pink rug. Before she goes to bed, Mum comes in.

'Glad you didn't throw this away,' I say, holding up a red leather-bound diary from 1987. She settles herself on the dressing table stool. 'Remember when I had to give that talk, when I tried to get elected?'

'I remember,' Mum says, 'you were upset for days after that.'

I find the page: *15th October 1987*. 'Had the most awful

day today,' I read, 'never going to do public speaking again.'

Mum heads for the door. 'Put you off for life. You've not been near a stage since.'

I collect my diaries, from 1983 to 1988, and put them in my suitcase.

At breakfast Mum's found some more things.

'Your art file,' she says, pointing to the large case leaning against the table.

I zip it open and run my fingers through the paper and card. Landscapes of the hills and country lanes around here. Most of them were done when I was going out with Robert Bridges, my first boyfriend. He had a red Ford Escort, and we spent most Sundays driving around here.

'Do you ever see Robert?' I ask, casually.

'Now and again,' Mum says, 'I think he's bought a house here.'

Robert never was the marrying type, but I was and I knew it at 16. I probably knew at 13. And when Mike Barrett said he wanted us to get married, after only knowing me for five days, in June 1988, I knew it was time to break up with Robert.

Fifty-One

Alison comes around again the next evening. Mum and Dad are at a fundraising dinner for the *Soroptimists*. We sit in the conservatory.

'How's it really going?' Alison asks. 'And you can tell me the truth now.'

'Not good,' I say, 'me and Mike are having a bad time.'

'Why?'

'I don't know.'

I feel bad complaining to her. Her late husband, Luke, died a couple of years ago. I know she still misses him. At least I still have Mike, healthy and alive. I know Alison would give anything to have Luke here, healthy and alive.

'When did it start?'

'He hired this woman,' I say, 'she's doing my old job now.'

'Can he do that?'

'He doesn't think I'm well enough,' I say, 'or reliable or capable.'

'And what do you think?'

'I don't know,' I say, 'I get upset a lot more now. Things just seem harder.'

I start sobbing. She puts her arms around me and my sobs become a wail.

'Hey?' she says. 'What's all this?'

'I'm okay,' I say, 'I don't know what's wrong with me.'

She reaches for her purse and takes out a small, tattered card. 'I went to see this lady, after Luke.'

I read the details: *Delia Mazur - Psychotherapist.* 'You think she can help me?'

She nods. 'Have you seen one before?'

'Sort of.' I'm thinking of the psychiatrists in the Unit. 'I'm not sure about this. Is she like a psychiatrist?'

'No,' she says, 'a psychotherapist, a counsellor. You can talk to her.'

I shrug my shoulders. 'I don't know.' I'm thinking of my discharge meeting.

'Give her a call,' she says, 'I'm sure she can help.'

In bed I imagine how Delia Mazur will be, if I see her. She'll probably tell me to pull myself together. That I need to toughen up, be more resilient, whatever that means. She'll tell me I've been incredibly selfish, and I need to put the family first. After everything they've done for me, it's time to start repaying them. That's why Alison has told me to see her. It's because she knows I need some tough love. I need to face up to hard truths.

Fifty-Two

Three days later I'm at the door of a very large house near the park, next to Holy Rood Catholic church. I remember it from when I was little. I watched lots of weddings here with Mum. It was at this church I saw the most beautiful wedding dress I've ever seen: a sleeveless fishtail dress in cream vintage lace. Seeing that dress, and the beautiful bride, with her hair in a chignon bun, made me determined that one day I'd wear an equally beautiful dress and wear my hair in a chignon bun. I felt envious as the bride and groom pledged to love each other and spend the rest of their lives together. How incredibly lucky those two people must be to have found each other, I thought, at twelve years old.

When the heavy front door opens, the woman I assume is Delia greets me with a wide smile. She's short, with salt and pepper hair in two plaits and stands on red and gold tiles in the ornate hallway. When she invites me in, I stand admiring the ceiling roses and religious icons.

'This was the presbytery,' she says, 'it's three apartments now.'

'I used to come to weddings at the church. When I was a lot younger.'

'Interesting. We can talk about that later if you want.'

She opens a door into a small side room. There are two soft leather armchairs each with a side table on which there is a box of tissues, a carafe of water and a glass. Delia sits in the armchair nearest the fireplace and rests her hands on her blue linen pinafore dress.

'So, how can I help you?' she asks. She has a soft friendly voice with a slight Eastern European accent. Around her neck she wears a small gold crucifix on a thin gold chain. I notice her black leather shoes over white socks.

'I was thinking you might be able to help me,' I say, 'I need some advice.'

She smiles. 'What type of advice?'

'I was meant to do a presentation to get a contract for a café but I couldn't do it. I was in hospital and this was to prove I was well again. But I let everyone down. I couldn't do it. So I mustn't be better.'

'Why were you in hospital?'

I start with the first time I felt the pain in my neck, right up until having the first meeting on the assessment ward.

'She thought I was lying,' I say, 'she said I had Munchausen syndrome.'

'That must have been frightening.'

'I kept telling them I was dying,' I say, 'and I wasn't. I feel so stupid now.'

'You were in a lot of pain,' she says, 'you were trying to tell them how bad it felt.'

'Yeah,' I say, 'I was sure I was dying. I just wanted to be out of pain.'

I wait, expecting her to tell me how self-centred I've been. I watch the large hand on the grandfather clock, in the corner, move forward. 'I want you to be honest with me,' I say, 'tell me where I've gone wrong.'

'Why do you think you've gone wrong?' she says, softly.

I reach for the box of tissues. 'I've made such a mess of things,' I say, 'I don't know how to put it right and everyone's so angry with me. It's just so hard.' I sink back into the low armchair. The cushion behind me presses into my lower back. I take a few deep breaths.

'Take your time,' she says, 'we're in no rush.' I tell her about Sophie and Jenny and what happened to them. 'And how did you feel about that?

'I was really upset,' I say, 'I'm still upset.' I reach for the glass of water. It's a heavy-cut glass tumbler, *Waterford Crystal*, I guess. I take a sip.

'What was in like in hospital?' she asks.

'A patient hit me on the ward,' I say, 'but the nurses didn't believe me. They said I fell back onto a chair.'

'They denied it?'

I reach for the box of tissues. 'Everyone keeps telling me to forget about it. What happened to me,' I say, 'but I can't.'

'Why do you need to forget?'

'I'm still here,' I say, 'and they're not.'

'And you feel guilty about that?'

I wipe a tear from the corner of my eye. 'I don't know what I feel.'

'You've been through a lot,' she says, 'you need to give yourself time to process it.'

I look at her, waiting for the criticism. 'I should have been stronger,' I say. 'Can you tell me how to be stronger?'

'You're being very hard on yourself,' she says, 'be kinder to yourself.' The grandfather clock indicates I've already used up 40 minutes. I sit forward again. My head is hurting, swimming with questions, and a few answers I wasn't expecting to hear.

Our time is up. 'Thanks for listening,' I say, handing her four crisp twenty-pound notes.

'That's my job,' she says, putting the cash under a round glass paperweight.

'But you were kind to me. You listened.'

She leads me into the hallway. 'Well now,' she says, opening the front door, 'you make sure to be kind to yourself, okay?'

Outside I can't see Alison's car so I go across to the church. It's an old red brick building, dominating its surroundings with a magnificent tall spire. The high oak doors are firmly locked. How many newlywed couples have stood here, full of hope and promise? Alison's car pulls up at the kerb.

'How was that?' she asks, as I get in.

'Not what I was expecting.'

'But was it helpful?

I massage my temples. 'I think so,' I say, 'but I have such a bad headache now.'

'Thought you would,' she says. I start crying. She reaches into the glove compartment and finds a packet of tissues. 'C'mon,' she says, 'let's get you home.'

Back at Mum and Dad's, Mum's watching *Emmerdale*, in the back room and Dad's in the garage. Mum turns down the volume on the TV.

'Well, how was that?' she says, sitting up.

'Emotional,' I reply, honestly.

'Did she upset you?' she says. 'I hope she didn't make things worse.'

'No Mum,' I say, 'she didn't upset me at all.'

She turns up the volume again. 'We didn't need all that in our day.'

I pick up today's copy of the *Express* and read a headline about a singer who's cancelled her world tour.

'So what did you do in your day? If you needed some help?'

She shrugs her shoulders. 'We just got on with it,' she says, 'we had no choice.'

I call Mike later that evening. He sounds happy to hear from me.

'So what have you been doing with yourself?' he asks.

'I went to see a counsellor today. A therapist.'

He chuckles. 'What for?'

'Just to talk. I think it helped.'

'Be careful,' he says, 'those types can do more harm than good.'

'She was very good,' I say, 'Alison recommended her.'

I go to bed but I don't drift off to sleep easily. I still can't get the thought of Mike going around Manchester, enjoying himself with Mary, out of my head. I call Alison.

'Everything okay?' she says sleepily.

'Fine,' I say. 'Are you still in touch with Robert?'

'Yes. Why?' I imagine she's grinning right now. She's always said Robert and me were made for each other. Even after I was married.

'Do you think he'd agree to meet up? For a drink?'

'Sure,' she says. 'He's always asking about you.'

Fifty-Three

Alison's at the front door at 6 pm the next evening.

'So did you manage to get hold of Robert?' I ask, casually, as we set off for the Royal Oak around the corner.

'Yeah,' she says. 'I've spoken to him.'

'And?' I'm impatient to know if he's going to be in the pub.

'He's coming,' she says, 'don't worry.'

Inside the Royal Oak, we take a seat by the unlit coal fire. This is where I had my first proper paid-for alcoholic drink outside home, at 17. It's not changed much in thirty years, except I can't see many underage drinkers tonight. The few customers who are in are at least our age, most are older. I look around the lounge. The last time I saw Robert I was 21, when I came home with Mike, the Christmas before we got married.

Alison comes back with another round of drinks. 'He's just walked in,' she says, turning discreetly towards the bar. I look over and notice a tall, thin balding man with glasses, wearing a lilac shirt and dark denim jeans. He buys a drink and walks over to our table.

'Robert,' I say, standing up.

'Ruth,' he says, 'you've hardly changed at all.'

He has, I think, but he still has that kind smile I always loved. He's wearing some lovely aftershave too. Alison takes her phone and goes out towards the beer garden.

'It's been a long time,' he says, 'how have you been?'

I hesitate for a moment, wondering if I should tell him what's happened. I take a large gulp of my gin and tonic.

'I wasn't well. I was in hospital.'

His smile disappears. 'Oh no,' he says, putting his pint on a beer mat, 'how are you now?'

I look at his hands, no rings. 'Getting better,' I say, 'slowly.' I wonder if I should tell him more, but I won't, not yet.

He takes another sip of his pint. 'Still married?'

'Just about. Celebrated our twenty-fifth in June and two teenagers - a boy and a girl.'

'Congratulations,' he says. He seems to be genuinely happy for me.

I smile and nod. 'Any family of your own?'

'No,' he says, 'never married.' At the bar, a man about our age looks over in our direction and winks at Robert.

'Girlfriends?'

'A couple,' he says, 'no one serious at the minute.'

Robert tells me he's lecturing at the university. 'The travelling was good,' he says, 'went on some great arena tours.'

'Sounds exciting,' I say. It's like we're both seventeen again. As if I've just come back from the Ladies, to check my hair, and he's waiting for me to carry on our conversation. It's like the past 30 years have never happened.

'I wrote to you,' he says.

'Mum told me,' I say.

'You never replied.'

'I had a new boyfriend,' I say, 'didn't think it was right.'

'Did you read any of my letters?' Alison comes back and I'm relieved. After I moved to Thornsea I told Mum to burn anything that looked like it came from Robert. His letters were always easy to identify.

'Do you remember when I did that talk at college and you two were in the wings?'

Alison gasps. 'Yes, yes, I do,' she giggles, 'you ran off the stage.'

'I was awful,' I say, giggling too.

'Well I thought you were brilliant,' Robert says, 'I couldn't have done that, back then.'

I stop giggling. 'Really? You really mean that?'

'Absolutely,' he says, 'I was proud of you. You had a go. Even though you were probably terrified.'

We spend the next hour remembering people who were in our year at St Ursula's and our teachers. Alison seems to have an encyclopedic knowledge of what happened to every one of them. When Alison goes to the bar I notice Robert's lovely eyes again.

'Have you ever been to Taos Pueblo?' I ask him.

He shakes his head. 'Nearly got there once. We were in Santa Fe, but we didn't have time. Why?'

'Oh nothing,' I say, 'just somewhere I'd love to go.'

'Me too,' he says, holding my gaze.

Alison comes back from the bar and claps her hands. 'Well isn't this lovely?'

When the bell rings for last orders, Robert gets up to leave.

'It's been lovely seeing you again,' he says, 'let's not leave it so long next time.'

'Yeah,' I say, 'it has been lovely. Sorry I left it so long.'

'We could come over to Thornsea,' Alison suggests, 'meet up over there.' I imagine telling Mike that my first boyfriend is coming to visit. I don't expect he'll take it very well.

'Maybe,' I say, with little enthusiasm.

Robert finishes his pint and puts his arms out for another hug. There's another long embrace. He was always great at giving hugs.

'Take care of yourself,' he says, patting my arm, one last time.

As we're walking home Alison can't stop grinning.

'He still really likes you,' she says, 'can't you tell?'

'No, he doesn't. That was a lifetime ago.'

Mum's in the back room, reading the *Express*, when I get in.

'Had a nice time?'

'Really nice,' I say. 'It's done me good, coming home.'

'So what you up to tomorrow?'

I bend to kiss her on the cheek. 'I'm ready to go home now,' I say, 'I'm missing Daniel and Ellie.'

'And what about Mike?' she asks. 'Haven't you missed him?'

'A little bit,' I say.

When I'm brushing my teeth I'm thinking of Robert. When I was 18, before I met Mike, I liked Robert, a lot. He was kind, but he could never make up his mind about what he wanted to do. Mike was different. He's always had a plan, always known exactly where he wants to be: next month, next year, next five years. I'm lucky to be married to him, I remind myself. And marriage can sometimes be hard work. I just need to work a bit harder.

Fifty-Four

Mike's on the platform when my train pulls into Thornsea.

He grabs my suitcase. 'Feeling better?' He strides ahead, pulling the luggage behind him. I walk quickly to catch up.

'It's done me good,' I say, 'had some good chats.' When we reach the car there's a bottle of *Dom Perignon* on the back seat. 'What are we celebrating?'

'We got the lease for the Manchester bar,' he says, smiling.

Before we turn into our drive I spot a couple kissing by the bus stop.

'What do you think about us having couples therapy?' I ask, still looking at the couple.

Mike laughs. 'Absolutely not. You're the one with the problems. Not me.'

In our drive, I reach for the door release. Mike flicks the locks and reaches for my hand. 'Before we go in,' he says, 'there's something I need to tell you.'

I know from his tone I'm not going to like it. 'What is it?'

'We've made Mary's contract permanent,' he says, looking out of his window.

There's an immediate tightness in my chest and I pull my hand away. 'Without speaking to me first?'

He flicks the locks open and goes around to the boot. He takes my suitcase and wheels it inside. I wait in the car.

My phone buzzes. It's a *WhatsApp* message from Mike: *I had no choice.* I stay in the car for ten more minutes. Then there's another message: *She might have left us if I hadn't.* Then another: *And David likes her.* Then another: *Are you coming in?*

When I do go in, Jean's in the kitchen.

'Had a nice break?' she asks.

'Lovely, thanks,' I say, leaning against the island.

'I've already told Ruth about the developments,' Mike says, smiling at me.

'It made sense to get it done now,' Jean says, 'make it all official.'

'While I was away,' I say, under my breath.

Mike finds the champagne bucket and fills it with ice.

'I've been very impressed with Mary,' Jean says, 'very

dependable and reliable. Always very calm, don't you think?'

'She's a real asset,' Mike says, 'just what we need.'

I take my suitcase into the utility room and load my dirty laundry into the machine. When I've switched it on I sit on the floor, leaning against the tumble dryer. From here I can listen to Mike and Jean talking about the Manchester bar.

Later, we order takeout from Mike's favourite Indian restaurant. While he's paying the driver, I get the plates while Jean gets the cutlery.

'You and Mike have been busy,' I say, 'while I've been away.'

'He was worried Mary might look for another job,' Jean says, setting the table. 'We didn't want to lose her. And David likes her.'

'So I hear,' I say. Mike puts the takeaway bags on the table. 'So what's your plan for me?' I ask.

He shrugs his shoulders. 'What do you mean?'

'What do I do now? Seeing as you've given Mary my old job.'

'There's loads you can do,' Jean says.

I look at them both in turn. 'Like what?' Neither of them respond.

After we've eaten, Mike takes the *Dom Perignon* into the garden and pops the cork. He runs back into the kitchen and fills five crystal flutes with the fizzing champagne.

'To the new Manchester bar,' he says, clinking my glass.

'To the Manchester bar!' we all cheer in unison.

Mike, Jean and I go into the lounge. He switches on the TV. I still haven't had a satisfactory answer.

'So what am I doing?' I ask again. 'Now you've given Mary my old job?'

Jean picks up this month's copy of Coastal Monthly.

'We'll need a big publicity campaign for Manchester,' Mike says. 'David expects it to be full on opening weekend.'

Jean looks up from the magazine. 'You can't ask Ruth to do that. She'll be way out of her depth.'

'You're right Mum. I should ask Mary. She'll get it done, no problem.'

I look at them both but Jean has her head down, reading the magazine, and Mike has his head down, tapping on his phone.

'I'll do it,' I say. I catch them giving each other a knowing glance.

'You're sure?' he says, looking up from his phone.

'There's a lot riding on this. We can't mess it up.'

'Leave it with me. I won't let you down.'

Jean raises her eyebrows and turns a page of the magazine. 'Like you did with the café presentation?'

'That was different. I can do this.'

'Let's give her another chance,' Mike says, 'everyone deserves another chance.'

Fifty-Five

In the morning I call Olivia. 'I need your help again.'

'Sure,' she says.

'We're opening a bar in Manchester, and I'm in charge of the launch. It's one of David's, so we have to get it right.'

'I'll help. On one condition.'

I was hoping we might get through this call without her mentioning it. 'You want me to speak next March?' I say. 'Is that what I have to do?'

She laughs. 'Got it in one.'

I let out a long sigh. 'Really? Do I have to?'

'How much do you need my help for the Manchester bar?'

I put my head in my hands. 'Okay,' I say, lifting my head, 'I'll do it.'

'Wonderful.'

'But can my talk be about something else?'

'Sure,' she says, 'what do you have in mind?'

'Don't know yet,' I say, 'but definitely not about what I've learned from meeting sports stars.'

As I'm emptying the dishwasher I get a call from Suzanna. 'We're taking our petition to the Unit,' she says, 'will you come along?'

'Of course,' I say. Mike and Jean don't need to know about this though.

Fifty-Six

I meet Suzanna and Terese on Thursday morning outside the main entrance to the Unit. Suzanna is carrying a large file under her arm.

'Eight hundred signatures,' she says, 'less than I hoped for, but it's a start.'

'Well done,' I say.

Terese stops and gently pushes Suzanna and I towards the foundation stone.

'We need someone to take our picture,' she says, 'so we can send it into the paper.'

I wave my hand. 'I don't need to be in it,' I say, stepping back. 'I can take one of you two.'

'Nonsense,' Suzanna says, 'you need to be in it too.' She grabs my hand and pulls me towards her. Terese stops a nurse as they're walking towards us and they agree to take the photo.

After the photo we head to the Unit's reception. Suzanna hands the file to a receptionist.

I take out my wallet. 'Let's go to the café. My treat.'

At our table Terese takes two small paper bags from her handbag. 'Gifts for you both,' she says, handing Suzanna and I a bag each.

Inside I find The Small Book of Compassion.

'Thank you,' Suzanna and I say in unison.

'Just to say thanks to you both,' Terese says, 'for all your help.'

I return my book to its paper bag and put it in my coat pocket, where it fits snugly. I remember the memorial stone and I'm annoyed for forgetting to bring some flowers.

'Before we all leave here,' I say, 'there's something I want to show you.'

Terese and Suzanna follow me to the memorial stone in the car park.

'They should have all the names engraved,' Suzanna says, climbing over the low-picket fence, 'they all need to be remembered.'

'I know one of them was David's auntie,' I say, 'Lizzie.'

Terese touches my arm. 'And I bet some shouldn't have even been in there.'

While Suzanna and Terese are chatting about the petition I'm remembering my time here. I still have so many questions that need answering.

On the drive home I make a detour and call at Doctor Berry's surgery. I sit in the car park, listening to the radio, wondering if I'm doing the right thing. I'm not sure I want to know what's been written about me. But I need to be brave. I go in and ask the receptionist if I can have access to my medical records. To my relief and surprise, she agrees.

A few hours later, back at home, I get an e-mail with a link to my records. I don't open it straight away.

The following day I'm the first one up, at 6 am. I haven't slept well and I know I can't put off reading the medical records any longer. I make a coffee and sit at my desk in the kitchen. The first file I open contains the notes between myself and the locums I saw in February. In the middle of the first page it's there: *Mrs Barrett is a challenging patient.* Is that what they were calling me?

When Mike comes downstairs I show him. 'Look,' I say, pointing to the words, 'they called me a challenging patient.'

He scans the screen. 'You probably were,' he says, yawning, 'you were being difficult. I remember that.' He makes himself a coffee, leaving me to read the other files.

'And there's something else,' I say, 'I've found something else.' He stands behind me and reads over my shoulder. 'Look,' I say, pointing to the screen, 'when Doctor Berry stopped my medication in December, do you think it could be linked?'

'How?'

I swivel my chair to face him. 'Me coming off the medication in December,' I say, 'did that start the pain in the New Year?'

He shakes his head. 'Doubt it,' he says, 'the doctors would have told you if it had.'

'But what if they didn't look at my notes? What if they missed it?'

He shrugs his shoulders. 'What difference would it make anyway?'

'They kept saying I was fine,' I say, 'they said I was lying about the pain.'

'You told them you were dying,' he says, 'and you weren't.'

'But I was in pain.'

'I don't know,' he says, 'I'm not a doctor and neither are you.'

Ellie comes into the kitchen, followed by Daniel. While they're getting their breakfast Mike comes over and switches off my laptop.

'Can we forget all this now?' he says, closing the lid.

'I'm just trying to get to the truth,' I say, quietly.

'Just be grateful you're okay,' he says, 'don't go looking for trouble where there isn't any.' Before I can reply he's already out of the kitchen. I watch Ellie and Daniel making toast and pouring milk into glasses. I know I'm lucky to still be here. Maybe Mike's right. Maybe what I need is to be with people who know nothing about what happened to me. Maybe I need to get back to Art Club.

Fifty-Seven

When I arrive at Art Club, the following Monday, Henry is his usual welcoming self. Today, we're painting a scene of the boating lake.

At break Henry chooses an album for us to enjoy: *The Complete Mahler Symphonies conducted by Leonard Bernstein with the New York Philharmonic.* As we listen to the first few bars Milly hands round a tin filled with homemade flapjacks.

'Are you free on Saturday?' she asks, as I take one. 'Want to come on a protest?'

Henry is behind her nodding vigorously. 'Say you'll come,' he pleads. 'It's lots of fun, and for a good cause.'

'A protest?' I say, wiping crumbs from my lips. 'I'm not sure.'

'Against the new road through the woodland,' Milly explains, 'it's important.'

I wonder what Mike will say. I know he won't be happy.

'C'mon Ruth,' Henry pleads again, 'for the environment.'

Milly hands around the tin of flapjacks again. They're buttery and delicious.

'Okay,' I say, 'count me in.'

I'm in the kitchen when Mike comes home. He goes straight upstairs without saying hello and when he comes into the kitchen he goes straight to the fridge. I can tell something is wrong.

'Everything okay?' I ask, hesitantly.

'We didn't get the café contract,' he says, taking out a plate of sliced chicken, left over from yesterday's roast dinner.

I try to sound positive. 'Never mind. It's probably for the best anyway.' He brings in his bag from the hall and takes out a copy of the County Herald.

'And this can't have helped.' He throws it on the countertop. 'You're in there with your friends.' He opens it at page five and points to a photo of Suzanna, Terese and I by the Unit's foundation stone. 'Your name's underneath the photo,' he says, 'what were you thinking?'

I read the description underneath our picture: *Suzanna Hardman, Terese Carlton and Ruth Barrett handing in a petition of nearly 1000 signatures requesting advocates for all patients of Thornsea Unit.*

'Oh,' I say, 'I didn't know they'd print my name.' He goes to the fridge again, takes out a jar of olives and pours some into a bowl. 'It wouldn't have worked anyway,' I say, 'we run bars, not hospital cafés.'

'But that could have opened up more things for us.'

'Sorry for messing it up for you.'

'Mary's disappointed too,' he says, 'she did a lot of research for that.' He goes out to the hall and comes back with a slim white envelope. 'Something to cheer us up,' he says, 'Captains Lunch at the Golf Club.'

I take two tickets out of the envelope and read the date. 'Sorry,' I say, handing them back, 'I've made plans for Saturday.'

'What do you mean?' What plans?' I don't want to tell him about the protest. Hopefully, he doesn't need to find out.

'It's something with the Art Club.'

'But we always go to this lunch, every year, without fail.'

I smile and shrug my shoulders. 'Not this year,' I say, 'I'm doing something else.'

'So what do I do with these?' he says, waving the envelope above his head. 'They're 50 quid each.' I go to the sink, facing towards the window.

'How about Mary?'

'Why Mary?'

'Why not?' I say, still with my back to him. 'You two seem to get on very well.'

'I'll take my mum,' he says. When I turn around he's not there.

Fifty-Eight

The Art Club's already full of people when I arrive on Saturday morning. As I take my jacket off, Henry thrusts a blank wooden placard into my hand.

'Paint yourself a placard,' he says, 'we set off at two.'

As more people turn up, Milly brings out a table and puts it outside on the pavement. The reggae music blasting from the speakers mixes with the sound of laughter and excited chatter. I've never painted a placard in my life. I've never been to a protest in my life. Unsure of how I should decorate my placard, I look at what everyone else is doing. I paint three trees on one side and a road with white markings on the other. Under the trees, I paint a big green tick and under the road, a big red cross.

At noon we gather outside, on the street, waiting for instructions. Henry moves to the front with a megaphone.

'Okay everyone,' he shouts, 'we'll parade down to the seafront then walk up to the Golf Club.'

'There's a big do up there today,' Milly shouts, 'so we

should get some attention.'

I turn to the woman standing next to me. 'Did he just say the Golf Club?'

'Yeah that's right,' she says. There's the tiniest possibility I might get spotted by Mike and Jean. Not wanting to risk it, I borrow a scarf from Milly. With a blue and pink scarf covering my hair and most of my face I set off for the Golf Club. Someone's brought a drum and we walk to the beat, chanting, 'Save Our Wood You Know You Should' and 'No More Roads No More Oil Love Our Nature Don't Let It Spoil.'

It takes about an hour to get to the Golf Club. Most passing motorists pomp their horns or give us a wave. When we arrive at the entrance I see the car park's full. The Captain's lunch must have started already and I breathe a sigh of relief I've avoided being recognised. The drummer starts a samba beat and before long I'm tapping my feet. The scarf falls from my face but I'm having so much fun, I don't bother putting it back.

Cars begin pomping their horns in long sirens. Six of the younger protesters are standing in the middle of the road.

Milly calls out to them. 'Don't block the road!' No obstructing traffic!'

The six move to the side and the cars start to pass

in a steady stream. One stops just in front of me and I recognise Mike's car straightaway. He's driving and Jean's in the passenger seat, staring at me. I hide my face behind my placard.

'Ruth, is that you?' Mike shouts through the window. I put the placard down.

He beckons me towards the car. 'Get in!' he shouts.

'Hi Ruth!' Jean shouts across from the passenger seat. 'What are you doing up here?'

I lay my placard on the ground and go over to Mike's window. 'Protesting,' I say, 'about the new road.'

Mike rolls his eyes. Jean takes out her phone and takes a photo of me.

'Get in the car!' he shouts. 'You're embarrassing yourself.'

'It's okay,' I say, gesturing to my fellow protestors, 'I'll walk back later with the others.' Cars behind are beeping on their horns again. Milly comes over to us.

'Everything okay?' she asks, bending down to the window. Jean waves at her, laughing.

'We're giving Ruth a lift home,' Mike says. I climb in the back seat, reluctantly.

'You sure you'll be okay?' Milly asks.

I wind my window down. 'I'll see you at Art Club. Thanks. I've had a brilliant time today.'

We drive to Jean's house in silence. When we leave Jean's, Mike continues, in silence. I try my best to make friendly chit-chat, telling him how much I love samba drumming now. When we park up in our drive, he releases his seatbelt and turns to me.

'What was all that about?' he says.

'I was just having fun,' I say, 'with my friends.'

He gets out of the car and slams the door. 'You're not the woman I married anymore,' he says, 'the old Ruth would never have done that.'

Fifty-Nine

I'm full of excitement when I turn up at Art Club the following week. I can't wait to chat about Saturday and how much fun it was. I'm hoping someone picked up my placard and brought it back. I want to keep it as a souvenir.

Henry doesn't greet me in his usual exuberant manner. Milly seems quieter too. During the tea break Milly hands round some cashew and date pieces while Henry chooses an album from the box: *Shostakovich Piano Concerto No.2 conducted by Dmitri Shostakovich.* It seems to match the scene we're painting: a stormy sea blending into a grey sky, seen through the black ironwork of Thornsea pier.

'Dad and I have some bad news,' Milly says, when we've all taken a piece, or two, from the tin.

Henry closes his eyes and moves his head to the melody. 'We're closing,' he says, 'our little project is over.'

Myself and my fellow artists gasp. I can't believe what

I'm hearing.

'Closing?' I say. 'No, no, you can't close.'

Milly nods. 'We've run out of money,' she says, 'lost our funding from the Council.'

I walk home from Art Club, slower than usual, that afternoon.

I'm in the lounge when Mike comes home. He gives me a bunch of yellow roses.

'What's all this?' I ask, wondering what I've done to deserve them.

'I'll get a vase,' he says, going into the kitchen.

When he comes back he places the vase on the coffee table, sits next to me and squeezes my hand. 'David's looking at places in London,' he says, 'wants me to go down there with him? You okay with that?' I rearrange the roses, spreading the gypsophila among the stems.

'Just you and David?'

'Err yeah,' he says, 'just me and David.'

'How long for?'

'Saturday night,' he says, 'be back Sunday.'

I tell him the news, about Art Club closing. He picks up the sports supplement from yesterday's Sunday paper and opens the magazine on a feature about a young male cricketer.

'Oh really?' he says, seeming disinterested.

'It's really sad,' I say, sighing, 'I'm really going to miss it.'

He turns the page. 'It didn't do itself any favours,' he says, eyes fixed on the article, 'getting involved in the road protest.' I pull the magazine out of his hand.

'You think that's why they lost it?'

'I know it,' he says, 'and can I have that back. I was reading that.' I take the magazine to the recycling bin in the utility room. He follows behind and grabs it out of my hand. I try to get it back but he grabs my wrist and holds it tight.

'Let go!' I shout.

He releases my hand and goes back into the lounge with the magazine. 'They're troublemakers, that lot,' he says, 'you need to stay well away.'

'They're not troublemakers,' I say, 'they're my friends. They're just standing up for what they believe in.'

Over dinner, I'm quieter than usual. I'm upset about Art Club closing. Surely, there must be some way it can be saved. But from what Milly and Henry said, it doesn't sound likely. I can't help but admire them, standing up for what they believe in. Organising a protest to protect the woodland, risking public ridicule, from people like Mike. Even risking their livelihood.

After dinner, while Mike's watching football in the

lounge, I go to my laptop. When he comes into the kitchen, at half-time, I've just pressed the Send button on my carefully composed e-mail.

'What you up to now?' he asks, peering over my shoulder.

'I've written to the Unit.'

'What about?'

'My complaint.'

'Why?'

'I want an apology for what happened?'

'An apology for what?' He goes to the fridge and takes out a box of Camembert. 'Nothing happened to you.'

'My assault,' I say, 'and they didn't believe me.'

He cuts a quarter of the Camembert and puts the box back in the fridge. 'For God's sake,' he says, slamming the fridge door, 'not that again.'

'It needs investigating,' I say, 'I don't want it to happen to anyone else.'

'You weren't assaulted,' he says, 'you fell!'

'And the pain?' I say. 'What about the pain? They didn't care about it. I had no painkillers.'

He rips the quarter of cheese in two and puts a chunk in his mouth. 'They said there was nothing wrong. It was all in your head.'

Sixty

It's three weeks before I get a response from the Unit:

Dear Ruth,

We acknowledge your complaint regarding an allegation of assault when you were a patient on Seagull ward in March. We have conducted a thorough investigation and are satisfied that no assault occurred.

As regards your comments that we failed to acknowledge your pain, we apologise if you felt this to be the case.

We consider this matter to be closed but if you wish, you may contact the Parliamentary and Health Ombudsman.

Later that evening, I show Mike the email.

'You need to forget about it now,' he says, peeling a tangerine, 'put it in the past.'

'I could contact the Ombudsman,' I say, 'see if they'll investigate.'

'Please, love, please,' he says, throwing the tangerine peel in the bin, 'you'll make yourself ill again.'

When he goes for a shower I call Suzanna. 'I saw our picture with the petition,' I say, 'did you get a reply?'

'Just an acknowledgement,' she says, 'I wasn't expecting much.'

'I got a reply to my complaint. They're denying it happened.'

'They hope we'll go away,' she says, 'but we have to stay strong.'

I look at the reply on my screen. 'Yeah, we have to stay strong.'

I know Mike will be furious when he finds out but I don't have a choice. I take out my phone and find Rebecca's number. My finger hovers over her number, my heart beating fast. I imagine what the article will look like when it's finally printed in the County Herald. She'll probably want a photograph of me. I could have it taken outside the Unit entrance, or at Sophie's bench, or at the Beach Road bar. And what will people think when they read about what happened to me? Rebecca picks up straight away. I take a deep breath.

'I'm ready to talk,' I say, 'about the Unit.'

There's a slight pause. 'Sorry Ruth,' she says, 'I can't do it.'

She's obviously misheard me. 'I've written loads of notes,' I say, 'I'll email it over to you. It's practically written already.'

'I can't do it,' she says.

'But I've written it now.'

'Sorry Ruth,' she says, firmly, 'I'm leaving the paper.' I hear Mike's footsteps coming downstairs and I go out into the garden.

'When?' I say, stepping onto the lawn.

'At the end of the week.' I go right to the bottom of the garden, to the trampoline. When I turn around, towards the house, Mike's watching me from the window at the sink.

'Where are you going?'

'Local TV,' she says, 'politics.' I look up into the evening sky. Surely there must be something she can do.

'So I'm too late?' I say.

'Sorry, Ruth,' she says, 'but let's keep in touch.'

I finish the call but stay outside. Mike's still staring at me from the window and I'm too angry with myself to go back inside. Instead, I kick the fallen leaves by the oak tree in the corner.

Sixty-One

On the Saturday, Mike's up at 6 am, ready for his trip to London with David. As I'm awake I go downstairs and make a coffee. When he comes into the kitchen he's wearing the navy suit and brown leather brogues he bought in Marbella.

'You look great,' I say, yawning, 'wish I was coming with you.'

He nods. 'Sorry love, he says, 'another time.' He kisses me on the cheek. 'David thinks we'll get more done if it's just us.' He makes a coffee and we sit opposite each other, the silence only broken by our sips. I study his face and wonder if he's telling the truth about London. His face gives nothing away. 'What are your plans for this weekend?'

'Catch up on some work,' I say, 'get the marketing plan finished.'

He kisses me on the cheek. 'Good plan,' he says, 'good plan.'

By seven he's out the door to catch his train. I wait 20 minutes and leave a note, telling Daniel and Ellie I'm at the Beach Road bar.

Once there I go straight to Mike's office. I find the key to his drawer on a hook on the wall. In the top drawer I find a few notebooks, a twenty-pound note, the Mont Blanc pen I gave him at Christmas and an *iPhone* charger. In the bottom drawer I find a white gift bag with a thick gold ribbon. I pull the opening back to see a box of *Godiva* chocolates inside.

There are no staff in yet. I go into Mary's office. Her drawers aren't locked. In the top one there's a black leather pencil case with her initials embossed in gold, half a bag of almonds, *Elisabeth Arden* hand cream and a *Burts Bees* lip balm. I go back to Mike's office and open his laptop. He's not changed his login or password. I go through his e-mails and find Mary's contract of employment, with her address. According to *Google Maps*, it should take me 20 minutes.

The house is on a pretty tree-lined road of ten houses. It's a 1930s semi, similar to Mum and Dad's. The curtains are closed but it's only 9 am. I park on the opposite side of the road. I can't see Mary's car but there's a *Ford Escort* on the drive.

After half an hour a couple come out, get into the car

and drive off. I wait until they've turned out of the road and set off back into town.

There must be a hundred cars in the railway station car park. I find Mike's car after five minutes but, no matter how many times I walk up and down the rows, I can't find Mary's anywhere. But there's another option, even if it means an hour's drive.

David and Cara's house is on a long country lane. There's not a parked car in site. I park opposite their gates and wait. For the first hour all I see is four middle-aged men on racing bikes and two riders on horseback. Finally, just after noon, the drive gates open and a *Range Rover* pulls out. It heads in my direction and I can clearly see David in the driver's seat with Cara next to him. I lean over into the well of the passenger side, hoping I'm not seen as they drive past.

My heart's racing as I drive home. When I get back I go upstairs and climb into bed. I've only had my eyes closed for a minute when there's a knock on the door, it's Ellie.

'You're back,' she says.

'Yes,' I say, sitting up and straightening my hair.

'You okay?'

'Fine,' I say, 'just getting some rest.' She closes the door and goes downstairs. I lie down. I'll just ask him. I'll just ask Mike how London was. That's a perfectly reasonable question for a wife to ask her husband when he's come back from a trip. He won't know where I've been today. He won't know I've seen David earlier.

It's just after 8 pm on Sunday when Mike gets back. I hear him in the hall but I stay in the lounge, reading Coastal Monthly. He goes straight upstairs and, ten minutes later, he comes into the lounge, in his dressing gown, his hair wet. He hands me a white gift bag with thick gold ribbon. It's the same one I found in his desk yesterday.

'Pressie,' he says, 'from London.' I untie the gold ribbon and take out the box of *Godiva* chocolates.

'Had a nice time?' I ask. 'How was it?'

He picks up the TV remote. 'How's the marketing plan coming along?' he asks. 'David wants an update.' I put the chocolates back in the gift bag and put it on the coffee table.

'I'm a bit behind,' I say, 'sorry.' He sits beside me and flicks through the channels.

'I thought you were on top of it all,' he says, 'what's the matter?'

'How was London?' I ask again. 'How was David?'

'Busy,' he says, staring at the TV.

'Where did you go?'

'I'm really tired,' he says, through a yawn, 'can we not talk about it?'

I try again. 'Where did you stay?'

'For God's sake!' he shouts. 'It was just business. Okay?!' He slams the remote onto the coffee table. It ricochets across the table, knocking over my half-full glass of cranberry juice. The juice splashes onto the white gift bag and makes a puddle of deep red on the oak top. I run into the kitchen and grab two tea towels hanging by the sink. When I come back Mike's knelt with his hand at the edge of the table in a futile attempt to stop the juice from dripping onto the carpet. I throw him the tea towels and he presses them onto the spill.

'What's the matter?' I say, rescuing my magazine, also mottled in cranberry juice.

'Sorry,' he says. He hands me the sodden towels, 'I'm shattered.' I take the tea towels to the sink in the utility room, turn on the cold tap and watch the red-stained water gush down the plughole. I go into the lounge and pick up the gift bag and magazine.

'We're you two up late?'

'Yeah,' he says, yawning again, 'you know David, he likes to party.'

I take the chocolates out of the gift bag and put the box, still unopened, in the kitchen peddle bin, covering it with vegetable peelings. Back in the lounge, I settle back into the corner of the sofa and rest my bare feet across his legs. He puts his hand on my foot.

'How do you think Mary's getting on?' I ask.

'Great,' he says, keeping his eyes on the TV.

'Do you think she'll stay?'

'Yeah,' he says, turning to me, smiling, 'I think she's loyal.' I pull my feet away. The quick movement triggers a cramp in my right calf. I let out a yelp of pain and rub my leg vigorously.

'Agghh!!' I scream. 'Ow! Ow! Ow! Ow!'

'You okay?' he says, as I'm rubbing my leg.

'Just cramp.'

'Nothing serious then?' he says.

'No,' I say, smiling, 'nothing serious.'

I leave him in the lounge and go upstairs.

When he comes to bed I'm sitting up reading The Small Book of Compassion.

'Everything okay?' he says, taking off his jumper. I put the book back in my drawer.

'Are we going to Marbella again?' I ask. 'In January?'

He sits on his side of the bed, with his back to me, taking off his socks.

'Let's give it a miss this year, eh?' He throws his socks into the laundry basket. I turn off my lamp and rest my head on the pillow.

'Should we go somewhere else then?' I say. 'Somewhere different?' He opens the door to the en suite.

'No,' he says, 'we're too busy for holidays right now.' When he gets into bed we lie with our backs to each other, but we're not touching. I'm so far over on my side, I'm almost hanging over the edge.

Sixty-Two

On Monday, when I wake, I have a heavy pressure on my head, as if I'm in a deep swimming pool and someone is pressing my head under the water. Mike's already up, I can hear him downstairs talking to Daniel and Ellie. When he comes upstairs I pretend to be asleep.

He taps me on the shoulder. 'Hey, sleepy head,' he says, softly, 'getting up today?'

'I don't feel too good.' I say, pulling the duvet over my head. He kneels down, by my side, and pulls the duvet down.

'You're not getting ill again are you?' he says. 'Do I need to call the doctor?' I pull the duvet over my face and turn over.

'I'll be fine,' I say, 'I don't need to see a doctor.'

'It's just you thought you had a pain last night,' he says.

I turn over. 'That was cramp,' I say, 'in my leg. Just leave me.' He goes into the en suite and I hear the shower door close. When he comes out I stay hidden under the duvet, not saying a word as he gets dressed. While I have my eyes closed I feel his hand on my shoulder.

'Are you sure you don't need to see a doctor?' he says.

'No,' I say, still under the duvet.

'I'll get Mum to come over,' he says, 'she can keep an eye on you.'

I hear Jean unlocking the front door around 10 am. She comes straight upstairs and knocks on the bedroom door.

'Ruth,' she says, loudly, 'are you okay?'

I pull the duvet down and shout out. 'I'm fine Jean, thanks.'

I stay in bed all Tuesday and all Wednesday, only coming downstairs to get food and water. Mike doesn't say much during that time, except that he's concerned about me and he's worried I'm getting ill again. I just tell him I'm fine. I'm just exhausted. And I am.

On Thursday morning I get a call from a number I don't recognise.

'Hello,' a man's voice says, 'am I speaking to Ruth Barrett?' I put him on loudspeaker.

'Who is this?' I say, looking at the number again.

'My name's Gordon,' he says, 'I'm from the Early Intervention Service.' I sit up, feeling my heart beat a little faster. ‘Your husband’s been in touch,’ he continues, ‘he’s worried about you.’ I throw the phone onto the duvet and throw a pillow over it. I can hear Gordon’s muffled voice calling out. ‘Ruth, Ruth are you okay Ruth?’ My hand is shaking as I pick up the phone.

‘I think he’s having an affair,’ I say, ‘Mike, I think he’s having an affair.’ There’s a silence from Gordon and I wonder if he’ll believe me.

‘Okay,’ Gordon says, slowly, ‘why...do...you...think...that?’ I swing my feet out of the bed and feel them sink into the sheepskin rug.

‘He said he went to London with David Fitzroy, but I know he didn’t.’

‘The footballer David Fitzroy?’ Gordon sounds surprised.

I go over to the dressing table and study my red face in the mirror. 'But I went to David’s house and waited outside his gates and I saw him in his Range Rover with his girlfriend. But he didn’t see me. So he couldn’t have gone with him.’

‘Okay Ruth,’ Gordon says, ‘I’ll be able to get you some help.’ I stare at my reflection in the mirror.

‘It’s okay,’ I say, smiling at my reflection, ‘thanks Gordon but I’m going to be okay.’

‘I can get you some help Ruth,’ he says, ‘I can make an

appointment for you to see someone.' I go to the balcony window. It's a beautiful clear day today and the sea is calm.

'No thanks,' I say, 'I think I'm going to be fine.' I hang up, without saying goodbye to Gordon. Then I block his number. I step into the shower and feel the hot water run down my back. I tilt my head back and, as the water soaks my hair, I imagine Mike and Mary, together. In the bedroom, I style my hair and take time doing my makeup. I pick out my navy funnel neck jumper and black denim jeans. Downstairs I pull on my black leather boots and black raincoat. Outside, there's a chill in the air. Before I set off for the bar I go across to Sophie's bench. I could just stay here, looking out over the beach, but I have to get this over with. I must ask Mike and it's best I do it now, this afternoon.

I go to Mike's office. I knock quietly and wait a few seconds, before he calls out. As I close the door behind me, he looks up, pushing back his chair.

'Didn't expect to see you?' he says, smiling. I sit in the antique wooden armchair on the other side of his desk.

'I had a call earlier,' I say, 'from Gordon.'

He nods. 'Good,' he says, 'and what did he say?'

'That you're worried about me.'

'I am, I mean, I was,' he says, 'that's okay isn't it?' I

shrug my shoulders. There's a long silence. I don't want to ask but I have to.

'Did you go to London with Mary?'

He throws his head back and laughs. 'No,' he says, loudly, 'of course I didn't.'

'You're sure? Because I know you didn't go with David.'

He pulls a face. 'What do you mean?' I pick up a brochure about fire extinguishers and flick through the pages.

'Who did you go to London with?'

He rubs his eyes with his fingers. 'No-one,' he says.

'You didn't take anyone to London?'

He shakes his head. 'No.'

'So why did you say you were going with David?'

'He cancelled at the last minute,' he says, 'but I went anyway.' I look up at the ceiling.

'You didn't take Mary to London?'

He laughs. 'I promise. I didn't take Mary to London.'

'Okay,' I say, looking straight in his eyes, 'if you say so.'

'So we're okay?' he says, smiling.

'I am, if you are.'

He nods, 'I am.' I get up and head for the door.

'And something else too,' I say, turning back.

'What is it?'

'I don't want Gordon calling me again.'

'Okay,' he says, nodding, 'I hear you.' His phone buzzes and he picks it up. I go into the bathroom where I hide myself in a cubicle for ten minutes. That went better than I was expecting. He told me he didn't take Mary to London and I believe him. I have no choice but to believe him. But now he knows I suspected he did. And, hopefully, that's the end of it.

I go downstairs and get to the car park without any staff seeing me leave through the back door. I set off for home and, as I carry on down Beach Road, I feel brave. I feel courageous for asking Mike about Mary. But more than that I feel relieved because he didn't take her to London. And I believe him.

Before I get home I cross over the road to Sophie's bench again. I sit, for 20 minutes, with my hands deep in my pockets still feeling brave and courageous. When I get up I go across to the noticeboard. The leaflet for the Leader at the Microphone event from last March is still there. My mind races forward to next March. I think I might have an idea for the topic. Back at home I call Olivia.

Sixty-Three

'A Patient's Perspective?' Olivia says, hesitantly. 'Sounds interesting.'

I'm sitting on my bed, a notebook on my lap, doodling long arrows with sharp tips, pointing in all directions. 'I got my medical records,' I say, 'from my GP surgery. They said I was a Challenging Patient.'

'Why?' she says.

I doodle a spiral in the middle of the page. 'I was in a lot of pain. I kept going back there, and to A&E.'

'Is that when you thought you were dying?' she asks.

'Yes,' I say, 'and I went to my GP's surgery and they kept sending me home.'

'That must have been scary,' she says.

'It was,' I say. I hesitate for a moment, before admitting, 'I ended up in Thornsea Unit.'

'Oh Ruth,' she says, 'I had no idea.' I draw an ornate key in the corner of the notebook.

'I was assaulted by a patient,' I say, 'the nurses denied

it.'

'Okay,' Olivia says, 'and that's what you want to talk about in March?' Continuing with the doodling, I draw a padlock to match the key.

'I was mistreated,' I say, 'I want people to know.'

'Okay Ruth,' she says, still hesitant, 'if that's what you want.' I lie back on the bed.

'You think I shouldn't do it?'

'Not at all,' she says, 'if that's what you want.' I get up from the bed and open my wardrobe door. I'll have to get a new outfit, of course, if I'm going to be on stage and filmed.

I nod. 'I do,' I say, looking in the mirror, 'I definitely do.'

'Okay,' she says, 'I'll get you in the programme.'

Downstairs, at my desk, I open my laptop and start to write my talk. The words flow out easily. March can't come around quickly enough.

Sixty-Four

I wait until New Year's Day 2018 before mentioning anything to the family. I take the opportunity while we're having dinner and discussing our resolutions.

'And what about you Ruth?' Jean says, finishing off her sherry trifle.

'Talk more,' I say.

Ellie laughs. 'Love it Mum.'

'Yes,' I say, 'I'm doing the Leader at the Microphone event again, in March.'

'Oh good,' Jean says, 'about the business?'

I shake my head. 'Not about the business, something different.'

'Oh dear,' Jean says. She turns to Mike. 'Do you know about this?'

Mike's lips tighten to a thin line. 'You're not going to make a fool of yourself are you?' he says, shaking his head.

'No,' I say, 'I won't.'

Sixty-Five

On the first Saturday in March, Mike, Jean and I are in the apartment, in Manchester. We're getting ready for the grand opening of David's second bar. The intercom buzzes and Mike goes into the bathroom. When he comes out, his hair has been combed, again, and I can tell he's applied more aftershave. When he opens the door, Mary's in the hall, wearing a short beige rain mac, dark blue jeans and black knee-length leather boots. She takes her mac off and I notice her sparkly *Lady Gaga* T-shirt. Mike can't take his eyes off her. She goes straight to Jean and they hug. I nod and smile at her, politely avoiding an embrace.

'We're just checking the guest list,' Mike tells her, 'most have confirmed.'

'Did we get an RSVP from Bruno Araujo?' Jean asks, reapplying her lipstick in a compact mirror. I open a lever-arch file and run my finger down the list.

'Yes,' I say, 'he's coming.'

'And is he bringing his stunning girlfriend?' Mike asks, taking the file from me. Mary slaps his arm, giggling. 'Sorry,' he says, turning and smiling at her. She giggles again but stops when she catches my eye. I look at Mike and he stops smiling too. 'C'mon my love,' he says, grabbing my hand, 'we'll see you two down there.'

As we wait for the lift he pulls me towards him.

'You look lovely tonight,' he says. I'm wearing my green taffeta cocktail dress. I was feeling happy with my choice of outfit earlier but, having seen Mary in her jeans, boots and T-shirt, I now feel overdressed.

'Did Mary not want to bring anyone tonight?' I ask, brushing a long dark hair from his jacket.

He shakes his head. 'She said not,' he says, pressing for the lift again.

'Does she have a partner?' I ask, casually.

'Think so,' he says, looking at his shoes, 'not met them.' The lift arrives and we ride down to the ground floor, holding hands.

When we get to the bar, a few of the guests have arrived before us. I stay by the entrance. There's a good mix of ex-footballers and ex-rugby players here with their partners. David and Cara come in and they each hug me.

'Well done Ruth,' David says, 'you've done an amazing job tonight.'

'Thanks,' I say, 'glad you're happy with it.'

'You look lovely,' Cara says. She's wearing a short strapless black cocktail dress and I feel better about my own choice of outfit.

I find a seat in the VIP section at the back and watch the party from a distance. Everyone's chatting, drinking and eating canapes. I'm relieved my hard work has paid off. Surely now Mike and Jean can see I'm well enough to get my old job back. I watch Mike move from the back of the room saying hello to the guests, moving towards Mary. He taps her on the shoulder and she turns around. He looks around the room and catches me looking at him. He raises his glass of champagne to me and smiles. I raise my glass of orange juice and smile back.

At ten o'clock I leave the VIP section to find Mike. He's chatting to Jean.

'Can you walk me back to the apartment?' I ask, putting on my coat.

He looks at his watch. 'But it's still early,' he says, 'we're just getting started.'

'It's been a long day.'

Jean laughs. 'What's the matter Ruth? Can't take the pace.'

'It's been a long week,' I say, 'getting all this ready for tonight.'

When we reach the street entrance of the apartment block Mike kisses me on the lips. 'Thanks,' he says.

I kiss him back. 'What for?'

'A fantastic night,' he says, 'David's really pleased with what you did. Well done.'

I climb into bed and check *Twitter* for mentions of the bar. There's a few tweets and photos. In one of the photos there's Mike, Mary and another couple of guests I don't recognise. All four faces squeezed close together, with beaming smiles. I feel utterly exhausted.

I dream I'm back in the dormitory of the assessment ward, in a wedding dress. Jenny and Sophie are my bridesmaids. I go to the small window with the thick iron bars and see a vintage *Rolls Royce* wedding car parked outside. Mike's waving at me to come down. When I go to the door, at the end of the ward corridor, there's a huge shiny padlock and a male nurse is telling me to get back to the dormitory. I go back to the window and see Mike's standing next to Mary. She's in a beautiful vintage lace wedding dress with a tiara. She waves at me and smiles.

When I wake in the morning Mike's getting dressed. He's sitting on my side of the bed putting on his socks.

'You okay?' he says, when I sit up.

'You came to bed late,' I say, 'where were you?'

'At the bar,' he says, 'chatting.'

I check my phone. It's 8.30 am. 'Who were you with?'

'David and Cara,' he says.

'And Mary?' I ask. 'Was she there too?'

I show him the photo I saved from *Twitter* last night. 'Looks like you were having fun?'

'Yes,' he says, 'she was.' He sighs, gets up and goes to the window. 'Want to come back here next weekend?' He opens the curtains and sunlight floods the room. I get out of bed and throw on my dressing gown.

'For my birthday?'

'Why not?' he says. 'No use paying rent on a place we don't use.'

Sixty-Six

The following Saturday, the day before my 48th birthday, we arrive at the apartment late afternoon. In the lounge, there's a bottle of *Billecart - Salmon Brut* in a silver bucket and two dozen red roses. I read the card tucked inside: *Happy Birthday, Love Mike xxx.*

I fill the champagne bucket with ice cubes. 'We had this at The Borough Hotel,' I say, 'on our anniversary.'

Mike puts his hand on the small of my back. 'Of course, how could I forget The Borough Hotel?'

'That's a lovely place,' I say, packing the ice around the bottle, 'I'd love to go there again.'

He opens the bedroom door. 'Want to come to bed?'

'Yes,' I reply.

I wake, about 7 pm, and roll over. Mike's fast asleep. I go into the bathroom to take a shower. The drain catcher is full of hair. As I kneel to pull long dark hairs out of it

I catch something glistening in the plughole: a diamond earring. I put it in a few squares of toilet roll and place it, carefully, in my dressing gown pocket. Before we leave for the restaurant I transfer the earring from my dressing gown pocket to my purse.

We go to a Thai restaurant in the cellar of an old building down a narrow side street. The manager nods when he sees Mike and comes over to us, smiling.

'He seems very friendly,' I say, when we're seated, 'does he know you?'

'No,' Mike says, 'he's just very friendly.' I look around the dimly lit restaurant. It's mainly couples.

'Been here before?' I ask, picking up the menu.

Mike shakes his head. 'No, never,' he says, putting a napkin on his knee, 'David recommended it.'

I wait until I've finished dessert before I mention the earring. While Mike's taking the first sip of his whiskey, I put it on the white tablecloth, next to his plate.

He puts the whiskey tumbler down quickly. 'Where did you find that?'

'In the shower,' I say, 'tonight.'

He picks it up, holding it over the small candle between us. 'Mum said she'd lost one.' I put my hand out to get it back but he's too quick for me. He pulls his hand back and puts the earring in the top pocket of his jacket.

'I can give to Jean,' I say.

He taps his pocket. 'No need,' he says, 'it's safe in here now. You might lose it.' We're interrupted by the waiter bringing the bill.

'And there was a lot of long dark hair in the drain,' I say.

He screws up his nose and eyes. 'What?'

'I had to clean it out,' I say, 'before I had a shower.' He shrugs his shoulders.

'I'll have a word with the cleaner,' he says, 'I hope they're not having showers when they should be cleaning.' He screws up his nose again. 'Disgusting.'

'That's what I thought,' I say.

In the morning, Mike brings me breakfast in bed, with a pile of presents: a bottle of *Marc Jacobs Daisy*, a pair of black knee-length leather boots, a silk dressing gown and a smartwatch.

'You can monitor your sleep with that,' he says, as I fit the watch to my wrist, 'do relaxation exercises.'

I take the instruction leaflet from the box. 'Just what I need.'

When he goes out to get the Sunday papers and some milk I get a call from Alison.

'Happy Birthday,' she says, cheerfully, 'what are you doing?'

'We're in Manchester,' I say, 'in the apartment.'

'You sound a bit down,' she says, 'everything okay?' I hesitate for a moment.

'If I tell you, please don't think I'm going crazy.'

'Of course I won't,' she says, 'what's happened?' I trace my fingers over the embossed heart on the birthday card he's just given me.

'I'm sure he's having an affair,' I say, 'I'm absolutely certain.'

She sounds shocked. 'Really?' Have you asked him?'

'I've tried once already,' I say, 'he'll just deny it anyway.'

When he comes back, he hands me a gift bag from *Harvey Nichols.*

'I forgot to give you this,' he says, kissing me on the cheek. Inside I find a box. Inside the box I find a pair of pearl earrings.

'Beautiful,' I say, smiling. He sits next to me on the bed.

'Life's good right now, isn't it?' he says, rubbing my back.

'Yeah,' I say, 'pretty good.'

'I'm proud of you,' he says, kissing the back of my neck.

'Proud?'

'How far you've come,' he says, 'putting all that stuff

that happened last year behind you.'

'Does that mean we get back to normal again?' I say. 'Just you and me. No Mary?' He moves his arm away.

'But everything's perfect right now,' he says, 'why spoil things?'

Sixty-Seven

On the morning of Saturday, 17th March 2018, I'm in a panic. I should be walking around in a state of Zen-like calm, totally prepared for my talk in the Grand Ballroom of the Railway Hotel. Instead, I'm pulling out drawers in the kitchen, looking for my bank card. Mike's finishing a bacon sandwich.

'Have you seen it?' I ask, in exasperation. 'It's not in my wallet.' He puts his plate in the dishwasher.

'I'll check upstairs.' he says, going into the hall. I carry on opening every drawer in the kitchen. Two minutes later he's shouting from the landing. 'Ruth! Get up here!' When I go into the hall he's holding the note cards I'm been using to practice my talk. 'Is this your talk?' he shouts. I thought I'd kept my notes well hidden. I run upstairs.

'Where did you find those?'

'C'mon Ruth,' he says, holding them up, 'assaulted?'

I follow him into the bedroom and try to grab my notes

but his hand is too high for me. 'Give them back,' I say, 'I need them for today.'

'You can't say this stuff.'

'Yes I can,' I say, still trying to get the cards from his hands.

'Dismissed your pain?' Everyone will think you're crazy.'

'They did,' I say, 'they didn't investigate properly.'

'You'll make a fool of yourself,' he says, throwing the cards on the bed.

I pick up the cards, scattered over the pillows and duvet. I put them back in order. Mike watches from the doorway.

I sit on the bed with the cards in my hands. There are three hours before I'm due on stage. Olivia's sent me the programme. I'm the first on. Next to my name is the title of my talk: A Patient's Perspective. This is the talk I've been rehearsing for weeks. Now I'm wondering if Mike's right and I'm about to make a spectacular mistake.

'Okay,' I say, 'I'll have to talk about something else.' He takes the cards from my hands, drops them in the waste basket, and goes downstairs. I'm due at the hairdressers in half an hour and I still haven't found my bank card. When I go downstairs, Mike's in the utility room, rooting through laundry baskets.

'I'll do the sports stars talk,' I say, 'the one I was meant to do last year.'

He raises his hands in the air, as if holding a trophy. 'Fantastic,' he says, 'much better idea.'

'Can you help me though?' I say, handing him ten blank note cards and a pen. 'Can you write it for me?' He smiles as he takes the cards.

'Of course,' he says. I go to the hall to check all the coat pockets, for a second time. As I reach into my raincoat, a piece of thick folded paper falls onto the floor. I pick it up and unfold it. 'Found it!' Mike shouts from the utility room. He comes into the hall, holding out my bank card. 'It was in the laundry basket.'

'From the Borough Hotel,' I say, holding out the unfolded receipt, 'when we went last year.' He puts his hand out to take it from me but I pull my hand back before he touches it. The date. I need to check the date again. 'Look,' I say, showing him, 'it says November, they must have made a mistake, we were there in June.' He grabs the receipt and, before I can take it back, he rips it into quarters. 'What date was that again?' I ask, as he goes into the downstairs loo. He says nothing. 'What was the date again?' I say, louder this time. I follow him and watch as he turns on the hot tap, holding the ripped quarters under the water. 'You went with Mary, didn't you?!' I shout, not even caring if Daniel and Ellie can hear me. 'You told me you went to London!' He drops the wet paper into the toilet.

'No,' he says, quietly, pressing the flush.

'You took her to the Borough Hotel?!'

'No,' he says, looking into the toilet pan. 'Keep your voice down.'

I lower my voice. And the earring in the apartment,' I say, 'that was hers too, wasn't it?'

He pushes past me. 'Don't get upset. Not today.'

I follow him into the kitchen. 'How could you?'

'We'll talk later,' he says, 'let me write this talk for you.' He tries to give me a hug but I push him away.

'No. I'll do my own talk now.'

'Not while you're upset,' he says, 'don't say something you'll regret.' I run upstairs to our bedroom. My shoulders rising and falling with shallow breaths. In the en suite I splash my face with cold water and examine my eyes, they're a little red. I feel sick. How could he? Of all the places to take her, he took her to The Borough Hotel. And I bet they drank *Billecart - Salmon Brut* together there too.

Ellie comes to the bedroom door. 'Everything okay Mum?' she calls out. I smile in the mirror and pat my face with a towel.

'Fine,' I call back. I go to the bedroom door.

'Were you and Dad arguing?' she says.

'No,' I say, smiling 'just a little disagreement.' I take the cards Mike dropped in the waste basket and put them in my bag. I hear the front door slam and when I go to the balcony I see his car leaving the drive. This morning, at breakfast, he said he'd definitely come to watch me do my talk. Now I'm wondering when I'll see him again.

Sixty-Eight

And now all the preparation and waiting is over. It's 12 noon and I'm here, on the stage in the Grand Ballroom of the Railway Hotel. The first speaker of Thornsea's 2018 Leader at the Microphone event. I wait a few seconds, for my eyes to adjust to the lights. I let my shoulders drop, smile and focus on my breathing. My feet, a foot apart, are keeping me firmly balanced. I look to my right. Olivia is in the wings, giving me a big wide smile.

'Don't forget to smile,' she mouths, pointing to her lips.

In the front row, I see Suzanna and Terese, sitting either side of two empty seats. Suzanna gives me a thumbs up. Terese has brought Teddy, he's sitting on her knee. She waves his paw.

I take a deep breath. I feel the ten small cards in my jacket pocket. I take them out, look at the top one, and read the title: A Patient's Perspective.

I look to my right again. 'Go on,' Olivia mouths, smiling again.

I look down at the two empty seats in between Terese and Suzanna and think of Sophie and Jenny. I put the cards back in my pocket, take another deep breath and look straight ahead. I have no prepared notes for what I'm about to say.

'The talk I'm about to deliver is different to the one I planned. That will have to wait till another day.'

I look down at the two empty seats again, count to five, then, taking a deep breath, I lift my head.

'A year ago two of my friends died within three months of each other. I hadn't known them very long. And I'm not exaggerating when I say, if it wasn't for them, I don't think I'd even be alive and speaking to you today.'

I catch Terese's eye. She's nodding and wiping a tear away.

'I've always considered myself pretty lucky. I live in a nice house, I have two wonderful children. I've been on some nice holidays. There's a golf resort we go to in Marbella, usually once a year. It's a five-star resort. You're welcomed by a concierge, left orchids and chocolates on your pillow, there are sommeliers advising you on the merits of a particular wine and there are some amazing restaurants, to suit every taste. You're really looked after there. Each time I've been away from home, no matter where I've gone, I've always gone with people I've known, family usually. I'm not used to travelling alone.'

I look down at Suzanna, she's smiling and nodding. I take a sip of water.

'Last year, I went somewhere new and I had to go there alone. I like to do my research when I go somewhere new: check out the rooms, read the online reviews on *Tripadvisor*. But not last year. Last year, I didn't have time to pack a guidebook or download a translation app. When I arrived, I didn't know the language. I didn't know what was expected of me. I didn't know who did what. On my first day, I was feeling scared and alone. I met another guest, a young woman. Her name was Sophie. That day I thought I'd lost my voice so she got a notebook and a pencil and we started chatting. I hadn't eaten. Sophie got one of the staff to bring me some soup with a straw.'

I wait and count to five.

'You may remember hearing about Sophie. There's a bench on the seafront now, dedicated to her memory. About a week later I made friends with another guest, Jenny. It was my birthday and, when Jenny found out, she arranged a little party for me.'

I wait and count to five again.

'You may remember hearing about Jenny. There was an article in the County Herald last year, about the result of her inquest.'

I take a sip of water. Suzanna gives me two thumbs up and Terese makes Teddy wave his paw at me.

'I never used to like speaking in public, I'm not sure I do now. But.'

I look over at Olivia in the wings. She nods. I take another deep breath.

'I'm here today to ask us all, me included, to consider what are we doing?'

I pause and look out into the audience. There's total silence.

'Because soon there will be another family who'll lose their loved one, just like Sophie and Jenny's families have lost their loved one. There'll be someone, like me, who'll learn they've lost a friend and be in shock. All of these people, who have been lost, will have been beautiful people. They might not have known it, they might not have seen it, but they were.'

I look down at Terese and Suzanna, they're holding hands across the two empty seats.

'All these people, who leave us too soon, will have been loved, even if they didn't always know it, or believe it. Each of these people do tiny, almost insignificant acts of kindness every day. Even if it's just making a cup of tea for someone, opening a door or saying hello. And each of these tiny things might have made another person's day just that little bit better, They might turn a frightening experience into something a little less frightening or a lonely experience into something a little less lonely.'

I close my eyes and count to five, breathing in and out on each count. When I open my eyes the first person I see is Terese, smiling.

'I'm sure you'll agree there are too many people losing their lives far too soon. And I wonder if we could take a moment right now to ask ourselves why? Why is this happening and what are we doing to stop it? Are we making sure people know just how much they are valued and loved? Are we making sure they know just how much they mean to us? And if they need help, if they go to the doctor, or to A&E or get admitted to hospital do they know how special they are and how much they are loved?'

I take another sip of water.

'Can't we just tell people how much they are loved and how beautiful they are, every day? No matter where they are?

Because our world is a little colder and a little darker because people like Sophie and Jenny aren't here anymore.

Thank you.'

Sixty-Nine

After the silence comes the applause. Terese and Suzanna start before it ripples across and back along each row. I beckon for Terese and Suzanna to join me. Terese shakes her head but Suzanna grabs her hand and leads her up the steps to the stage.

'Thank you,' Suzanna says, hugging me, 'thank you.' Terese face is streaming with tears, as she gives me another hug.

'Thanks so much,' she says. My legs are trembling. Olivia comes walking out from the wings and grabs my hand. I hold onto her arm to steady myself. The four of us walk off the stage into the wings and through to the dressing room.

'Well done,' Olivia says.

'Was that okay?' I say, sitting down in front of the dressing room mirror. 'It's not what I'd prepared.'

'Brilliant,' she says, 'what made you change it?'

'The empty seats,' I say, turning to Terese and Suzanna,

'they were for Sophie and Jenny weren't they? When I saw you'd got tickets for them, I changed what I was going to say.'

Terese smiles. 'The tickets were for my two boys,' she says, 'but they were late.' All four of us burst into laughter. I pick up my hairbrush and makeup from the table and put them in my bag. There's a tap on my shoulder: it's Alison with Robert.

'Great job,' Alison says, 'well done.'

'What? How?' I stutter. 'I had no idea you two were coming.'

Robert gives me one of his big friendly smiles. 'That was great Ruth,' he says, nodding, 'what you did up there was amazing.' I'm overwhelmed with emotion.

'Let's go to the Swann,' I say, 'this is all too much.'

Alison insists on getting the first round in while the rest of us find a table. Robert and I sit close together.

'It's so lovely to see you again,' I say, 'I can't believe you came all this way, just to hear me do my talk.'

I walk with Alison and Robert to the railway station. When I say goodbye to Robert he holds me really tight.

'You were amazing today,' he says, 'really amazing.'

I walk home, down Railway Street, happy. Happy that

I've done my talk, and that I didn't make a spectacular fool of myself. Happy I've been in the company of some great friends all afternoon.

Mike's in the lounge when I get in, watching the preamble to the Liverpool - Watford match. I pick up the remote control and switch off the TV.

'Think we need to talk,' I say, sitting on the sofa opposite.

'I'm watching the match,' he says, 'can't it wait?'

'No,' I say, 'this is important. You and Mary. We need to talk about it.'

'It meant nothing,' he says, picking up the remote from the coffee table and switching on the TV. 'She knows that.'

'So it's over?'

'Yes,' he says, not looking at me,

'But she still works for us.'

He shrugs his shoulders. 'I'm not going to sack her. She's a good manager.'

'So what about us?'

'We keep on going,' he says, looking directly at me. I leave him in the lounge and go upstairs to the bedroom. In the bottom drawer, next to the bed, I find the old diaries I brought back from Elsford.

Seventy

I spotted Mike Barrett on the first morning of our holiday in Thornsea in June 1988. Alison and I stayed at the Orchard Hotel on Marsham Crescent. On that first morning he was standing in the doorway, between the kitchen and dining room, surveying his kingdom of twelve tables. Twenty hotel guests were in various stages of eating their breakfast among *Eternal Beau* crockery and starched lace tablecloths. He looked confident. I giggled when I told Alison I liked a man who looked like he was in charge. He was tall, with broad shoulders, a strong defined chin, clean shaven. His thick brown curls framing his kind face.

I was delighted when I saw him coming into the bar on the second evening. Alison and I were at a table in the bay window. I saw him looking around the room and hoped he was looking for me. When he saw me, he smiled and I smiled back. In less than ten seconds he was at our table.

'So what's brought you two to Thornsea?' he said,

pulling a stool from a nearby table. It was the eyes that did it - he had the lightest of light blue eyes.

'We're celebrating the end of our exams,' I said, trying my best to look relaxed.

'Clever as well as beautiful,' he said, pushing his stool further towards me, 'tell me more.'

Alison nursed her rum and coke while we continued our conversation.

'So what do you two girls like to do for fun?' he said.

'Well, I like to draw,' I said. Then I felt embarrassed and hoped I didn't sound too boring.

'Great,' he said, 'you can draw my portrait sometime.' He turned to face the wall and contorted his face into an exaggerated pose, lowering his head and lifting his eyebrows. I threw my head back, laughing. 'I'm serious,' he said, turning back to me.

'Maybe tomorrow night,' I said, lifting my half-pint of cider.

He kissed my hand. 'It's a date.'

He was there again at breakfast the next day, in the doorway. I smiled and he winked and smiled back. I felt we were sharing a secret code, one which the other guests, even Alison, wouldn't crack.

Alison and I spent most of that day sunbathing at South Beach. I tried to sketch the pier but the image of

Mike, standing in the doorway or kissing my hand, kept interrupting my focus.

He was in the lounge bar that night, sat at the table in the bay window, when we came in.

'That guy's here again,' Alison said, when we went to get a drink at the bar.

'I know,' I said, trying to hide my relief and excitement. 'Do you mind?'

Alison gave me a look which I knew meant *Actually I do.*

'Just for tonight,' I said, 'we'll go somewhere else to-morrow night, just us two, I promise.'

'I'm here for my portrait,' he said, as we put our drinks down at his table. I ran upstairs for my sketchpad and pencils. I spent a long time getting the angles and the shapes as close to his likeness as possible. I shaded in his hair, eyes and lips in colour. 'When can I see it?' he said, after I'd been sketching for 10 minutes.

'I'm not done yet,' I said. I loved how still he was, allowing me to examine and savour his features. When I had finished I flipped the sketch pad to show him.

He took the sketch pad from me. 'That's brilliant. You're really good.' I smiled, pleased to receive his praise. 'Can I keep it?' I pulled it out of his hands.

I giggled. 'No chance.'

'Will you come for a walk on the pier with me tomorrow night?' he said, stroking my hair.

I shook my head. 'I promised Alison I'd go out with her tomorrow night, on our own.'

He put his hand on my knee. 'I'll wait in the bar till you get back, we can go then.' He moved his hand round to the small of my back and pulled me towards him. I could smell his aftershave.

'Okay,' I said. He gave me a long lingering kiss.

I'd been going out with Robert for four months but, in truth, I hadn't thought about him once since the start of my holiday. Robert had told me, on our very first date, he didn't want any kind of commitment. He planned to go to university after his A Levels. He told me of his plans to travel around the world and couldn't see himself settling down and having a family. Because of that, I decided I'd never go to bed with Robert. If he wasn't going to offer any commitment I certainly wasn't going to risk any pregnancy. But Robert was good company and I enjoyed going for drives in his blue *Ford Escort.*

I kept my promise to Alison and the next evening we went to the South Beach Nightclub, just the two of us. When we got back I saw Mike through the bay window of the hotel bar, sitting alone.

In the morning Alison was up and reading a book when

I got back to our room.

'He's asked me to be his girlfriend,' I told her excitedly.

She raised her eyebrows, 'Go on.'

'His mum has a bridal wear shop, here in Thornsea. She's going to help him open his own bar.'

'So he's got money?'

I smiled. 'And lots of ambition.'

On the last morning of the holiday I woke Alison, trying to sneak back into our room. I couldn't wait to tell her he'd told me he was going to marry me, just an hour before, while we were in bed.

He came to the train station to wave me off. Alison made an excuse about needing to buy something from the station café.

'When are you coming back?' he said, after a long kiss.

'As soon as I can,' I said.

Back in Elsford, I phoned Mike straightaway.

'I'm missing you already,' he said.

My heart leapt when I heard his voice. 'Same here.'

'I can send you some money. So you can get the train back to Thornsea.'

Two weeks later I was on my way back to Thornsea. I did that trip every other weekend for the next six months. He did the return journey to Elsford twice during that time. He said it was hard to get time off work at week-ends.

When I moved in, with Mike and Jean, she let me work in her shop in exchange for my rent. I loved watching the brides-to-be coming in and choosing their dresses, that's when I wasn't upstairs steaming and pressing for her.

When he proposed, after 18 months, I said yes straight away. When I told Mum and Dad they were happy I'd found someone as nice as Mike. They liked the fact he had a clear idea about where he was going.

I became Mrs Barrett in the June after my 22nd birthday. It was a church wedding. I wanted a religious service, like the ones I used to watch with Mum. Mike didn't mind either way. Jean was on the flower festival committee, at the Parish Church, and the vicar let us get married there. The reception was in the Grand Ballroom of the Railway Hotel.

We didn't go on honeymoon. Mike said we shouldn't waste money when we were saving up for our own place.

'Anyway,' he said, 'Thornsea in June could be just as lovely as anywhere abroad.'

Seventy-One

When the Liverpool - Watford match is over I go downstairs and take my coat from the hook. I go into the lounge. When Mike sees me he sits up and stretches his arms above his head.

'Great match,' he says, 'did you see it?

I put on my coat. 'We need to talk,' I say, 'can we go for a walk?'

He rolls his eyes. 'If you insist, but there's nothing to talk about.' While we're still in the hall Ellie comes downstairs.

'You two okay?' she asks, searching our faces.

'Of course,' Mike says, smiling, 'just taking a walk.'

We cross over the road and head towards the pier. We walk, side by side, neither of us saying anything. When we're opposite the Beach Road bar, he stops and looks across the road. It's busy tonight.

He reaches for my hand. 'Want to call in for a *Guinness*?'

'No thanks,' I say, putting my hand behind my back, 'let's carry on walking.'

When we get to the bench near the coffee van, at the top of the pier, I sit down. Mike stands.

'Well,' he says, looking left and right along the promenade, 'what do you want to talk about?'

'You and Mary,' I say, 'was it serious?'

He sits next to me. 'It's over with Mary, you were ill. You've got to understand how difficult it was for me.' We wait for a group of young women in St Patrick's Day hats to go past. He gets up and starts walking back towards our house. I run to catch up with him. Each time I reach his side he speeds up and walks a little faster, until I'm jogging next to him. When we reach Sophie's bench he stops and sits down. I sit down too, but there's a good metre between us.

After ten minutes he slides over to my side. 'It meant nothing,' he says, reaching for my hand.

'You'll have to sack her,' I say, 'she can't stay working for us.'

'Okay,' he says, 'I'll get rid of her.'

'And I can have my old job back?'

'Yes.'

'And you'll let me back into the systems you locked me out of?'

'Yes,' he says. I get up from the bench and start walking home. He follows, a few metres behind.

When we get home, I go upstairs but not to our bedroom. Instead, I go to the spare room and turn down the duvet. Mike follows me in. 'What's this?' he says. 'You're sleeping in the spare room?'

I have my back to him, closing the curtains. 'I think we need to separate.'

He raises his voice. 'But I thought?'

I turn back to him. 'It's for the best.'

'Not now,' he says, his arm across the doorway, 'just as things are getting good for us. Let's move. Have a fresh start.'

'No.'

'Move near David and Cara.'

'It's been a long day,' I say, closing the door to him. 'We can tell Daniel and Ellie tomorrow.'

In my dream, I'm on stage in the Grand Ballroom of the Railway Hotel. I'm just about to do my talk. When I turn to my right, Sophie and Jenny are in the wings. I walk down the steps and sit in one of the empty seats in the front row. They each give a talk to the audience. When they finish I join in the applause. A short woman runs to the front of the stage and hands them a huge bouquet. When the woman turns around, it's Jean.

Seventy-Two

I wake, in the morning, in the spare room. It takes me a few seconds to remember why I'm not in our double bed. I check my watch: 10.23 am. When I go out onto the landing I hear Mike in the kitchen talking to Daniel and Ellie. There's a strong smell of bacon wafting up the stairs. I go into the en suite to splash my face with cold water. At the dressing table, I brush my hair and apply lip balm.

In the kitchen my family are sitting at the island. Mike's wearing the blue pinny Ellie gave him at Christmas. There are six cream dishes in the middle, containing the vital ingredients of a Mike Barrett special cooked breakfast: scrambled egg, mushrooms, tomatoes, bacon, sausage and hash browns. I remember getting these dishes as a wedding present from Mike's Auntie Anne, we only use them on special occasions.

'Perfect timing,' Mike says, as I grab a mug out of the cupboard. 'I was going to wake you.'

I take my seat, next to Ellie, opposite Mike. He hands

me the dish of mushrooms and smiles, a sheepish smile. I don't want to tell the children but I know the sooner I do, the better for all of us. I cough to clear my throat.

'Me and your Dad have something to tell you,' I say, looking at Mike. He shakes his head and narrows his eyes.

'Not now Ruth,' he says, 'we're having breakfast.'

'It's best if we tell them now,' I say, 'please.'

Ellie puts her fork down. 'Are you two separating?'

'Yes,' I say, nodding.

Daniel takes another spoonful of scrambled egg from its dish and a piece of toast from the toast rack. 'That's why you were in the spare room last night.' Then, looking at his sister, 'Told you so.'

Mike nods. 'But nothing's going to change,' he says, 'not until you've both got your exams done.' He stares at me.

'I'm sorry,' I say, reaching over to Ellie's hand. 'It's bad timing, I know.'

Ellie pulls her hand away, leaves the kitchen and runs upstairs. Daniel follows her.

'Happy?' Mike says, getting down from his stool. 'Upsetting your children?'

I stay, sitting at the island. 'Of course not, but what option do we have?'

'Forgive and forget,' he says, taking his plate to the

dishwasher. 'It doesn't have to be like this.' I go upstairs and find Ellie and Daniel in the top lounge. They're huddled together on the sofa. I sit on the coffee table facing them.

'Things haven't been easy,' I say, 'since I got ill.'

Daniel has his arm around Ellie. 'I know,' he says, 'I understand.'

Ellie sniffs. 'Do we have to move?'

I put my hand on her arm. 'Of course not, we'll still be a family.'

She sniffs again. 'How?' I leave my children on the sofa and go downstairs. Mike's in the garden, by the trampoline. I walk across the lawn and stop at the swing.

'Might as well take this down now,' he says, kicking the metal legs. I sit on the swing.

'And I want the Beach Road bar.' He looks up, the corner of his top lip quivering, his hand on the trampoline net. He blinks, turns and walks up the garden. I follow behind. In the kitchen, we clear away the breakfast things, in silence. It feels so final, like we'll never clear up together after a Sunday cooked breakfast again.

'That's all you want?' he asks. 'The bar?'

'The bar and this house,' I say. 'You said you wanted to move away from Thornsea anyway.' He shakes his head and goes out into the hall. I lean on the sink and look out through the kitchen window. In the flower beds, tulips are emerging from the dark soil. It won't be long before I see them bloom.

Seventy-Three

Thursday 12th July 2018

There's a small crowd outside the new café at 50 Beach Road, watching a wide piece of heavy green tarpaulin blowing gently in the breeze. Daniel stands on a step ladder, holding a corner of the tarpaulin. Ellie stands on a step ladder at the other side of the window.

I tap on the microphone. 'Ladies and gentlemen,' I shout, 'thank you for coming.'

There's a ripple of applause and I nod to Daniel.

Ready?' Daniel shouts to Ellie.

'Ten!' Ellie shouts.

Everyone joins in. 'Nine! Eight! Seven! Six! Five! Four! Three! Two! One!'

To shouts of 'Woop Woops' and 'Yeahs' from the crowd, they pull down the tarpaulin to reveal the sign:

CAFÉ COMPASSION

I nod to Terese, she's holding Teddy close. She pushes the front door with Teddy's paw and there's a loud cheer from everyone behind her. From the pavement, I hear squeals and gasps as the queue files in. I take a moment to admire the new sign, hand-painted by Milly.

Henry walks towards me, holding a cardboard box. 'Where do you want the music?' he asks.

'First floor,' I say, 'you can take the lift.'

'Can't wait to see the studio,' Milly says, following behind. I follow them in, eager to hear everyone's reaction.

The old wooden booths, high leather banquet seating and bar have gone; donated to a furniture recycling charity. The photos of sports stars have been taken down; given away to customers on the night the old sports bar closed for good. The hard seats have been replaced by squishy tan leather sofas. Low tables hold lamps with soft lighting. On one wall there are three giant prints: Jenny from her 40th birthday, Sophie from her last Christmas Day and Lizzie, aged 17, between her two younger sisters. On the back wall, a dozen paintings frame each side of a chalkboard displaying today's menu. On the first floor all but one of the pool tables have been removed. In their place, a space for Art Club with eight high stools around a huge table. The once boarded-up bay window has been cleared of the black MDF, revealing the view of Thornsea seafront. And, on the second floor, an office and counselling room.

Chrissie and Sam, our new café manager and chef, are serving sandwiches and cake.

Mike comes over to me, smiling.

'Thanks for coming,' I say.

'We wanted to see what you'd done,' he says, looking at the pictures on the walls.

'How's Jean?'

'Still a little upset about you having this place,' he says. Mary's at Mike's side now, hooking her arm through his.

'Are you ready?' she says. 'We need to get back to Manchester.' She turns to me. 'Well done Ruth.' This is no time for resentment. Plus, it was Mary who persuaded Mike to let me have the Beach Road bar, after Jean told him not to.

'Thanks Mary,' I say. And mean it.

Rebecca beckons me towards her. 'Ready for your piece to camera?' I follow her outside and she points to a cross marked in chalk on the pavement. 'Have we got the sign in there?' she says to the camerawoman, setting up her tripod. Rebecca moves the microphone towards me. 'We'll try to get you on the early evening news.'

I stand with my feet firmly on the ground, ready for my interview.

'Now tell me Ruth,' Rebecca says, 'what are your hopes for your new café?'

‘I want people to come here and know there’ll always be someone to chat to,’ I say, ‘get something to eat, get a hot drink, draw, paint, cook, laugh.’

She nods. ‘And what inspired you to open it?’

‘The friends I made in Thornsea Unit,’ I say, ‘Sophie and Jenny. This place wouldn’t be here if I hadn’t met them.’

‘And the name?’ she asks. ‘Where did you get the name from?’

I take out a small book from my bag. ‘From this,’ I say, showing The Small Book of Compassion to the camera. ‘It was a gift from Sophie’s mum, Terese. It really helped me.’

When the interview’s over I turn to see Robert coming towards me with a huge piece of cake. He puts his arm around my waist.

‘Happy?’ he asks, pulling me towards him.

‘Very happy,’ I say, resting my head on his shoulder. ‘Really, very happy.’

Milton Keynes UK
Ingram Content Group UK Ltd.
UKHW010801290224
438643UK00005B/5/J